JUL 06 2010

An Honest Love

**Center Point
Large Print**

Also by Kathleen Fuller
and available from Center Point Large Print:

A Man of His Word

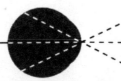

**This Large Print Book carries the
Seal of Approval of N.A.V.H.**

An Honest Love

KATHLEEN FULLER

CENTER POINT PUBLISHING
THORNDIKE, MAINE

This Center Point Large Print edition
is published in the year 2010 by arrangement with
Thomas Nelson Publishers.

Scripture quotations are from
the King James Version of the Bible.
This novel is a work of fiction. Names, characters,
places, and incidents are either products of the author's
imagination or used fictitiously. All characters are
fictional, and any similarity to people, living or dead,
is purely coincidental.

The text of this Large Print edition is unabridged.
In other aspects, this book may vary
from the original edition.
Printed in the United States of America
on permanent paper.
Set in 16-point Times New Roman type.

ISBN: 978-1-60285-741-4

Library of Congress Cataloging-in-Publication Data

Fuller, Kathleen.
    An honest love / Kathleen Fuller.
        p. cm.
    ISBN 978-1-60285-741-4 (library binding : alk. paper)
    1. Middlefield (Ohio)—Fiction. 2. Amish Country (Ohio)—Fiction.
    3. Amish—Social life and customs—Fiction. 4. Large type books. I. Title.
    PS3606.U553H66 2010b
    813′.6—dc22
    2009051522

To Tera

Pennsylvania Dutch Glossary

ab im kopp: crazy
boppli: baby
bruder: brother
bu: boy
burre: boys
daed: father
demut: humility
danki: thank you
Dietsh: language most commonly used by the Amish
dumm: dumb
dochder: daughter
dummkopf: dummy
familye: family
frau: wife, Mrs.
fraulein: unmarried woman, Miss
geh: go
gschenk: gift
gut: good
guten morgen: good morning
gutguckich: handsome, good-looking
gut nacht: good night
guten owed: good evening
Hallicher Grischtdaag: Merry Christmas
haus: house
herr: Mr.

hochmut: pride
kapp: an Amish woman's prayer covering
kinn: child
kinner: children
lieb: love
maed: girls
maedel: girl
mann: man
mami: mother
mei: my
mudder: mother
nee: no
nix: nothing
onkel: uncle
rumspringa: the period between ages sixteen and twenty-four, loosely translated as "running around time." For Amish young adults, *rumspringa* ends when they join the church.
schwester: sister
schee: handsome
sehr: very
sohn: son
wunderbaar: wonderful
ya: yes
Yankee: a non-Amish person
yank over: to leave the Amish faith

Chapter One

*E*lisabeth Byler cradled her nine-month-old niece in the crook of her arm while she fumbled with a baby bottle. Powdered formula was normally easy to prepare, but with Ester squalling and Velda—

"Velda?" Elisabeth glanced around the kitchen, then ran into the living room in search of her other niece. "Velda Anne! Where are you?" She looked behind the couch and one of the armchairs, gripping the baby to her side.

Elisabeth ran up the stairs to Velda's bedroom, shouting her name several times. She panicked, unable to find her little eighteen-month-old niece in any of the bedrooms. "This is the last time I'm babysitting for Moriah and Gabe!" Ester's cries grew louder.

A check of the bathroom proved fruitless, so she ran down the stairs to the back door, hoping, praying with all her might that Velda was outside and hadn't strayed too far from the house. She flung the door wide and took a step outside—

"Oof!" She'd run into a solid wall. Of muscle, she realized as she stared at the front of a light blue shirt and black suspenders. She looked up and saw the face of Aaron Detweiler. "Oh, thank

God you're here. Velda Anne's missing! You've got to help me find her!"

Aaron's expression was inscrutable. She shoved the baby into his arms. "Watch her while I *geh* find Velda."

"You don't have to do that—"

"Are you crazy? Of course I do!" Elisabeth moved past him, wringing her hands together. "Velda! Velda Anne Miller, you come here right now!"

"Elisabeth."

She spun and faced Aaron. "What!"

"She's right here." He shifted the baby to one arm, then pointed at the little girl clinging to one leg of his gray, broadfall trousers.

Elisabeth looked down at Velda, who stared back at her, sucking her thumb. Her black *kapp* was askew on her head, and strands of light brown hair rested against her plump cheeks.

Elisabeth rushed over and squatted down on the ground, clutching the child to her chest. "Where have you been?" She looked up at Aaron. "What are you doing with her?"

"She came out to the blacksmith shop."

"*Da.*" Velda wiggled out of Elisabeth's grasp. She pointed at the shop behind Elisabeth. "*Da.*"

"Guess she was looking for her *daed.*" Aaron shifted Ester in his arms.

Elisabeth's panic subsided, replaced by anger. She met Velda's wide, innocent gaze. "Don't you ever, *ever* run off like that again!"

Ester, who had quieted down while Aaron held her, started howling again. At the same time Velda's bottom lip began to tremble. *"Da!"* She burst into tears.

Aaron turned and walked into the house. Elisabeth picked up Velda and followed, watching him as he calmly walked over to the sink, as if he dealt with screaming babies on a daily basis. Within a minute Aaron had not only made the bottle, he had gently nudged the nipple into Ester's mouth, silencing her cries. He held the baby in the crook of one arm as if she weighed no more than a football.

Elisabeth put her niece down and leaned against the kitchen table, letting her heart rate slow. She tried not to stare at Aaron, but he seemed completely unaffected by the commotion. And there was something mesmerizing about seeing such a large man feeding a little baby. The bottle looked like a toy in his hand. She tried to remember back two years ago when Aaron Detweiler had been a scrawny kid of seventeen who had just gotten out of jail after serving time for dealing drugs. So much had changed since then. Not only had he grown a couple inches taller, he'd also filled out, probably due to the physical exertion of being a blacksmith.

Pulling her gaze from Aaron and Ester, she glanced around the kitchen for Velda, who had disappeared again. Her sister's firstborn had been a complete angel until she'd turned fifteen months. Since then the child had become a complete terror, and Elisabeth could barely keep up with her. Elisabeth started for the living room again, her patience as thin as parchment paper. "Velda Anne, I'm warning you—"

"Down the hall." Aaron took a step forward, his boot thudding on the floor.

"What?" Elisabeth asked from the living room.

"Velda went down the hall."

She leaned back and poked her head back into the kitchen. "How do you know?"

"Watched her go." He looked down at Ester just as her little chubby arm slipped from the bottle and hung over his muscled forearm.

Elisabeth groaned and walked to the short hallway adjacent to the kitchen, just in time to see Velda duck into the bathroom a few feet away. By the time she reached her niece, Velda had already started pulling the toilet paper off the roll, letting it fall in airy, folded layers at her feet.

"Velda, *nee!*" Elisabeth rushed to her and snatched the paper out of her tiny hands. She quickly rolled it up. "That's naughty, Velda!"

"*Da,*" Velda said, then dashed out of the bathroom.

Elisabeth raced after her, scooping her up in her arms as soon as they reached the kitchen. Aaron and Ester had disappeared, but she couldn't worry about them right now. She sat the child down in a chair and bent down in front of her.

"Now you listen here, Velda Anne Miller. No more disappearing. You march into the living room and play with your toys, and do not leave until I tell you to. Understand?"

Velda stared, and Elisabeth knew her niece didn't understand at all. She took her into the living room and put her inside a playpen next to the couch. She surrounded her with a stuffed bear and two board books. "Play with your toys."

Elisabeth turned around and took a step toward the stairs but stopped when she heard a book hitting the wood floor. She looked back at Velda who held the other book poised for flight.

"*Da!*" Velda said.

"Your *daed's* not here, remember? He and *Mami* went to visit your *Aenti* Rachel. She's in the hospital, and she just had a *boppli*." Elisabeth put the heel of her hand to her forehead. "Why am I explaining this to you? It's not like you understand what I'm saying."

Velda dropped the book and pointed to a wooden toy chest next to the playpen. "*Na!*"

With a sigh Elisabeth opened the lid of the chest and searched for a toy that might resemble a *na*, whatever that was. After three failed attempts, she held up a raggedy, faceless doll, the one she had given Velda shortly after she was born.

"*Na! Na!*" Velda waved her arms and jumped up and down in the pen. When Elisabeth handed her

13

the doll, Velda held it close, plopped down in the pen, and put her thumb in her mouth.

"Finally." Elisabeth moved the playpen toward the center of the room, made sure Velda couldn't climb out of it, then went to search for Aaron and Ester. She hadn't heard a sound from the baby since Aaron had fed her. As she made her way to the bottom of the staircase, she heard the heavy tread of Aaron's boots as he came down.

"She's asleep." He walked past her toward the kitchen, holding an empty bottle. Elisabeth followed closely behind.

Aaron went to the sink and added the bottle to the dirty stack of cups and plates. She hadn't had a chance to wash the breakfast dishes and it was nearly noon.

"Want some help?"

She looked at Aaron, stunned by his offer, and more than a little embarrassed. First she couldn't handle the children, and now it looked like she couldn't even take care of a simple kitchen chore. He probably thought her completely incompetent. "*Nee*," she snapped, sounding harsher than she intended.

Something flickered in his blue eyes. Before she could figure out what it was, he stepped away from her, then turned and left without saying another word.

Elisabeth turned on the water and stared at it pouring out of the tap, regretting her sternness with Aaron. Squeezing a couple drops of dish-washing detergent into the hot water, she started washing the breakfast dishes. But as she wiped the first glass, she gazed out of the window for a long moment, letting the slight summer breeze cool her embarrassment. When she finished the dishes, she would go out to the shop and apologize to Aaron. He'd helped her out, and that certainly didn't deserve her rudeness, even if she was a bit jealous of how easily he handled the children.

With the tips of her damp fingers, she rubbed her forehead. This was the third time she had babysat Moriah's daughters, and each time she felt more inept. If she couldn't handle her nieces for a few hours at a time, what kind of mother would she be? A terrible one. And her failure to keep Velda under control and Ester fed and content today made that clear. It wasn't the first time she worried about having children . . . or wondered if she even wanted any. Not that she would ever tell anybody that. That would be akin to heresy, an Amish woman announcing that she wasn't sure she wanted children.

She thought about Aaron and how he had made it look so easy. How'd he get to be so good with children? She would have never expected it of him. Of course, Aaron had been around Velda and Ester before. Aaron's older sister was married to Elisabeth's older brother, so Aaron had been to at

15

least one of the Byler family gatherings. But he hadn't interacted with the children much—or with many of the adults for that matter. She didn't know what to expect when it came to Aaron Detweiler. But she had to admit she was grateful he'd been there to lend a hand.

As she finished the last plate, her sister Moriah came in the door, followed by Gabriel. Gabe set a few plastic bags filled with groceries on the table, then kissed Moriah on the cheek. "I have to *geh* back to work," he said, staring into her eyes.

"I know. *Danki* for coming with me to see Tobias' *boppli*."

"I wouldn't have missed it." Gabe smiled. He leaned down and kissed her lips.

Elisabeth reddened and averted her gaze. She cleared her throat. "I'm standing right here," she said, lifting her voice an octave.

Gabe moved away from his wife, his face turning the same shade as the tomatoes in their garden. "Sorry. I didn't realize you were here."

"You asked me to babysit."

"I meant in this *room*." He looked at Moriah and gave her a tight smile. "See you later."

Moriah nodded. "*Ya*. I'll have supper ready when you come in."

Gabe gave another slightly embarrassed look at Elisabeth, then disappeared out the door. Moriah looked at her sister, clearly not as self-conscious as Gabe had been. Which wasn't surprising, considering Moriah had grown up with five brothers and sisters, while Gabe had grown up with only one brother, an identical twin who had died in a car accident only three years ago.

"Where are the *maed*?" Moriah asked, removing her black bonnet and revealing her starched white prayer *kapp*.

"Ester is upstairs taking a nap, and Velda is in the living room, playing in her playpen."

"I'll *geh* check on them."

"Okay. I just have a couple more dishes to dry."

Moriah went into the living room as Elisabeth finished wiping the damp dishes with a clean kitchen towel. A few moments later her sister reappeared. "Velda's asleep too." Moriah smiled. "You must have worn them both out."

"I think it was the other way around."

"*Kinner* can be exhausting, can't they? But they are such blessings." Moriah walked over to Elisabeth, beaming.

Elisabeth tilted her head. "Okay, I know that look. Spill it."

Moriah giggled. "I haven't told Gabe yet, but I can't keep the news a secret any longer."

Her mouth dropped open. She could tell by the bright glow on Moriah's face and the excited tone of her voice what the news was. Good grief, her sister was a baby-making machine.

"I'm pregnant!" Moriah clasped her hands

17

together. "Isn't that wonderful? Gabe will be thrilled. He wanted a large family, and we're well on our way."

"Congratulations," Elisabeth said, mustering a smile. "That's . . . *wunderbaar* news."

"*Danki*, Lis." She hugged her sister. "*Danki* for being happy for me. But don't tell anyone about it yet. I want to let Gabriel know first."

"My lips are sealed." She smiled, trying to elevate her mood to mirror some of Moriah's excitement. But the thought of babysitting three of their *kinner* made it near impossible.

Moriah picked up a couple of freshly dried plates and put them in the cabinet. "You should see Rachel and Tobias' *boppli*. He looks just like his *mami*."

Elisabeth smiled. "Uh oh." she said, rolling her eyes, "I'm sure Tobias had something to say about that."

"*Ya*, he promised their next *boppli* would look like him." Both Moriah and Elisabeth laughed, both knowing that the spark in Tobias and Rachel's marriage came from their competitive natures.

Elisabeth handed Moriah a glass. "Have they decided on a name?"

"Finally. It took them the whole day. It's not like they didn't have months to think of one."

"I'm guessing they probably spent all that time arguing over who got to choose the name."

"I'm sure you're right. But whoever did, they picked a *gut* one." She looked at Elisabeth. "Josiah Andrew."

"That is a nice name. I'll have to go over and see them once Rachel comes home." *Just as long as they don't ask me to babysit.* She gave Moriah the last of the dishes. Once they were put away, Elisabeth asked, "Do you need help with anything else?"

"*Nee.* I appreciate you watching the *maed.* Hope they weren't too much trouble."

"They were . . . lively." She wasn't about to admit she'd nearly been bested by an infant and a toddler. Her family thought her flighty enough as it was. Sure, she was often late getting ready for church, and sometimes she forgot things, like leaving the cap off the ketchup or not adding baking powder to a cake. Still, she was getting better about that—or at least she was trying to.

Taking one last look at Moriah, who had started putting the groceries away, Elisabeth thought about her sister's news. First Moriah had her two children, with a third on the way, and now her brother Tobias just had his first child with his wife Rachel, Aaron Detweiler's sister. It wouldn't be long before the next Byler, Lukas, would start thinking about marriage and a family. Unlike her, Lukas was great with his nieces. Fortunately, her youngest two siblings, Stephen and Ruth, were too young to think about all that. At least she wasn't the only one in her family who didn't have babies on the brain.

As she left the house, she saw Aaron exiting the Miller's blacksmith shop with a large wooden crate, a few horseshoes visible on top. He moved slowly, forearms and biceps straining, as he walked behind the shop. At the same time she heard the creak of the shop door open. She turned to see Gabe walk outside.

"Glad I caught you before you left," he said, walking toward her. Any embarrassment at getting caught kissing his wife earlier had disappeared. Instead, he had a serious look on his face. "I want to talk to you about something."

"*Ya*?" The summer sunlight beat down on them. She shaded her eyes with her hand as she regarded her brother-in-law. "What about?"

"I wondered if you'd be interested in a job. God has seen fit to bless our small business, and with *daed* officially retired, I need someone to help out part-time." As Aaron approached the front of the shop, Gabe motioned for him to join them.

Elisabeth watched Aaron remove his straw hat and wipe the perspiration from his forehead, revealing a mop of dark blond hair. She looked back at her brother-in-law as Aaron neared. "Gabe, I have no idea how to make horseshoes."

Gabe laughed. "*Nee*, Elisabeth. Not with the blacksmithing. I need someone to do the books and help with ordering. Also taking orders from customers, keeping the paperwork straight—office details. Moriah said you're *gut* with numbers."

Elisabeth lifted a brow, surprised that Moriah had mentioned that to Gabe. She'd been bored out of her mind in school, and no one had ever been happier to graduate after her eighth grade year than she was. But math had been her best subject and the only one that hadn't put her to sleep.

"It's part-time, only three days a week," Gabe continued. "But you can pick your days and set your own hours. Are you interested?"

"I'm definitely interested!" She had spent a good part of the last two years since graduation working with her mother at home, helping with the gardening and canning, and keeping the household running smoothly. Unfortunately, those tasks didn't give her much satisfaction. During the past year she had decided to go out and find a job, a quest that had been more difficult than she'd thought, as opportunities were scarce. "Did Moriah tell you I was looking for work?"

"She mentioned it. She said you were having a tough time."

"Gabe, I don't want you to create a job for me."

"Oh, trust me, I'm not." He looked at Aaron. "We were just talking the other day how we needed to hire someone."

Aaron nodded. "You're looking at the current bookkeeper. I'd be more than happy to hand the paperwork over to you."

Elisabeth looked at Aaron. "And let me guess, you'd rather be working at the forge than the desk?"

"Definitely."

"So?" Gabe gave her an expectant look. "Do you want the job?"

It didn't take long to make up her mind. "*Ya*, I'd love to come work for you. When should I start?"

Gabe pushed his hat back on his head. "I said you could make your own hours, so you tell me."

"I'll come in day after tomorrow. I promised *Mami* I'd help her can spaghetti sauce tomorrow. We have tomatoes coming out of our ears. I can bring a few jars with me, since we'll have more than enough."

Gabe grinned. "Great. When you get here, Aaron can fill you in on his 'special' filing system."

She turned to Aaron. "What's so special about it?"

Aaron smirked. "You'll see."

Chapter 2

*A*nna Esh twisted the brand new key in the lock, frowning when it didn't turn. She reinserted the key and with a little effort, finally got it to unlock the door of Esh's Amish Goods. With a small shove she forced open the door and peered inside.

She surveyed the small gift store and let out a long sigh. She and her mother had purchased the shop a week ago, and there was still much to do before it was ready for business. Changing the name for one thing. As of today the store would be known as Esh's Amish Goods, and the new sign would be delivered next week. The gift shop was in a great location—a small shopping center located next to the Middlefield Market. Business would be brisk, especially on Mondays when the flea market was open. Its prime location a street over from the Middlefield Cheese Shop, another popular destination for tourists, couldn't hurt business either.

She walked over to the glass countertop and set down her bag with her lunch and paperback novel inside. The display case beneath the glass held a few cheap knickknacks, part of the inventory the previous owners had left when they sold everything to Anna and her mother and then moved back to their retirement home in Florida. At first Anna had been hesitant about the venture, not only of buying the business but of moving from Maryland to live with her great uncle Zeb, her late father's much older brother. Leaving the Amish community she grew up in hadn't been easy. But since her father's death three years ago and Uncle Zeb's accident last month, not to mention her broken relationship with Daniel . . .

She shook her head, sending thoughts of the past away. When she and her mother had made the decision to move to Middlefield, she had vowed to focus on forging a new life, not on remembering her painful past.

Anna picked up her bag and opened the dirty white door that led to the back of the store. Her gaze took in the small office and storeroom, noticing the peeling yellow paint on the walls and the chipped linoleum floor. The entire store smelled musty. Although the temperature inside was cooler than outside, it was still warm. The previous owners had closed the store five years ago, but they hadn't had a single offer until Anna expressed interest. She could see why. Besides repainting everything, she had to replace the back door, fix the leaky toilet in the tiny bathroom, and order more inventory and shelving. And that was just the beginning.

But despite all the work involved, she loved the place.

Placing her bag on the dented metal desk, she grabbed a rag and a can of all-purpose cleaner, ready to tackle the dust and grime that had formed on every surface of the store. As she walked back into the store, she hummed a hymn she'd sung in church last Sunday, occasionally singing a German word of praise.

"Excuse me, *fraulein*."

At the sound of the deep voice, she jerked up

her head, nearly dropping the cleaner. Standing inside the front door was a young Amish man. Unnerved, she gripped the can tightly.

"I'm sorry. I didn't mean to startle you." He shoved his hands in his pockets. "I knocked on the door a couple times, but I guess you didn't hear me. It was unlocked, so I came right in."

"That's okay." She struggled to regain her composure, something she found difficult to do with this nice-looking, dark-haired man standing only a few feet away. She hadn't seen him before, and as she took in his face, she noticed his hazel eyes, their unusual color apparent even in the dimness of the store. "I suppose I shouldn't have left the door unlocked. We're not ready for business yet."

"*Ya*, I know. I spoke with your *mudder* a couple days ago. She said you hoped to open the store in a couple of months."

"That's the plan. We should have the repairs and renovations done on the shop and have enough inventory by then.

He grinned, revealing perfectly straight teeth. "I'm hoping I can help you out with that. I've got the toys and other things your *mudder* ordered out in my buggy."

Anna frowned. She had no idea what he was talking about. "I'm sorry, *Herr* . . ."

"Byler. Lukas Byler. Call me Lukas."

"I'm sorry, Lukas. I don't know anything about the order."

"Your *mudder* didn't mention it to you?"

"*Nee*." Anna made a mental note to discuss the matter with her mother when she came in later. They couldn't order things without discussing them first, or at least telling each other about it. Finances were tight, and they had to watch every nickel and dime.

"I guess there's some sort of misunderstanding then." A puzzled look entered his eyes and he stroked his clean-shaven chin. He moved his hand from his face and looked at her. "Is your *mudder* here? She can probably help clear things up."

"She won't be back until late this afternoon."

"Then I tell you what. What if I bring in the goods, you take a look at them, and I'll come back tomorrow morning. Then you can let me know if you change your mind."

"If my *Mami* ordered the items, then I'll pay for them." Anna didn't want the man to go away empty-handed just because she and her mother hadn't communicated. That wouldn't be fair to him. "Just bring them inside and put them over there." She pointed to an empty space near the front door.

He nodded. "Be right back."

Anna sighed. She hoped her mother hadn't negotiated too steep of a price with Lukas. She also hoped that he wasn't bringing her a pile of junk she couldn't sell. There were several stores in the area that sold cheap, plastic goods at high

26

prices. She didn't want Esh's Amish Goods to go that route. She had envisioned having high-quality, yet reasonably priced, handcrafted goods like quilts, small pieces of Amish furniture, and perhaps some decorative ironwork and home-made pastries, jams, and jellies for sale. She wished to sell only authentic Amish goods to patronize and support the Amish cottage indus-tries. But her mother had a soft heart and Anna could see her ordering a bunch of high-priced, useless items so she could avoid saying no.

When Anna saw Lukas heading toward the shop with a huge cardboard box, she hurried to open the door for him. "I have one more in the buggy. *Geh* ahead and take a look at what's in here while I fetch it."

She peeked inside the box, her mouth opening in surprise. Kneeling down, she pulled out a doll-sized rocker, made in the Amish style out of hickory wood. As she inspected the piece, she took in its sturdy construction. Each small, flat spindle was hand-carved then tightly fitted with a mortise-and-tenon joint. The curved rocker run-ners had been sanded perfectly smooth, then var-nished to prevent splintering. She set it gingerly next to the box and then pulled out two more small chairs before noticing a couple of rectan-gular wooden train whistles that had been coated with clear lacquer. She picked one up and felt the smooth, shiny surface. Turning the whistle over, she saw a small stamp imprinted on the bottom: Byler and Sons Carpentry Company.

At the creaking sound of the door, she jumped up to help Lukas with the other box. "These are just some miscellaneous things," he said, setting the box on the floor as the glass door fell shut. "A few garden plaques, a couple of knickknack shelves. I also made two clocks in the shape of Ohio. Yankee visitors seem to love those."

Lukas grinned.

Anna's eyes widened. "You made all these?"

"Most of them. My brothers and *daed* helped with a few, but they don't really care for working on the small stuff. I usually make them on my own."

"I'm impressed." She picked up one of the garden plaques with the word *thyme* burned into the smooth, light colored wood. A thin, straight wooden stake was attached so that a gardener could put it in the ground next the herb. "You're quite gifted."

He cast his gaze to the ground, but said nothing. He showed *demut*, the humility expected of all Amish. She'd always appreciated that trait.

She tried to focus on the matter at hand. "What price did you and my *mami* settle on?" When he told her, she froze. "Are you sure?"

"*Ya.*"

She looked at the toys in the boxes again. "That's way too low."

He shrugged. "I don't make them for the money. I enjoy doing it and the Yankees and other folks like buying them."

"*Ya*, but you could get so much more for these if you wanted to. Are you sure that's the price you want me to pay?"

"Anna, if you don't stop questioning me, I'll lower the price." His mouth formed a small half smile.

She frowned. "How did you know my name?"

"Your *mudder* mentioned it the day I came in here. She also said she was sorry I'd missed you." He gazed at her, the intensity of his hazel eyes deepening. "I'm glad I didn't miss you this time."

Lukas noticed the blush that bloomed on Anna's cheeks after he paid her the compliment. Goodness, she was a pretty *maedel*, with blonde hair around her heart-shaped face and faint brown freckles across the bridge of her nose and the tops of her cheeks. But the thing he'd noticed right off was her height. She was only about an inch shorter than him, and he liked that he could look her directly in the eyes when they spoke.

He also appreciated her eye for quality. He wasn't into bragging about his own work, but he always put in his best, even when he was working on his hobby of making toys and other small items out of wood. He'd been selling those items at Mary Yoder's Amish Kitchen for a couple of years, and when he'd seen that Trinkets and Treasures was reopening, he decided to try to sell them here. As he made the toys, he imagined the delighted faces of children playing with them.

"Let me get the checkbook," she said, not looking at him directly. But he could see a tiny smile playing at the corners of her pale pink lips. Cute.

He watched as she went to the back room, the ribbons of her white prayer *kapp* trailing behind her slender shoulders. He pushed his hat off his forehead and wiped at the perspiration gathering there. He naturally assumed she wasn't married. Her mother had said the two of them had moved here from Maryland four months ago, but that didn't mean she didn't have someone back home. Or maybe there was someone in Middlefield she had taken a fancy to.

As he stood by the glass counter, he shoved his hands into his pockets and took in the store. Although it was the beginning of August and the sun shone bright in the early morning sky, the single window on the east side of the store only gave a little bit of light. Puffy white clouds hovered, threatening to block that sunlight, dimming the already dark room.

He hadn't paid much attention to the gift shop before the Eshes had taken over, and he knew little about it other than that it had been run by Yankees who hadn't dealt too much with the local Amish. He glanced up at the two gold-pendant chandeliers suspended from the ceiling. The lights hadn't been turned on and wouldn't be, since using electricity wasn't the Amish way. Somehow Anna would have to get some more light in the store.

"I know it's dark in here." She emerged from the back room, speaking as if she'd read his thoughts. "I need to pull out the electric lighting and put in a few gas powered lights. I thought I might be able to get away with the natural light streaming through the window, but I don't think that will work every day."

"Especially in the winter. We have some dreary days here in Ohio."

"Same in Maryland. I'll figure something out." She flipped open the checkbook and started writing. When she finished the check, she tore it out of the book and handed it to Lukas.

He took a quick glance at the check. *Esh's Amish Goods* it said at the top. Then he noticed the check number. 103. A brand new account. He remembered when his father had first started his carpentry business. Lukas had been young but old enough to recall there had been a couple of lean years at first. He suspected Anna and her mother were experiencing the same restricted finances as they started their new venture. "I could help you out." He pocketed the check. "With the lights and electric."

She lifted a light blonde brow. "I wouldn't ask that of you. I'm sure you have enough work to do."

"I can come by during lunch. It's no bother, and I'll have the fixtures and electric wires out in no time. Also, if you need some display shelves I could make you a few."

Anna hesitated for a moment. Her pause convinced him that money was on her mind. Then she shook her head. "I appreciate the offer, but to be honest . . . I don't think I could afford your work. If your shelves are as *gut* as your crafts, which I suspect they are, you'd be well out of my price range."

Her words pleased him, making him redouble his efforts to convince her. "Not if I use scrap wood." He leaned forward, pressing the issue. "Which I have plenty of back at the shop."

"I don't know. Seems I would be taking advantage of your kindness." She lifted her chin and her expression became stern. "*Danki* for the crafts, Lukas. I know they'll sell very quickly."

On the verge of being dismissed, he had to figure out a way to help her. "I don't think you're taking advantage of anything, especially when what I'm proposing will help both of our businesses."

She stepped out from behind the counter. "What do you mean?"

"I can build your shelves in exchange for putting some business cards in your store and maybe a label telling where the shelves came from. You could sell them to your customers if you wanted, and we'll split the proceeds."

Putting her hands behind her back, she said, "That does make *gut* business sense."

"Then shall we shake on it?" He held out his hand.

"I haven't said *ya*, yet."

"But I can tell you're going to." He moved his hand toward her, gratified when he saw the ghost of a smile twitching at the corners of her mouth. She slipped her delicate hand in his. He noticed the warmness of her palm, and he didn't want to let go.

"And if you don't mind," she said, still shaking his hand, "I'll take you up on the offer to pull out the electricity and put in some gas lighting. I'll pay you, of course."

"Of course." But he didn't intend to take a penny from her.

"Zeb, you really should be at home. Resting."

"I don't need you tellin' me what to do, Edna Esh."

Anna stopped washing the store-front window and glanced over her shoulder at her mother and uncle arguing behind the counter. Uncle Zeb had insisted on coming to the shop today and helping out, even though his doctor had told him to take it easy for the next few months after he'd fallen off the ladder in March. Luckily he hadn't broken anything when he landed on his back, only compressed some vertebrae. Still, he'd spent a few days in Geauga Hospital, giving the nurses fits. At that point the hospital personnel had called Edna, Uncle Zeb's next of kin, and practically begged her to take him home.

"Zeb, Anna and I can't help you if you ignore what we say." Edna put her hand on his thin shoulder.

He shrugged it off, his back bent into a slight C shape. "Didn't ask for your help. Was doin' just fine until you came along."

"You could barely stand up."

Zeb scowled but didn't contradict her.

"I promised the hospital I would keep an eye on you." Edna moved to stand in front of Zeb, her hands on her full hips. "And that's what I'm going to do. Anna and I are capable of getting the store ready for opening day. Now, get in the buggy and I'll take you home. Melvin Yoder should have never brought you here in the first place."

"He was being neighborly."

"Because he saw you limping on the side of the road. He said he couldn't let you walk all the way over here, and he was right. I'm glad he did pick you up." She let out a long sigh.

"You can't expect me to stay home and do nothin'." He slid away from her, the soles of his work boots scuffling against the smooth cement floor.

"That's exactly what I expect you to do. I wish you would listen to me for once."

"An' like I said before, I ain't takin' orders from you."

Noting the escalating tone of their voices, Anna went to them. "*Mami's* right, *Onkel* Zeb. You should *geh* home and rest your back. That's the only way you're going to get better."

"*Mei* back is fine." Stepping away, he looked at her, his blue eyes surrounded by deep wrinkles in his permanently tan skin. "Just like I told that doctor. Don't trust them anyway. Yankee docs, what do they know about Amish people?"

Anna wanted to say they knew plenty, but at that moment the door opened and Lukas walked in, a heavy tool belt slung over his shoulder. From the looks of it he'd brought every tool he owned. "*Guten morgen.*" He looked straight at her, then smiled.

Attraction zinged through her but she tried to ignore it. She hadn't expected to see him so soon after making their agreement yesterday. "Hello, Lukas."

"We're so glad you're here." Edna's frustrated expression suddenly melted faster than ice cream on a summer day. "Anna told me you offered to take care of the power. *Danki* again for your help."

"Glad to do it." He walked further into the store and nodded at *Onkel* Zeb. "*Herr* Esh. Nice to see you."

Zeb ignored Lukas' greeting, turning to glare at Edna and Anna. "So you'll let this *bu* help you but not me?"

Anna detected a note of hurt in his gruff tone. "*Onkel* Zeb, it's not that we don't want your help—"

"You think an old *mann* can't do his share."

"*Nee*." She looked to her mother, catching the flustered expression in her eyes. Why did her uncle refuse to listen to reason?

"Just got finished tellin' these womenfolk I'm fine." His gaze narrowed. "But all they want to do is put me out to pasture."

"Zeb, that's not true and you know it," Edna said.

Without missing a beat Lukas jumped in. "Well, if you've got the time to spare, I can use all the help I can get."

Edna shook her head. "I don't think that's a *gut* idea."

"Well, I do." Zeb shuffled over to Lukas. "I've been takin' out fancy Yankee wirin' since before you were born, Edna Esh. Could do the job with my eyes closed."

"That's not the point and you know it—"

"Why don't we start in the back?" Lukas gave Edna a quick nod and led Zeb toward the back office. A moment later Lukas stepped out of the office, pulling the door almost closed behind him. In a lowered voice, he said. "I'll make sure he doesn't overdo it." He winked at Anna, then disappeared into the office again.

Anna couldn't help but smile. Somehow she knew her uncle was in good hands.

"He's a fine young *mann*." Edna leaned against the counter, relief washing over her features. "Not too many people can handle Zeb that easily." She turned to Anna. "He's quite *schee*, too, don't you think?"

"I'm not interested." Anna turned away from her mother and returned to the front window, her good humor dissipating. "I'm sure Lukas isn't either."

"Oh, I doubt that." Edna came up behind her. "It looked to me that he's *definitely* interested."

Anna turned to her mother. "Don't, *Mami*."

"Don't what?"

"You know what I'm talking about. I'm not ready, or willing, to get involved with someone again."

"Oh, Anna." Edna's voice lowered and turned soft. "I know Daniel hurt you deeply. But you have to forgive him sometime."

"I have." She nearly choked on the words, even though they were the truth. She had been raised to forgive others, seventy times seven if necessary. "Forgiving isn't the problem."

"Then you have to move on. You're twenty-four years old, *dochder*. Time to be thinking about marriage and a family."

"What if that's not what I want?" She turned her attention back to the window and started wiping it with a paper towel dampened with cleaner.

"You wanted that at one time."

"Not anymore." She moved the towel back and forth over the glass with such force the towel started to fray. "This new business holds so many possibilities, and I'm excited about that. I love the idea of being independent."

"Now you sound like Zeb."

"Maybe I'm more like him than you think."

Edna moved to stand alongside her. "*Nee*. I think you're hiding."

"And I think you're prying."

"Well, at least there's one thing you and Zeb have in common."

"Which is?"

"Stubbornness." She smoothed the skirt of her navy blue dress. "You are both *sehr* stubborn, and there's no talking to you." Turning around, she walked back to the counter.

Anna pressed her lips together and stared out the window. Esh's Amish Goods was one of a small strip of stores that faced the side of a large quilt shop. She imagined a steady stream of customers coming into the store. She loved the idea of not having to depend on anyone. She would be her own person, with her own money and her own business. That was what she wanted.

But if that was the case, then why didn't she feel satisfied? She refused to believe her mother was right—that she was hiding her true desires for a husband and family. That had been her dream once, before Daniel Hochstetler had crushed it into a thousand pieces by breaking their engagement last November. They had been together for over three years, although she had been in love with him for much longer than that.

With a shake of her head she cleared her thoughts. After Daniel had left her two days before their wedding, then married someone in another district only months later, she had redefined her goals. God must have agreed with her choice, because He had given her this new opportunity. Moving from Maryland to Middlefield and purchasing this shop had been almost seamless, save for Uncle Zeb's cantankerous attitude.

"Anna."

She turned around at the sound of Lukas' voice. She had been so deep in her own musings she hadn't heard him approach. He had come up directly behind her, and now they were face-to-face, so close she could see tiny flecks of gold interspersed with the green in his hazel eyes. She felt her pulse thrum and blurted out, "You're done already?"

"*Nee*. It's a bigger job than I thought. Plus we

still have to take out the fixtures." He glanced up at the ceiling at the gold-pendant lights. "Too fancy for the shop, don't you think?"

He had left his hat in the back room, and his black, wavy hair hung down to his eyebrows and over his ears. "*Ya*," she said, tearing her gaze away from him. "They are too fancy." She strode past him to the opposite counter.

"Once Zeb and I get them down and finish with the wiring, we can hook up the propane."

She turned around. "Are you sure he's not bothering you?"

"Bothering me?" Lukas chuckled. "He knows this stuff inside and out. I'm glad he wanted to help out. He tells me what to do, and I do it."

"Sounds like my uncle. He's great at giving orders, just not so *gut* at taking them."

"He's a *gut mann*. A little gruff, but who wouldn't be after falling off a ladder? Especially at his age."

"So you heard about his accident."

"He filled me in."

"That doesn't surprise me. But I don't think he's gruff only because of the accident. According to *Mami* he's been crabby pretty much his entire life. Or so she tells me. I hadn't met him until we moved here. He's almost twenty years older than my father was."

"Was?"

"He died a few years ago."

"Oh. I'm sorry." Lukas shoved his hands in his pants pockets, the tool belt dangling around his trim waist.

"I appreciate you working with him. Not everyone can handle *Onkel* Zeb."

"I will say he's unusual, being a lifetime bachelor and all that. But the Lord created all kinds of people, because He knew we all had to be a little different or we'd drive each other *ab im kopp*."

Anna grinned, unable to help herself. Lukas Byler was definitely different than Daniel, not only in looks but in manner. Daniel had been shy and reserved, at times even unsure of himself. That description definitely didn't apply to Lukas, who exuded confidence and was quick with a smile. A very attractive smile.

Not that any of it mattered, because she didn't want to be attracted to Lukas. She couldn't afford to be attracted to him.

Chapter 3

Aaron grunted as he lifted another crate of horseshoes into his buggy. It must have weighed about eighty pounds, and he was thankful he had a vehicle to transport it in. His feet had been his transportation for the past couple of years, but when he took over the farrier part of the business for Gabriel last fall, he finally broke down and bought one. Many of their clients lived within a few miles, and though he could borrow Gabe's buggy when he needed to go to a job, having his own was quicker and more practical.

He walked back to the shop and saw Gabe busy at the forge, pounding out another horseshoe. "Why don't you knock off for the day?" Gabe brought the hammer down on the hot metal, the clanging sound vibrating through the shop. "There's only a few more of these left to do." He looked up at Aaron. "How many horses do you have to shoe tomorrow?"

"I think about fifteen, but I'm taking twenty pairs with me." Gabe and his father, John, had not only taught Aaron how to make horseshoes and other useful items out of metal but also how to shoe horses. Aaron actually enjoyed being a farrier more than he did a blacksmith, but those two jobs went hand in hand. He looked forward to Tuesdays when he had a chance to work with the horses.

"Better to be prepared." Gabe put down his tongs and wiped the sweat off his forehead.

"Are you sure you don't need me to stay?"

Gabe shook his head. "*Nee*. I'm going to finish up these shoes, then close the shop for the rest of the afternoon."

"When's John due back from Indiana?"

"Next week." Gabe picked up the tongs again. He took the horseshoe from the anvil and put it back in the forge. "But he's extended his visit twice, so we may not see him for another month or so."

"I'm glad he's enjoying time with his *familye*."

"*Ya*, I am too. Retirement seems to suit him, and to hear him tell it, he's healthier than he's ever been. Although I'm sure he's staying busy with his sister's *kinner*. *Daed* can never be idle for too long." He pulled out the shoe and put the red hot metal on the anvil. "Speaking of *familye*, your sister was asking about you. She wondered if you planned to come visit her and the *boppli* in the hospital. I didn't know what to tell her."

Aaron paused. "I don't want to bother them."

"I don't think Rachel would see it as a bother. Sounded to me like she would appreciate you stopping by."

"All right. I'll head up there later on." Aaron was glad his sister and the baby were doing well. He hadn't always gotten along with Rachel, but after she'd married Tobias—and since he'd given up his wild and illegal ways—they were on better terms with each other.

His four brothers were several years older than him, so they had never been close. Three of them lived nearby in West Farmington, and one lived in Pierpont, about an hour away. He didn't see them very often, although his mother had often babysat the grandchildren when they were younger. Aaron had done little to cultivate any type of relationships with his nieces and nephews, or his brothers and their wives. In turn, they hadn't wanted much to do with him during his teen years. Not that he blamed them. More regrets to add to an ever-growing list.

Back in his buggy, Aaron made his way toward his parents' home. He saw another buggy in the distance, but instead of making its way down the paved road, it was pulled to the side. When he drew near enough, Aaron pulled his horse to a stop behind it to offer his help. He jumped out and walked up to the driver's side of the buggy. "Do you need some . . ." His voice trailed as he saw Elisabeth Byler inside.

"Oh, I'm glad to see you!" Elisabeth breathed a sigh of relief as she poked her head out of the buggy. She said a quick prayer of thanks that God had sent help, especially Aaron, who would know exactly what to do about her predicament. "Daisy threw a shoe a little while back."

He stopped when he reached the driver's side, then faced her. "Is she hurting?"

"She's limping, but I don't think she's in a lot of pain. I pulled over as soon as I could."

Aaron nodded. "*Gut.* I've got shoes and tools in my buggy. We'll get her fixed up quick." As he stood on the shoulder of the road, several cars dashed by, stirring up a breeze strong enough to flutter the brim of his straw hat.

"*Danki*, Aaron." She moved to step out of the buggy when he touched her arm.

"What are you doing?"

"Going to find the shoe."

"*Nee*. Stay in the buggy. I'll find it."

"That's all right, I don't mind looking for it."

"Stay here. Too many cars flying by."

His tone firm, she nodded and hopped back inside. Elisabeth peeked over the edge of the door and watched him search for the shoe. When he found it, he strolled to his buggy, apparently oblivious to the traffic racing by. He climbed inside, then disembarked, holding a black object in his hand, and went straight for the horse. Now she could tell what he held—a small protective leather boot that would allow her to drive home without damaging the horse's foot. After murmuring a few words to the horse, he crouched down and placed the boot over her left foot. When he stood up, he put his hands on his hips and called out to Elisabeth. "I'll meet you at your house."

Goodness, she'd never noticed how broad his shoulders were. Not that she'd ever thought of Aaron in romantic terms. That would be ridiculous. But she had to admit he was a nice looking man, and she couldn't help but see the way his light blue shirt sleeves, rolled to the elbow, revealed muscular forearms sprinkled with blond hair. Just like all the other Amish men, he wore black suspenders and broadfall pants, pegged at the ankles, along with a yellow straw hat that cast a shadow over his face.

She grasped the reins as he started to walk away. "*Danki* again. I really appreciate this."

He gave her a brief nod and went to his buggy.

Twenty minutes later she pulled into her driveway, with Aaron not far behind. She bypassed the house on the left and her father's woodshop on the right and headed straight for the barn. When she jumped out of the buggy and peeked outside the entrance, she saw that Aaron had parked near the woodshop, in the spot where Lukas normally parked.

She watched Aaron pull out a worn buttercolored leather bag bulging with tools, then retrieve a couple horseshoes from the back of his buggy.

"I really appreciate you doing this," Elisabeth said, meeting him at the entrance. When she saw Aaron move to detach the horse from the rigging, she followed him. "Here, I can do that."

He shook his head. "I don't mind." He patted Daisy's chestnut-colored flanks. She let out a low snort. "She's a beautiful horse."

"*Ya*, she is. *Daed* got her a few years ago. You won't find a gentler horse than our Daisy."

With deft movements Aaron removed the horse's harness, then positioned her in her stall so he could access her foot. He slipped on a pair of leather leg coverings with the split in the middle and walked over to balance the horse's bent leg on his thigh. Aaron's hands seemed to fly as he scraped and cleaned her hoof, removing dirt, tiny pebbles, and small pieces of asphalt picked up from traveling paved roads. He grabbed one of the shoes lying on the ground nearby and matched it to the bottom of the horse's foot. Seeing that it didn't fit, he took the shoe and began bending and shaping it with his bare hands.

"You aren't using her old shoe?" Elisabeth asked.

"*Nee.*" He glanced up at her. "It was pretty worn. She would have needed a new one soon." Within minutes the shoe matched Daisy's hoof perfectly.

Impressive. She'd had no inkling he possessed that kind of strength.

He put a couple of small nails in his mouth, then quickly pounded them in, one at a time, through the shoe and into the hoof. The first time she'd seen a horse get shoed she had been a young child and had burst into tears, not realizing that the horse didn't feel a thing and that the shoes were necessary to preserve the horse's feet.

After he pounded the last nail, Aaron gently put Daisy's foot down, then stood up. "*Gut* as new," he said, more to the horse than to Elisabeth. He walked to meet the animal's head and stroked her nose. "*Gut maedel.*"

"How much do I owe you?"

47

He shrugged, still petting Daisy's nose. "*Nix.*"

"Are you sure? At least let me pay for the shoe."

Aaron scratched the back of his neck. "It isn't necessary."

"Tell you what. How about if I bring you a batch of my oatmeal cookies when I come to work on Wednesday? Well, they're actually not *my* oatmeal cookies, but my *mami's* recipe, and they're delicious. Best you'll ever have, I promise."

He tilted back his hat, his forehead beaded with perspiration from the exertion of shoeing the horse. "You don't have to do that, Elisabeth."

"I know, you've made that abundantly clear." She stepped toward him. "But I want to. I can't let your good deed go unrewarded. Besides, I still kind of owe you for yesterday."

He frowned. "Yesterday?"

"Helping me out with Velda and Ester, remember?" She sighed and dragged her toe across the barn's dirt floor. "I didn't have everything quite under control. And I wasn't very nice to you, either. I apologize for that."

"You were doing fine." Aaron picked up his tool bag and slung it over his shoulder. "Everyone knows Velda is a handful."

"Really? I thought it was just me."

"Nah. She's a pistol, that one. And I'd seen *mei mudder* make lots of bottles for my nieces and nephews when I was younger, so that wasn't a big deal."

48

It dawned on her that this was the most she'd ever heard Aaron speak. Intrigued, she wanted to keep him talking. "How many do you have?"

"Twelve. They don't live too far from here, but I don't see them very often." He glanced down at the ground for a moment before meeting her gaze again, discomfort evident in his eyes. "I've got to *geh*." He headed for the exit.

"Aaron?"

He paused, then turned around, almost as if he were reluctant to face her again. "*Ya?*"

"Do you like raisins or chocolate chunks in your cookies?" She crossed her arms and smiled at him.

"Elisabeth—"

"Chocolate chunks it is. Those happen to be my favorite too."

She detected the corner of his mouth lifting ever so slightly, the closest she'd ever seen him smile. Feeling victorious, she gave him another grin as she passed him and went into the house. But before she went inside, she glanced over her shoulder to see him loading his tools in the buggy, his profile now the picture of solemnity.

As he pulled away she went inside the house, the screen door shutting behind her. "*Mami*, I'm home!"

"In the kitchen."

Elisabeth followed her mother's voice to the kitchen in the back of the house. The spicy aromas of tomato, garlic, and oregano hung in the air. "You've started the spaghetti sauce?"

"Just the first batch." Emma Byler adjusted the gas heat underneath the large stockpot of simmering red sauce. "We'll finish up the rest tomorrow. Line up the jars for me on the counter, please."

"Okay." Elisabeth took several glass quart jars from the table and put them on the counter as her mother instructed. She placed a large funnel beside the first jar.

Emma gave the sauce a quick stir with a long-handled wooden spoon. "So how are my *wunder-baar* grandbabies today?"

"*Gut.*" Elisabeth leaned over and inhaled, taking in the delicious scent emanating from the pot. Her mouth watered. She'd love to dip a slice of bread into the thick sauce, but her mother wouldn't appreciate the crumbs she'd leave behind.

"Did you have any trouble with them?"

"*Nee.* Everything was fine. They had breakfast, and played, and Ester had her bottle before they both took naps. Then Gabe and Moriah came home."

Emma peered at Elisabeth over her wire-framed glasses, which she had just started wearing this past year. "I'm glad to hear it. Those two can be a handful sometimes. I remember the last time I took care of them, Velda Anne just about ran me ragged. I love that *kinn*, but she's got an independent streak in her, that's for sure."

"The morning went by without any problems." She spun around and sat down at the kitchen table, biting her lip on the tiny fib.

Emma turned around and joined Elisabeth. "I wish I could have watched them, but I had to visit Sarah Lapp today. She's got the cancer, you know."

Elisabeth nodded. "Is she feeling any better?"

"Not really. I did a little cleaning today and made dinner for her family. They need a lot of prayer. No one knows how long Sarah has, and we're all praying for a miracle."

Elisabeth made a mental note to pray for Ben and Sarah Lapp. Sarah, a young mother of four, had been diagnosed with cancer several months ago. She said a quick prayer of thanks that everyone in the Byler family had their health.

"So tomorrow we'll can the rest of the sauce, then Wednesday we can put away some pickles. Sometimes it just never seems to end. So I'll need your help." Emma sat back in the chair and wiped her forehead with the back of her hand. Despite the open window, the kitchen sweltered. Still, Emma's appearance remained neat and tidy, her *kapp* perfectly straight and not a hair out of place. "But when we're done we'll have lots of food stored up, praise God. "

"All right. Oh, wait. I almost forgot." Elisabeth

grinned. "I won't be able to help you on Wednesday. I've got a job."

"You do?" Emma smiled. "That's terrific, Elisabeth. Where will you be working?"

"For Gabe. In the blacksmith shop."

Her smile dimmed, replaced with wariness. "Please tell me you won't be working at the forge."

Elisabeth laughed. "*Nee.* I'm sure he won't let me near the forge, not that I want to do that hot, messy work anyway. He's asked me to work in the office. Doing the accounts and keeping track of invoices. Filing. Stuff like that."

"That sounds like a great opportunity for you. And how *wunderbaar* you're working for *familye.*"

"*Ya.* Apparently it was Moriah's idea. She told Gabe I had a head for numbers."

"Which you do. She must have thought you would do a *gut* job."

Elisabeth put her elbow on the table and leaned her chin on her hand. Her mind wandered back to earlier that day. Moriah probably would have taken back her recommendation if she had seen how Elisabeth handled Velda and Ester.

"Is something wrong?" Emma tilted her head as she looked at Elisabeth.

"*Nee.*" Elisabeth sighed. "Well, maybe."

"What is it?"

Normally Elisabeth wouldn't voice her doubts about something aloud, but this time she couldn't help herself. "Working for Gabe and Moriah is a big responsibility."

"It is."

"But I'll be dealing with money, and the blacksmith shop is their livelihood. You know I'm not the most organized person in the world."

"True."

Elisabeth rolled her eyes. "You don't have to agree with me so quickly."

Emma chuckled. "I'm only being honest, *dochder*. But don't be hard on yourself. I've noticed you've been better about being on time to church the past couple of months."

"I've been trying."

"And while you had a hard time in school, you've been a huge help to me since you graduated. I know I can count on you to do anything I ask, and do it well."

"But what if I make a mistake?"

"You're bound to. We're not perfect people, none of us are. If you make a mistake, own up to it and learn from it." Emma stood up, smoothing the skirt of her gray work dress. "You'll be fine, Elisabeth. Don't worry about it. Pray for the Lord to give you a clear mind while you're working. And to wake you up on time in the morning."

Elisabeth sat back in her chair and smiled, most of her doubts dissipating with her mother's encouraging words. Yet as she helped her mother can the spaghetti sauce then make supper, a smidge of anxiety niggled at her. Even though the job was part-time, there would probably be plenty of opportunities for her to screw up. And while she had been on time to Moriah's this morning, and even to church this past month, that didn't cancel out all the Sundays she'd been late, making the family wait for her to get ready. Or the times she'd lost her homework or made poor grades on a test because she'd forgotten to study. Then there was the day she neglected to close the gate after feeding the cows. They had walked right out of the barn and into the neighbor's pasture, two of them taking time to snack on the Mullet's daisies. That had happened only two weeks ago.

However, that was in the past. She was seventeen, almost eighteen now. Time for her to grow up, to be responsible and take life more seriously, like the rest of her family. Including Tobias, now that he was married. Her oldest brother had always been at least a little similar to her, slightly more carefree than her solemn-minded siblings. But since his marriage to Rachel, he had left some of that waywardness behind. If Tobias could do it, so could Elisabeth. She would hold down this job and excel at it. She would show them. Most of all, she would prove it to herself.

Aaron already had the forge going and was getting his materials out to work on a wrought iron sconce when Elisabeth rushed through the door ten minutes late for her first day at work. Gabe hadn't arrived at the shop either, which was surprising, considering he was always punctual. Gabe owned the business, so he could show up anytime he wanted to. Elisabeth, however, was a different story, especially since she had barely started the job.

"I know I'm late!" She sounded breathless, and her cheeks were flushed. "I'm sorry. I promise it won't happen again." Her gaze traveled around the shop. "Where's Gabe?"

"He's running late too."

Her expression relaxed a bit. "Thank goodness."

"But normally he's here. Be sure you're on time Friday. Gabe doesn't abide tardiness. He's a fair boss, but he has high expectations."

"*Danki* for the warning." She looked up at him, her blue eyes filled with pleading. "You're not going to tell him, are you? Because I really don't want to get fired on my first day."

Seeing as he was the last person to point out someone else's mistake, he said, "*Nee*. I won't say a word."

She let out a sigh. "*Danki, danki.* You've saved me again." She held up a white plate covered in plastic wrap. "I'm glad I brought extra cookies. Actually, that's why I was late. I forgot them at home and had to turn back." She held the plate out to him. "Want one?"

He glanced at the cookies. "Later."

"Okay, take one or three whenever you want. Where should I put my things?"

She spoke so fast he could barely keep up with her, and she'd already walked past him, heading to the back of the shop. He quickly followed.

"I'm assuming the office is in here?" she asked, standing in front of an oak door with a small, square window cut into it. But she didn't wait for him to answer; she walked right in. "Oh my. Gabe was right, this place is a mess."

Aaron glanced around the office, thinking it wasn't too bad, despite the crooked stacks of papers littering the desk and the dust on top of the filing cabinets. But he had to admit she was right; it did need some tidying up. He dusted off one of the three wooden pegs hanging on the wall to the left of the doorway. Probably a good cleaning wouldn't hurt either. "You can hang your stuff here."

Then he watched her remove her black bonnet, revealing a white *kapp* underneath that topped her pale blonde hair. He took the bonnet from her and hung it on the peg.

"Here's the desk," he said, feeling dumb for pointing out the only other piece of furniture in the room besides the chair and a short stack of filing cabinets. "The account books are in this filing cabinet, and the cash box is in the bottom drawer. I'm sure Gabe has a key for you."

She clasped her hands together, looking eager to get started. "What's that system you and Gabe told me about?"

"Oh, that would be this." He pulled out the top drawer of the filing cabinet, which was filled with Ziploc bags that held receipts, purchase orders, and other paperwork. "There's a bag for everything," he said, pulling one out. "Let see, this one holds receipts from, um, three years ago."

She walked over and peered into the cabinet, frowning. "How do you know where anything is?"

"It's written on the bag." He showed her the words written in faded marker on the label. He could barely make out the print, but it was there. "See?"

Elisabeth squinted. "Oh, *ya*, now I can. For a minute there I thought I might need glasses. Where did you say the file folders are?"

"I didn't." He glanced around for a few moments. "I know we got a box of them here somewhere. Just can't recall where I put them. Oh, wait." He crouched down underneath the desk, then retrieved a brand-new box of folders. He blew on the top of the box, sending more dust flying. She really did have her work cut out for her. "Here you *geh*."

She accepted the box from him, then set it on top of one of the leaning stacks of papers. "Are all the cabinets filled with baggies?"

Aaron nodded. "The desk drawers too. I've also got a couple boxes of papers over there." He pointed into the far corner of the office. "Those date back years. Seems Gabe and John didn't have a much better system than I did."

"It's going to take me forever to sort through all this. Not that I'm complaining. I don't mind this one bit." She tapped her finger on her bottom lip. "I just need to figure out where to start."

He watched her as she continued tapping, noticing for the first time how delicate her hands were. She wore a light green dress, which complemented her fair skin. During his teen years he had thought Amish clothing to be drab and frumpy, especially the Amish dresses. When he had gone through his *rumspringa*, he had spent time with plenty of girls who had dressed far less modestly and had no problems wearing short skirts and baring tops that showed a lot of skin. As a fifteen- and sixteen-year-old, he had enjoyed the view. But now that he was older and had joined the church, he had a new appreciation for the modest dress of Amish women. Their clothing left everything to the imagination, which he found far more appealing.

Not that he'd ever had such thoughts about Elisabeth. He hadn't paid much attention to her growing up. They were a couple of years apart and, of course, had run around with different people. Besides, she was so innocent, sheltered by her family, something she didn't seem to mind. He, on the other hand, was far from pure. They had little in common, other than being related to Tobias and Rachel.

Gabe walked in the office, breaking into Aaron's thoughts. "Sorry I'm late. Moriah and Ester aren't feeling well, so I was up most of the night with the *boppli*." He put his hands on his hips and did a quick scan of the small space. "I see Aaron has already showed you everything."

Elisabeth nodded. "I promise I'll get the place in tip-top shape."

With a chuckle Gabe said, "I know you will. That's why I hired you." He turned to Aaron. "Lukas stopped by last night. He had an order for six sconces from Anna Esh. She and her *mudder* took over that little shop, Trinkets and Treasures, and she wants to sell some of them in her store. I thought it was a *gut* idea."

Aaron nodded. "We better get started." He looked at Elisabeth, who held a baggie full of yellow, white, and pink papers. "Any other questions?"

She shook her head and smiled. "I've got it under control."

But just as Aaron turned away, he saw her expression change from confident to doubtful. Which surprised him, since Elisabeth always seemed to be sure of herself, except for the other day when she babysat Velda and Ester.

Gabe had already left the room, and Aaron had intended to follow right behind him. Instead he paused. "Elisabeth?"

She turned to him, her bright smile back in place. "*Ya?*"

"If you need anything, let me know. Okay?"

"That's nice of you, Aaron, but I'll be fine. I can do this."

As he left the office he thought he heard her whisper the same words again.

Chapter 4

"*T*here. Toilet's fixed." Lukas stood up in Esh's Amish Goods' small bathroom and put his wrench back in the tool belt on the floor. He turned to Anna, who was standing in the doorway. "You're lucky; it was a slow leak. I thought you might have to replace the subfloor, but it's fine. You'll still need some new flooring in here, though."

Anna nodded, stifling a sigh. Another expense she hadn't budgeted for. It was October, and Esh's Amish Goods was open for business. Since she and her mother had bought the store, her bills had mounted and her savings had dwindled. Business hadn't been as steady as she'd expected, or needed, it to be. She also hadn't received a lot of help from her mother, who still had her hands full with Zeb. Just the other day he'd been caught up on the ladder again, trying to fix the broken latch on one of the windows, and this morning he had insisted on mucking out Marge's stable. He refused to part with the old cow, even though she no longer gave milk and was too tough to eat. She was more like a pet than anything else, but a pet that required work, and she and her mother were both afraid he would overdo it and hurt himself again.

So while her mother was busy keeping Zeb out of trouble, Anna had spent almost every waking moment at the store, save for Sundays. Hopefully someday she could hire someone to help her out, but right now she couldn't afford it.

She looked at Lukas, trying not to stare at the dimple that deepened on his right cheek when he smiled. She also tried not to notice his broad shoulders. Or the warmth in his eyes when their gazes met, which had been frequently, since he'd volunteered to help with more repairs in the shop. Over the past few months he had spent several evenings and every Saturday afternoon fixing and replacing almost everything in the store. She wondered where he got the energy to do the labor in addition to his carpentry job. More importantly, why he would even bother? But she was grateful he did. If he hadn't, her business would have gone under before opening day.

"Do you know what kind of floor you want?"

She looked at Lukas. "Something inexpensive." She eyed the old yellowed linoleum, which was stained and buckling in a couple of places.

"I have a friend who puts in flooring." Lukas stepped out of the bathroom and faced her. "I'll talk to him and see if he can give you a discount."

"Lukas, I appreciate it but—"

"Let me guess. You'd rather pay full price."

She couldn't help but laugh. "*Nee*, I'd rather not." Her mirth faded. "You've done so much already."

Tipping back his hat, he said, "Glad to do it."

"And I'm grateful, I really am. But I'm afraid I'm taking advantage of you."

"I'm the one who should decide that, don't you think? And I've decided you're not taking advantage. So let me talk to Nathan and see what I can do about the flooring."

"But I haven't paid you for replacing the door yet."

He gazed at her for a moment, as if he were deep in thought. "Tell you what, there's a singing Sunday night at my house. Say you'll attend and we'll call it even."

His invitation caught her off guard. She hadn't been to a singing in years, mostly because Daniel had never enjoyed them. She loved to sing, and for a brief moment she considered saying yes. But she couldn't. "I'm sorry," she said, turning away from him and facing her desk. "I can't come."

"Why not?"

Was that disappointment she heard in his voice? She turned around and saw that his grin had faded, his hazel eyes peering at her intensely. She looked away. "I'll be busy with the store."

"On a Sunday?" He shoved his hands in his pockets. "You'll have to come up with a better excuse."

"Then how about this. I'm too old to go to singings."

His brow lifted. "Too old? You're kidding, right?"

She tilted up her chin. "*Nee*, I'm not. I haven't been to a singing in a long time."

"All the more reason to come. You'll have a great time. My sister Elisabeth will be there. I know you two will get along great. She'll probably talk your ear off, though, so consider yourself warned. My *mudder* is also making her famous Ho Ho cake. You haven't lived until you've tasted it."

"Lukas, I'm not going." Why couldn't he just take no for an answer? She went to her desk and pulled out her checkbook. "How much do I owe you for fixing the door and the bathroom?"

He came up behind her. "Anna."

Unable to resist his gentle tone, she faced him.

"How about you tell me the real reason you don't want to *geh*."

"I already did."

"You gave me an excuse, not the truth."

She placed her hands behind her on the desk and leaned back. "Why is it so important that I go?"

"I've never been one to tiptoe around things, Anna. I'm straightforward, and what you see is what you get. You've probably figured that out by now."

She nodded, transfixed by the way his intense expression pinned her in place.

"While I haven't minded at all helping you out, I'll admit I had other reasons." He stepped toward her. "I wanted to get to know you better. And now that I've started doing that, I don't want to stop."

She felt her pulse quicken. Even when she and Daniel had decided to get married, he had never been so open with his thoughts or feelings. She took a moment to collect her thoughts and try to calm down her heart rate. Finally, she spoke. "I appreciate that, Lukas. It's, um, nice of you to say."

He frowned. "That wasn't the reaction I was looking for."

She took a deep breath. "I'm sorry. But . . ."

"But what?"

"There are things you don't know about me that might change your mind. Like my age, for one thing."

His brows knitted together. "What does that have to do with anything?"

"You're young—eighteen or nineteen, right?"

"Wrong. Almost twenty."

"Still young. How old do you think I am?"

"I don't care."

"I do. I'm nearly twenty-five."

He let out a low whistle. "Wow. Practically a senior citizen."

"I'm serious, Lukas."

"I am too. If you think it matters to me that you're five years older, you're wrong."

"Then here's something that will matter to you. I used to be engaged."

Surprise registered on his face, but he barely paused. "Tell me about him."

"What?"

"Tell me about the *dummkopf* that was foolish enough to let you get away. Although I might have to find him and thank him."

"Lukas, this isn't a joke."

"I'm not laughing." His expression remained somber. "Tell me what happened."

The compassion in his voice and expression nearly brought her to tears. She was surprised she had any left; she'd shed so many after Daniel broke up with her. She looked away. "I don't know." How it pained her to say the words out loud, to admit that she had no idea why her fiancé had ended their engagement less than a week before the wedding.

"He broke his vow to you?"

She hesitated, then nodded before standing

up. "He came to see me a few days before the wedding. I thought everything was all right between us. We'd been together for a long time, almost four years. I was happy, and I thought he was too. But he said he couldn't marry me." Her throat caught. The pain of his last words still lingered.

"He said it was him, not me. That he wasn't ready for marriage. Then he wished me the best and left." She looked at Lukas. "He moved to another district shortly after. A few months later I heard he married someone from that church."

"Anna, I'm sorry."

Lifting her chin, she said, "So now you understand why I can't *geh* to the singing."

Lukas shook his head. "*Nee*. What I understand is that you're scared of getting hurt again. And after what that jerk did, I don't blame you."

"He's not a jerk."

"Sounds like one to me. I'm surprised you're defending him."

She crossed her arms over her chest. "We're supposed to forgive, aren't we?"

"*Ya*." His tone softened. "We are. I don't mean to sound harsh, but the thought of someone hurting you . . . you don't deserve that, Anna."

She didn't like the way her emotions were responding to him. She stepped to the side. "It's late. We should both be getting home. Just let me know how much I owe you so I can write you a check."

Lukas didn't say anything. Instead he turned and retrieved his tool belt from the bathroom. He gave her a long look, then walked out of the office.

Surprised, she followed him. "Lukas, wait."

He turned around, his expression as serious as she'd ever seen it. "I won't take your money, Anna."

"But—"

"I don't know how it is in Maryland, but here we help each other."

"We did the same."

"Then there's nothing more to discuss. Unless you've changed your mind about Sunday."

She hesitated for a moment. A part of her wanted to say yes, to go to the singing with Lukas and not worry about her growing feelings for him. But Daniel's betrayal kept popping into her thoughts, a stark reminder of what could happen if she acknowledged her feelings. "*Nee.* I haven't."

Disappointment colored his features. "Then there's nothing more to say."

She threaded her fingers together behind her back. "I guess not."

Without another word he left.

Anna went to the door and watched him get in the buggy. Dusk had already descended, cloaking the sky in gray and purple light. As his buggy pulled away, she put her hand on the door, feeling the coolness of the glass against her palm. Several dead leaves skittered across the parking lot, pushed along by the fall breeze. She leaned her forehead on the door, unable to shake the feeling she'd just made a huge mistake.

As she turned to go inside, a dull ache suddenly spread across her lower abdomen. She winced. Since the age of sixteen she'd experienced similar pain, but it had gotten worse over the past few months during her monthly cycle. Most times she could ignore it, but lately that had become more difficult. She'd always hoped it would go away as she grew older, but instead the pain had steadily increased.

Anna went to her office and sat down at her desk. She opened the side drawer, pulled out her purse, and searched for a bottle of pain reliever. She shook out two pills in her palm, then took them with a sip of water she always had nearby. Usually after thirty minutes the pain would subside. It was something she had come to expect a few days every month.

Ignoring the ache, she began to straighten up her desk before she went home. She picked up the checkbook, thinking of Lukas again. Even though she had turned him down, he still hadn't wanted her money. Mentally she calculated how much he'd saved her business over the course of two months. Just the labor alone was enough for her to say a prayer of thanks for his generosity.

And to make her feel guilty.

She exhaled. For everything he'd done for her and Esh's Amish Goods, he'd asked so little in return. The least she could do was show up at the singing. Besides, it might be fun. She'd been so focused on her work and family since moving to Middlefield, she really hadn't had a chance to get to know people in the community, especially those close to her age. And if she went to the singing, she wouldn't be obligated to Lukas anymore. Well, not completely. She still planned to pay him for his work. She'd force him to take a check if she had to.

Twenty minutes and a tidy office later, she felt much better. The pain reliever had kicked in, and she felt good about her decision to go to the Bylers' Sunday evening, even though the thought of seeing Lukas there made her palms grow damp. If only she'd met him before Daniel. Everything would be different. But she hadn't, and she believed that God had a plan for her life, and her experience with Daniel happened for a reason. She had to protect her heart. Somehow she'd have to make him understand.

"Who tied your tail into a knot?"

Lukas looked at his sister Elisabeth with a puzzled expression then turned over one of the chairs in the kitchen. It was wobbly, and he needed to fix it before people started showing up for the singing. The table, handcrafted by their father years ago, took up a large part of the room but had comfortably seated their family of eight for years. "What are you talking about?"

"You're so crabby today." She scraped a large dollop of mayonnaise from the jar and plopped it on top of a huge bowl of chicken salad.

"Elisabeth, I've barely been around you today." They had both been busy getting ready for company. Since it was Sunday they weren't doing actual work but finishing up minor details. Elisabeth had decided at the last minute the chicken salad needed "a little something extra," but other than that they were prepared for their guests, who would start arriving any minute.

"I know I haven't seen you much, but when I have you've been scowling. You're face will freeze like that if you're not careful."

"You don't still believe that old wives' tale, do you?"

"*Nee.* But you never know, you could be the first." She looked at him and grinned. "Then you'll only be half as *gutguckich* as all the *maed* think you are."

Lukas didn't answer her. He didn't care what other girls thought of him. He only cared about one. And that one didn't want to have anything to do with him, only his repair skills.

He frowned. That wasn't entirely true. But that didn't help stem the bitter disappointment he still felt from her rejection the other day.

70

"See, there you go again." Elisabeth started stirring the salad, cradling the bowl against her chest as she faced him. "You haven't been sucking on lemons, have you?"

"Drop it, Elisabeth." He checked the bottom of each chair leg then discovered the problem. He pulled out his pocket knife and started scraping the wood.

"This wouldn't have anything to do with Anna Esh, would it?"

"Why would you think that?"

"Oh, I don't know," Elisabeth said in a singsong voice. "Maybe because you're with her almost as much as you're here at home?"

"I'm not *with* her; I'm doing work at the store."

"And at her house."

"So?" He set the chair down and pushed it back and forth, checking the stability. It still wasn't even, so he flipped it back over and tried again.

"A *mann* wouldn't work so hard for a *maedel* unless he was sweet on her."

"Or unless he knew she didn't have any help." His frown deepened. His sister could be like a dog with a bone sometimes. She didn't know when to let something go. "It's none of your business anyway."

"You're my *bruder* and I care about you."

"I'd believe you, except I know the truth." He checked the chair again, glad to see he'd fixed it this time. He stood up and looked at Elisabeth. "You're being nosy."

71

She continued stirring the chicken salad with a long-handled wooden spoon. "I'm hurt you would accuse me of such a thing."

"Even if it's the truth?"

She gave him a look then glanced at the bowl. "Oh, *nee*! I put too much mayo in this!"

"You should have left it alone."

"It's all soupy." She set the bowl on the counter then went to the pantry and threw open the door.

"Put some more chicken in it."

"I don't have any more chicken. I used it all up yesterday." She put her finger to her lips as she scanned the ingredients in front of her, her brows knitting into a line. "You think potato flakes would work?"

"Potatoes in chicken salad?" His stomach lurched at the thought.

"I'm trying to improvise!" Her hand went to her forehead. "Why did I think I could improve on *Mami's* cooking?"

Lukas walked over and peered inside the bowl. Chunks of chicken and sliced celery seemed to float in a sea of mayonnaise. While he had no problem fixing a toilet or building cabinets, he didn't cook, and he had no idea how to salvage the salad.

Elisabeth shut the door. "I'll have to ask her what to do. I should have just left it alone."

"Elisabeth, it's not that bad. It's just chicken salad."

"That's the point. I screwed up something so simple. Again."

Lukas didn't know what she was talking about, but before he could ask her, she flew out of the room in search of their mother. He looked around the kitchen at several dishes and desserts his mother and sisters had made yesterday. Their guests would also bring food, so there would be a lot to go around and probably plenty to spare. He didn't know what she was getting so upset about, but at least she'd stopped talking about Anna. Now if only he could stop thinking about her.

He spied his mother's Ho Ho cake on the counter, pushed far in the corner. He'd recognize that familiar foil-covered pan anywhere. After taking a quick glance around the room, he snuck over to the pan and lifted the corner. Just one little taste; no one would know. Grabbing a fork out of a nearby drawer, he moved in for a bite when he heard the back door slam. Quickly he ditched the fork and covered the cake before turning around.

"Hi."

He turned around, stunned to see Anna standing in his parents' kitchen. The word *hello* caught in his throat.

"I hope I came in the right way. I wasn't sure."

Finally he found his voice. "It doesn't matter. We use both the front and back."

"*Gut.*"

He stood still for a moment, taking in the fact

that she had shown up. She looked lovely, as usual, with added rosiness to her cheeks from the chilly weather outside. Then he noticed her holding a covered casserole dish. "Here," he said, going to her. "Let me take this."

"*Danki.*"

While he set the dish down on the kitchen table, he said, "I can take your bonnet and shawl too."

She unpinned the black shawl around her shoulders, then removed her bonnet. He watched her reach up to touch her white *kapp* for a moment. What had made her change her mind?

He hurried to the mudroom just outside the kitchen and hung up her bonnet and shawl on one of the pegs nailed to the rack on the wall, afraid if he took too much time she might leave. When he walked back into the kitchen, he saw her and Elisabeth standing near the counter, talking, his sister still upset.

"Do you know how to fix chicken salad?" Elisabeth asked.

Anna nodded. "I've made it many times. My *Onkel* Zeb loves it. I think he'd eat it for all three meals if he could."

"*Nee*, I'm not talking about making it. I mean *fixing* it." She held up the bowl and showed Anna. "It's ruined."

Anna peered into the bowl. "It doesn't look too bad. Why don't you use it as dip?"

"Chicken salad dip?"

"Sure. Do you have some crackers?"

Elisabeth's features relaxed. "*Ya*, some of those round buttery ones." She went to the pantry and pulled out a sleeve of crackers. "I'll put some of the salad in a small bowl, then the crackers on a plate." She smiled at Anna. "What a great idea."

Lukas smiled and walked up to the women. "Need someone to do a taste test?"

"You can wait." Elisabeth retrieved a plate from the cabinet. "Like everyone else." She set the plate on the counter and picked up the crackers.

"Elisabeth!" Their mother's voice sounded from the living room. "I need your help for a minute."

She handed the crackers to Anna. "Would you mind setting these out?"

Anna nodded. "I'd be happy to."

"*Danki*." As she left the kitchen she called out over her shoulder, "Don't let Lukas get into the Ho Ho cake. He's already tried that once today."

"How did you know?" Lukas yelled back.

Elisabeth poked her head back into the kitchen. "You've been sneaking bites from Ho Ho cakes since you were a *kinn*. Everyone knows that." Then she disappeared.

Anna opened the wax paper tube of crackers and began placing them on the plain white plate.

"So now you know one of my deep dark secrets. I can never resist a Ho Ho cake."

She gave him a half smile but didn't say anything. Lukas watched her for a moment. "I'm glad you came."

She paused briefly, then continued putting out the crackers, arranging them in concentric circles.

He moved opposite her and leaned his hip against the counter. "What made you change your mind?"

"You."

A surge of happiness shot through him. He grinned.

"I wanted to square things between us. I have a check in my purse to give you before I leave."

His grin faded. That wasn't what he'd wanted to hear. "Anna, I won't take your money."

She put the last cracker on the plate and faced him. "I figured the labor costs based on what is typically charged for the jobs you performed, so I think you'll agree it's a fair amount."

Her intelligence was impressive and one of the many things he liked about her. Right now it was also irritating. "You're not listening to me. I didn't help you out for the money."

"I understand that, Lukas. And I know that it's our way to give our time and talents to others. You've been generous to me with both." She glanced away for a moment before looking back at him. "But I don't need your help anymore. I want to make sure I've covered my obligations."

Lukas shook his head. She was the most stubborn woman he'd ever met. "You're not obligated to me, Anna. I don't know what else I can say to make you understand that."

"And I don't know why you won't accept that this is how it is."

"Is it?" He stepped toward her, closing the distance between them. She averted her gaze. "Anna, be honest with me. If you and that other *mann*—"

"Daniel. His name was Daniel."

"Daniel," he said, his tone tinged with derision, resenting the man that had hurt her so deeply. "If Daniel wasn't between us, would you feel the same way?"

She frowned. "Daniel's not between us. He's married and living in Maryland. He's not in my life anymore."

"Are you sure? Because it feels that way. And you haven't answered my question. Is Daniel the only thing keeping us apart?"

"There's our age difference."

"That doesn't wash with me. Five years is nothing."

"You say that now, but what about when I'm fifty and you're forty-five?"

"Still doesn't matter. I wouldn't care if you were ten years older, Anna. I would still like you. I would still want to help you and your *familye*. And I would still want to court you."

She crumpled the empty cracker sleeve in her hand.

"All I'm asking for is a chance."

"I . . . I can't. Not now."

At least she hadn't shut him down completely, as she had in the past. "What about friendship? Can we at least agree to be friends?" At the doubt on her face he said, "I promise I won't push you for anything else."

She looked him in the eye. "I would like to be friends."

"Then friends it is." He took a step back from her. She had given him a thin cord of hope to cling to, and he wasn't about to let go.

He heard voices coming from the living room. "Looks like more people are here."

"*Gut.* I'm looking forward to meeting them."

"Then as your new friend, I would be happy to introduce you."

At her smile, his hope grew stronger. He'd have to be satisfied with what she could give him, although it wouldn't be easy. But he wouldn't abandon asking the Lord to change her heart.

Chapter 5

*E*lisabeth stood inside the office and peered out of the door's small window and into the blacksmith shop. She could still hear the sharp clanging of the hammer hitting the anvil as Aaron pounded on a long strip of metal. The process of transforming a rod of iron into something useful fascinated her.

Her first weeks on the job had gone smoothly, for the most part. While her fears of making a monumental mistake that would cost her job were unfounded, she had made a few minor errors, the latest one last week. She'd gotten delivery dates confused for two Yankee customers who both ordered the same number of horseshoes for their respective farms. But she'd corrected her slip-up before Gabe found out.

She took another bite of her green apple and continued to observe Aaron, his back to her as he pounded the metal into shape. Gabe had left earlier that morning to help one of his neighbors fix a broken plow. It was turning out to be a slow and boring day, which was unusual for a Saturday.

Aaron set the hammer down and turned to the side, his body angled away from the forge and more toward her. He slipped off one of his leather gloves and wiped his forehead with the back of his hand, then picked up a glass of water on a table nearby.

Dying to talk to someone, Elisabeth saw the opportunity. She opened the door and walked into the shop, breathing in the familiar scent of burning charcoal and piping hot iron. "Ready for lunch?"

He turned to her, his face streaked with sweat and smudged with charcoal. He glanced up at the battery-operated clock on the wall. "It's not even ten thirty."

"Oh." She hadn't thought to check the time. "Then maybe you'd like to take a break. I have an extra apple in my lunch bag." She held up her half-eaten apple.

"I'll wait for lunch." He took a long swig of water, then set it back down. He started to turn back to the forge but paused. "Did you need something?"

"*Nee*." She ran her finger along the edge of the table, grimacing when she saw the grime on her finger. She put her hand behind her back. "Just hanging out."

"Finished with your work?"

"Um, *ya*."

He faced her. "Maybe you should *geh* home then."

"But what if we get a customer? Gabe's not here and you're busy at the forge."

"I can handle it. I've worked alone before."

She frowned. "That can't be much fun."

"Actually, I prefer it."

His words didn't surprise her. Aaron personified the word *loner*. Even after working with him several days a week over the last few weeks, she didn't know him any better than before. Not that she hadn't tried. She'd invited him to eat lunch with her more than once, but he never took her up on her offer. She had asked him to come to the singing at her house, but he never showed up.

At least Lukas' friend Anna had come and saved her from screwing up the chicken salad. Turned out everyone liked it as a dip, and one of her friends asked her for the recipe. Elisabeth had liked Anna immediately and admired her for having her own business. She understood why Lukas was sweet on her, even though he had insisted to her later that night they were just friends.

What she didn't understand was Aaron's reluctance to visit with her and her friends, or any young people at all. Just last Sunday it had been her family's turn to host church, and while Aaron had shown up for the service, he didn't stay for the fellowship afterward. She'd even sought him out right after church ended, but he had dashed out the door before she could catch up with him.

"Why?" she asked, the word out of her mouth before she could stop it.

"Why what?"

She hadn't meant to voice her question out loud, but now that she'd blown it she might as well find out the answer. "Why do you prefer to be alone?"

"I just do." He spun around and slid his glove on his hand.

She walked around to the side of the forge. Heat radiated from it, warming her skin. "That doesn't make any sense."

"Does to me." He didn't look at her, he merely picked up the hammer and started pounding but then stopped and put the end of the rod into the fire.

"No one likes to be alone all the time."

"I'm not." He cast a sideways glance. "You're here."

"I mean away from work. What about friends?"

He yanked the rod out of the fire and plunked it down on the anvil. "Elisabeth, you must be really bored." Sparks flew as he slammed the hammer down on the rod.

"But—ow!" A spark landed on her cheek and she jumped back from the forge.

Aaron dropped the hammer and went to her. "Are you okay?"

"I'm fine." But the burning sensation sharpened. She put her hand on her cheek.

"Let me see." He whipped off his gloves and bent down slightly to peer at her face.

She removed her hand, the skin on her cheek still burning. "Does it look bad?"

"You have a red mark right here." His finger brushed against her cheek. Then he yanked away his hand and stepped back from her. "Sorry."

She wasn't sure exactly what he was sorry for —accidentally burning her cheek or touching it. For one split moment she was sorry for neither.

Wait a minute. This was Aaron. Her coworker. A man she barely knew anything about. Why would a split-second gesture done merely out of concern affect her at all? Aaron was right;

she had to be bored out of her mind for her imagination to run crazy like that.

"Some ice will cool the burn." He went back to the forge, then glanced at her, not picking up the hammer until she moved away.

"It's already feeling better." She took a few more steps back. "Sorry. I shouldn't have been so close."

Aaron didn't say anything. Instead he started pounding. A bead of sweat ran down his face.

Dismissed, she spun around and headed back to the office. Pulling a small mirror out of the top drawer of her desk, she checked her face. The sting had already diminished, and the red welt was hardly noticeable. She was grateful the burn hadn't been worse.

Elisabeth turned around and leaned her backside against the desk. She should just go home like he suggested. Better than being at loose ends here and getting in the way. Gabe would fire her for sure if she caused any trouble. He wasn't a harsh man at all, quite the opposite. In fact, after his twin brother had died a few months before Velda was born, Gabe had stood by Moriah's side. Eventually, Gabe and Moriah had married, and they were one of the happiest couples Elisabeth knew. But he had a business to run, and she didn't want to do anything to jeopardize that. She enjoyed her job and wanted to keep it.

She put her black bonnet on over her *kapp*,

pinned her shawl around her neck, then grabbed her lunch bag and purse. She did have a few chores to finish up at home before getting together with some of her friends later on that night, so taking off early wasn't a bad suggestion.

As she left the office, she had an idea. On her way out the door she walked past Aaron, making sure she steered clear of the forge. When she called his name, he answered her but didn't look up.

"A bunch of my friends are getting together tonight at the Troyers' over on Bundysburg Road. They've got a big barn and we're setting up a corn toss tournament. You should join us."

"I'm busy."

"Doing what?" She raised her voice to be heard above the noise at the forge.

He gave her a quick look, his blue eyes impassive. "Stuff."

"Okay, what kind of stuff?"

"Personal stuff, all right?" Impatience entered his tone.

"You don't have to get all snippy about it. I'm just trying to be nice."

He paused and took a deep breath. "Sorry. *Danki* for the invite, but I can't make it."

"How about tomorrow night, then? There's a singing—"

"Elisabeth, I'm not interested." He looked back down at the anvil and started working again.

Her feelings pricked, she left the shop and went to her buggy. She thought about stopping in the house to talk to Moriah, but she wasn't in the mood. Instead her thoughts were on Aaron. Maybe he did have his own group of friends he hung around with that she didn't know about. That was highly possible, as she didn't know *everything* that went on in their community.

Then a thought occurred to her. What if he had started using drugs again?

No, that wasn't possible. She'd been there when Aaron had joined the church. The day he gave that commitment to the Lord in front of everyone he'd promised to put worldly things behind him. Since then, as far as she could tell, he had done exactly that. Besides, Gabe would have noticed if Aaron had been involved in drugs again.

Although she fought to dismiss her suspicions, they didn't go completely away. She wanted to think the best of him, and other than his stand-offish demeanor, he gave her no reason not to.

Judge not, that ye be not judged . . .

The scripture popped into her brain, a reminder that she had no business speculating such things about Aaron. She certainly wouldn't want her friends or anyone else judging her actions or thinking awful things about her without basis.

"Sorry, Lord," she said out loud, over the sound of cars passing by her as she steered the buggy down the road. Her father had put the winter curtain over the front of the buggy to keep out some of the cold, but she could still see puffs of her breath suspended in the air as she spoke. "You're right, I should know better."

Yet even though she put a halt to her suspicions about Aaron, she couldn't get her mind off him completely.

"Where's Elisabeth?" Gabe asked as he entered the shop a short time later. "Her buggy's not parked in the driveway."

"She left." Aaron tossed aside the piece of iron he'd been working on all morning. Three hours wasted, because he'd ruined the end by pounding it too thin. He could use it for something else later, but it was useless as a spindle for the decorative fencing he needed for an order due by Christmas.

Gabe picked up the rod and inspected the end. "What happened?"

"Misjudged the thickness." Aaron hated to admit the mistake, which shouldn't have happened considering his experience. Since being given the chance to work for the Millers almost two years ago, he had wanted to prove his worth, first as an employee and then as a blacksmith. Gabe had taken a chance by hiring an ex-drug dealer with a jail record, and Aaron didn't ever want him to regret that decision.

"Happens to the best of us." Gabe set the piece

down on the nearby counter. "Why did Elisabeth leave? I thought she was staying until three."

"Slow day. We haven't had a single customer. She said she finished her work, so I told her to *geh* home." Never had he been so relieved as when she left. Besides distracting him from his work, she'd been nosy. And relentless, especially about inviting him to join her and her friends, people he didn't even know. While he was glad she'd taken over the tedious office operations of the business, he hadn't expected her to be so friendly. That was something he wasn't used to, not since he'd turned his back on the Yankee world and joined the church.

Not to say the Amish were unfriendly. That wasn't the case at all. But folks made it easy for him to keep his distance. Most men his age were like him, busy with work. Or, unlike him, busy courting and thinking about marriage. He'd never been one to hang out with the Amish crowd at singings and frolics as a teen. Those activities were what the "good" Amish kids did, the ones who joined the church early on and married young, who stayed in the church and raised families. He didn't fit in with them then, and he wouldn't fit in with them now.

So Elisabeth's efforts to bring him into her fold of friends were pointless. Someday she'd get the message. He hoped.

But that wasn't what bothered him the most.

Not even close. What took his thoughts away from his work for the rest of the morning after she left was when he'd touched her cheek. He'd done it out of concern that the burning spark might have flown in her eye. Yet for the briefest of moments he'd felt a spark within him as his gaze met hers. He'd spent the next couple hours trying to ignore his reaction, but judging from the messed up iron rod, he'd failed.

No one could deny Elisabeth Byler was a pretty woman, something he'd noticed more than once before today. But just because he appreciated her looks didn't mean he was attracted to her. Even if he was, he wouldn't let her know. Elisabeth was destined to marry a good Amish man, one who'd never strayed into the devil's playground, much less wallowed in it like Aaron had.

So he chalked his reaction up to loneliness. He'd had a steady girlfriend for several months before he'd been arrested, and he'd missed Kacey something fierce while he'd been in jail. But he had to make a choice, and he'd chosen the safety of the Amish community, a decision he didn't regret. Over time his feelings for Kacey disappeared but not his desire for companionship. But what Amish woman would want an ex-con for a husband?

Definitely not Elisabeth Byler.

"Aaron?"

Spinning around, he looked at Gabe, who had

taken off his coat and already hung it up in the back. "*Ya?*"

"You all right? You seem in deep thought."

"I'm fine. Just thinking about not making another mistake."

Gabe nodded and pulled on his leather gloves, preparing for work. As the day progressed, Aaron forced himself not to think about Elisabeth or the past. Yet try as he might, he couldn't block the loneliness from his mind or his heart.

"What a *wunderbaar* day!" Edna pulled back the curtains in the window in the front room of *Onkel* Zeb's house. Bright November sunlight streamed inside. "Not a cloud in the sky or a flake of snow on the ground." She turned around and looked at Anna seated on the couch. "A great day to be outside in the fresh air, even if it is a little chilly."

"Better than staying cooped up inside." Zeb walked inside the room, scratching the side of his belly. He hitched up his trousers. "When's that Byler *bu* getting here?"

"He'll be here when he gets here." Edna turned around and faced Zeb. "Don't be so impatient."

"Only if you'll stop being so bossy."

Anna rolled her eyes, happy that she would be leaving for work soon so she wouldn't have to listen to her mother and uncle's ceaseless bickering. She left them arguing in the living room and went into the kitchen to pack her lunch. As she washed her hands in the sink, she looked out the window to see Lukas turning in to the driveway.

A small tickle formed in her belly, as it had lately every time she saw Lukas. Since the singing at his house nearly a month ago, he had been true to his word, and they had developed a natural, enjoyable friendship. He stopped by work at the end of the day a couple times a week to take her home, since she and her mother took turns using the buggy. Today he had taken a day off work to help her uncle fix several broken slats in the barn. How could she not love his selfless generosity?

She froze. *Love.* Had that word really popped into her mind? It had, but certainly not in a romantic context. Even though she thought about Lukas a lot when they weren't together, it didn't mean she'd changed her mind about their friendship. The fact that her time at work seemed to crawl by on the days he picked her up wasn't a sign that she felt any different toward him than she always did.

Picking up the towel by the sink, she dried her hands and kept looking out the window, watching as he parked the buggy and jumped out. His dark blue coat was buttoned up halfway, revealing a light blue shirt underneath. He adjusted his yellow straw hat before reaching in the back of the buggy for his tool belt. Although it had to be heavy, he slung it over his shoulder like it weighed next to nothing.

She checked the clock on the kitchen wall. If she didn't leave within the next few minutes, she would be late for work, which meant the store wouldn't open on time. But when she heard the back door open she didn't move, knowing he would appear in the kitchen in a few seconds.

Just as she heard the thud of his shoes on the kitchen floor, a sudden pain stabbed her abdomen. She doubled over from the intensity of it.

"Anna?"

She could barely hear Lukas's voice through the haze of pain.

"Anna, what's wrong?"

A crash sounded in her ears, and Lukas was suddenly at her side. Then just as quickly as it hit, the agony subsided. Slowly she stood up, gazing into Lukas's worried face.

"I'm okay." She gripped the side of the sink and straightened. Only then did she notice how close he was standing to her, and that his hand was on her shoulder. Their eyes met.

"Are you sure?"

"*Ya.*" Then she realized she had another problem besides the way she was reacting to him. She couldn't tell him the source of her pain. Her monthly problems were something she couldn't even share with her mother, much less with Lukas. But how could she explain what just happened?

"You're not sick, are you?" He didn't remove his hand from her arm, something she was acutely aware of.

"*Nee*." Then she realized that would be a good enough explanation for him. "Well, maybe a little sick to my stomach."

"What on earth was that noise?" Edna came into the kitchen then halted. Her eyebrows flew up at the sight of Anna and Lukas so close together.

Lukas immediately jumped back. "Sorry, *Frau* Esh. I dropped my tool belt." He walked to the back entrance of the kitchen and picked it up. "Anna was telling me she's not feeling well."

"You're sick?" Edna went to her. "You do look pale. Why didn't you say anything?"

"I'm okay, really. Just a little nauseated." She chewed the inside of her lip, waiting to see if her mother believed the fib.

"Then you should stay home from work. The store will survive being closed one day."

"*Nee*, not on a Saturday." She turned to her mother. "I'm fine, really. I probably just need something to eat."

Edna frowned. "We had breakfast an hour ago. You're still hungry?"

Anna looked from her to Lukas, who still looked concerned. It amazed her how one little fib led to so many others. "*Ya*. I am. But I packed a big lunch, so I'll be okay." She rushed past Edna and grabbed her lunch and purse off of the kitchen table. "I'll be back in time for supper." She gave Lukas a quick glance, then dashed out the door before her mother asked any more questions.

Taking a deep breath of crisp November air, the tension started draining out of her. She hated telling lies, even small ones, especially to her mother. But she'd had no alternative. Ignoring her guilt she started to climb into the buggy.

"Anna, wait."

She paused as Lukas strode toward her. A familiar fluttery sensation went through her.

He came up to her, once again standing close. His hazel eyes met hers. "Let me drive you to work."

His kindness only intensified the fluttery feeling. "*Nee.* I can drive myself. I'm already feeling better." At least that part was true, as her pain had disappeared.

"Still, I'd like to take you. I can come by and pick you up after work. I wouldn't want you to be on the road if you got sick again."

"Lukas—"

"I'm not taking *nee* for an answer." He opened the door for her.

"What about the barn?"

"It can wait."

"Then what about *Onkel* Zeb? He's not nearly as patient, you know."

"Your *mudder* said she'd take care of him."

"So my *mami* told you to drive me?"

He shook his head, then took her lunch bag from her hand. "I told her I was driving you." He held out his hand. "You don't want to be late."

She looked at his hand, then slipped her hand in his. His fingers were rough and scarred from work, but she loved the feel of his palm against hers.

There was that word again. *Love.* Although standing next to him, enjoying his nearness and the way his eyes held hers, the thought of loving Lukas didn't seem as frightening as it used to. Instead it seemed a very real possibility.

"Anna." His voice was low and husky, sending a shiver through her body. Then he cleared his throat and released her hand. "I better get you to work."

Disappointment wound through her as she climbed in the buggy. They drove to Esh's Amish Goods in silence, and she wondered what he was thinking. She couldn't tell by looking at his impassive profile.

When they reached the store, there were already a couple of cars in the parking lot. She grabbed her lunch and purse and got out of the buggy.

"I'll pick you up at five," he called out to her.

She nodded, then paused, unable to tear her gaze away from him. "*Danki*, Lukas."

Finally he smiled. "My pleasure."

As she rushed to the shop to greet her waiting customers, she snuck another look at Lukas pulling away, knowing she would be counting the minutes until she could see him again.

Chapter 6

*E*lisabeth stood in the corner of the Mullets' large living room, taking in the blissful expression on her friend Carol's face as she gazed up at her new husband. Christian Weaver appeared equally happy as he bent down and whispered something in her ear. She laughed, and they both got up from their seats at the wedding table and started to mingle among the guests again.

A sigh escaped her lips. Christian and Carol were so much in love, everyone could see it. The irony of the marriage wasn't lost on her either. Carol had been smitten with Elisabeth's brother Tobias for a long time, and Rachel Detweiler and Christian had actually been engaged at one point. But when Tobias had come to his senses and told Rachel he loved her, she'd broken up with Christian. To his credit, Christian had taken the breakup well, and soon he and Carol had started seeing each other. Now both couples were happy and had remained good friends, with Tobias and Rachel at the wedding along with the rest of the family.

Elisabeth wondered if she'd ever have that kind of love. She wasn't in any hurry to get married, and she definitely wasn't ready to think about children, but she did hope that when she met the right man, he would look at her with the same expression her brother had for his wife, and Christian had for Carol.

She pulled her gaze away from the couple and scanned the room, sipping a cup of delicious hot apple cider. She'd been relieved from kitchen duty a short while ago and was now waiting to take her turn at one of the dining tables. Until then she was content to hang back and people-watch. Although she enjoyed visiting with all her friends and family, sometimes it was nice to stand back and be an observer.

Moments later she spied Aaron standing near the staircase, alone as usual. She wasn't just surprised that he had attended the wedding but that he'd stayed for the gathering afterward. She watched him shift from one foot to the other, tugging at the top of his collarless shirt. Her eyes widened a bit as she took in his crisp white shirt, black pants, and vest. She had seen him in those clothes on Sundays during church, but for some reason he looked especially nice today. He also looked as uncomfortable as a pig in pantyhose.

She couldn't let him suffer alone. With a smile she walked over to him. "Hi, Aaron."

He barely glanced at her. "Hi."

"Whatcha doing? Hiding out?"

His blond brows furrowed. "*Nee.*"

"Sure looks like it to me. You're over here on

your own while everyone else is out there visiting." She gestured to the packed room where people were standing around talking or sitting at a few tables eating. "Or are you trying to be incognito?"

"Neither. What I'm trying to do is enjoy the fellowship."

"You have a funny way of showing it. To enjoy fellowship you usually have to engage someone in conversation. Which you aren't doing."

"I am now."

"Because I walked over here."

"Uninvited, by the way."

"If I waited for you to invite me, I'd be old and gray." She moved closer to him until their shoulders were nearly touching. "Why are you so mysterious, Mr. Detweiler?"

"Why are you so nosy, Ms. Byler?"

"I prefer inquisitive."

"You're definitely that."

"And as an inquisitive person, I'm filled with questions. Like why you're here in the first place."

"The Weavers are family friends. Of course I'd be at Christian's wedding."

"I don't mean the wedding part." She lifted up her mug of cider and took a sip. "I'm talking about this. Usually you tuck tail and run whenever more than three people are in one place."

He gave her a surprised look, as if he couldn't

believe what she said. She couldn't believe she said it either. Memories of her school teacher threatening to tape her mouth shut suddenly came to mind. Perhaps now would be a good time to do just that. "I'm sorry. That wasn't nice."

He shrugged. "Whatever."

Frustration started to rise inside her. "That's part of your problem, Aaron. You don't seem to care about anything. Wait, I should say *anyone*. You definitely care about your job."

"Thanks for at least giving me that." He faced her. "If you're done pointing out my faults, I'll be tucking my tail now and leaving." Shoving his hands in his pockets, he stalked away and headed for the front door.

Oh boy, she really screwed that up. Elisabeth set her mug down on one of the stairs and followed him outside. The chilly winter air seeped through the thin fabric of her dress, but that didn't matter. Her comments had been out of line. What had gotten into her?

She saw him climbing into his buggy and ran over to it. He had just picked up the reins when she reached him. Grabbing the door, she thrust it open and climbed in.

His eyes widened. "What are you doing?"

"Stopping you from leaving." She crossed her arms over her chest and hugged her body, trying to keep warm.

"Why would you do that?"

"So I can apologize. I'm truly sorry, Aaron. Sometimes my mouth moves faster than my brain."

"Really? Hadn't noticed."

His droll response almost made her smile. "I definitely don't believe that." Her body started to shake a bit from the cold, but she didn't move to leave. She wouldn't until she knew he forgave her.

"You shouldn't be out here," he said, glancing at her dress. "Not without a coat."

"Neither should you."

"I forgot it inside."

"Then you'll just have to go back and get it. And while you're there, eat some food, and go back to enjoying yourself before I ruined everything."

Aaron released the reins. "You didn't ruin everything." He paused, looking down at his feet. "I wasn't having that great of a time anyway."

"Then we need to fix that." She reached out and grabbed his hand.

Aaron looked down at the delicate hand inside his. One thing he could say about Elisabeth Byler, she was definitely full of surprises.

"Let's go inside before we both freeze," she said, tugging on his hand. Then she released it and exited the buggy, clearly assuming he would follow her.

Which he did. He'd been stupid to bolt out of the house without getting his coat. But he'd been even more of an idiot to let her words get to him. She apologized for being mean, but she hadn't been mean at all. She'd been honest, and that hurt more than any callous words could.

She'd already dashed inside the Mullets' house by the time he reached the front steps. He welcomed the warmth that greeted him as he stepped inside. He hadn't been to a wedding since his sister Rachel's, and he'd spent most of that day plastered against the wall, too, observing everyone else having a good time. He'd been happy for his sister, but he still felt like an outcast among his own people.

Time hadn't changed those feelings too much. No one brought up his past anymore, but it hung over him like a thundercloud. Every once in a while he thought he caught a few people looking at him suspiciously, as if they were expecting him to slip back into his old ways and start dealing drugs again. Which proved not everyone had forgiven him. Sometimes he wondered if even God had. He'd spent the past two years trying to come to terms with the fact that he would probably spend a lifetime earning back the trust he'd broken.

"There are two empty seats at one of the tables."

He hadn't even noticed Elisabeth coming up beside him. "What?"

"We'd better go sit down or we'll never get anything to eat." She tugged at his shirtsleeve, and he had no choice but to follow her.

They both sat down at a table of four, the other two seats occupied by the bride's grandparents who had nearly finished eating. The man looked up at Aaron and frowned. His eyes narrowed until his thick gray brows pushed together into one bushy line.

Aaron shifted in his seat. "I'm not all that hungry, Elisabeth." He moved to get up, but she put her hand on his arm, pinning him in his seat.

"You're not going anywhere until you have a slice of my *mami's* pot roast. It's the best in Middlefield, isn't it *Herr* Mullet?"

The man nodded, still squinting at Aaron. Bits of bread were stuck in his long gray beard.

"Elisabeth, I think your *mudder* has topped herself this time." The short, plump woman sitting next to Mr. Mullet smiled at them both. "I don't know how she gets the meat so tender."

"Me either. I wish I had half of her cooking talent."

"I'm sure you're a fine cook."

"Who are you?" Mullet punched his fork in the air in Aaron's direction.

"Zachariah, please." Looking horrified, Mrs. Mullet put her hand on her husband's forearm and guided his fork back to his plate. She leaned over and whispered in his ear. "That's Aaron Detweiler."

101

Aaron wanted to disappear underneath the old man's scrutinizing gaze. He seemed to stare at Aaron for eternity. He could only imagine what *Herr* Mullet was thinking, probably realizing he was breaking bread with a former criminal. He wouldn't be surprised if the man and his wife got up from the table and left.

"Detweiler." Mullet said the name slowly, like it was a piece of gristle he couldn't chew completely. "Aaron Detweiler." Then he finally turned to his wife.

Aaron scooted his chair back. He didn't need this. If these people didn't want to sit with an ex-con, he'd do them the favor by leaving. He moved to get up.

"Oh, now I know who you are. Sarah's youngest boy." Mullet leaned back in his chair and smiled, his stern expression completely disappearing.

"How many times have I told you to get your eyes checked?" Mrs. Mullet looked at Elisabeth, then at Aaron, clearly exasperated. "Stubborn *mann*. He can't see two feet in front of him."

"Can too." He speared the last piece of pot roast on his plate. "Been a long time since I seen this *bu*."

"He comes to church," Mrs. Mullet pointed out. "Every service."

"That don't mean nothing. Lot's of people come to church. We have a big district. Can't expect me to remember every single person."

Mrs. Mullet sighed. "I don't know what I'm going to do with him."

"There ain't nothing wrong with my hearing, Alma, and I heard that!"

Aaron glanced at the Mullets, then at Elisabeth, who was staring down at her lap. One of the hairpins holding her *kapp* in place was crooked. Her shoulders started to shake, and he could tell she was trying to contain her laughter.

For the first time that afternoon he allowed himself to relax a bit. The Mullets, finished with their dinner, excused themselves and left the table. When they were gone, Elisabeth burst into giggles.

"That was hysterical." She brought her hand up to her mouth, her eyes glittering with humor. "*Herr* Mullet staring you down like that. And all because he can't see."

"That's not why I thought he was staring me down."

"You're kidding. Everyone knows Carol's grandpa is practically blind. The only reason he knows who I am is because the Mullets are family friends. I've known them all my life." Her smile faded. "Wait a minute. You're serious, aren't you?"

He stood up. "I'll get us something to eat."

Elisabeth watched Aaron make his way to the dining room, where two long tables had been set up end to end, laden with a variety of numerous dishes. Behind the tables several women served heaping helpings of food. As Aaron waited his turn, she studied him, wondering why he had reacted to Mr. Mullet that way. Even as he stood in line, he seemed to separate himself from everyone else, not speaking to anyone unless spoken to.

It didn't take him long to go through the line, and soon he came back carrying two plates. He set the plate in front of her. "Wasn't sure what you liked, so I got a little bit of everything."

She looked down at a thick slice of her mother's pot roast, smothered in rich brown gravy, fluffy potatoes, buttery corn, creamy celery casserole, and a fresh slice of bread. Her mouth watered as the aromas reached her nose. "Perfect. *Danki.*"

He lowered his head and dug into his meal as if she weren't there.

Despite her hunger, she kept looking at him, wondering if she would ever figure him out.

"What?" he said, glancing up, his mouth full of food.

"You never answered my question."

He swallowed his food. "Which one? You've been so *inquisitive* today, I lost track."

"Ha ha. Why did you think *Herr* Mullet was staring at you?"

"Does it matter?"

"*Ya.* And I'm not eating until you answer me."

"You're assuming I won't let you starve."

"Oh, I know you won't let me starve."

He regarded her for a moment. "Okay, but I'm answering you only because *I'm* starving, and the Mullets were right, this pot roast is fantastic."

She grinned. His response was a small victory but a victory nevertheless. "I'm listening."

"My past is not exactly a secret around here. People pretty much see the words *drug dealer* stamped on my forehead whenever they look at me."

"That's not true." Elisabeth looked at him. "I don't, and obviously the Mullets don't either."

"But that's what I thought. So there's your answer." He picked up a slice of bread slathered with butter. "Now, can I eat in peace?"

"I suppose." She took her fork and slid it into the tender pot roast. "So is that why you keep to yourself so much? You think everyone thinks badly of you because you were in jail?"

"So much for the peaceful part." He kept his gaze on his plate. "And I don't think everyone thinks badly of me."

"I know for a fact the Mullets wouldn't think that way because *Herr* Mullet's brother Nathaniel got arrested years ago for stealing a neighbor's horse."

He looked up at her. "Really?"

"*Ya*. That was when I was a little girl. I remember him spending time in the pokey for a while."

The corner of his mouth lifted. "The *pokey*?"

"Isn't that what they call jail?"

"Who calls it that?"

"I don't know, I thought I heard someone say it."

He shook his head, a genuine smile on his face. "The pokey. I've heard a lot of names for jail, but never that one. "

She wiped her mouth with her napkin. "Maybe I read it in a book. But I'm pretty sure I heard it somewhere, because I don't read too many books."

"Me either. Never been much of a reader. Rachel's a different story. Always saw her with a book in her hand."

"That's my sister Ruth. I can't believe she hasn't gone blind from it."

"I don't think you can go blind from reading, Elisabeth."

"I know that, Aaron." She lifted a brow at him. "It's an expression."

"I know it's an expression, I just didn't know if you knew."

"Well, I know, okay?" Her good humor started to fade. "I'm not stupid."

Aaron set down his fork. "I never said you were."

"I'm sure you were thinking it."

"Elisabeth, I have never thought you were stupid. It's amazing what you've done with the office. Everything is organized, the accounts are always balanced, and you've done a great job keeping track of the orders. That takes smarts."

She blushed at his compliment. "*Danki*, Aaron. That's nice of you to say."

He tore a chunk off his piece of bread. "I'm not being nice, I'm being honest."

"I'm glad you think I'm doing a *gut* job. I was worried I'd screw up."

"Well, you were late on the first day." His lips formed a smile, a rare occurrence.

Tilting her head, her grin widened. "You have a nice smile, Aaron. You should smile more often."

He cleared his throat and glanced away. She thought she saw his cheeks redden. He scooped up the last bite of mashed potatoes on his plate. Certain he would bolt as soon as he finished eating, she asked, "What was jail like?"

Aaron froze for a moment, mid-chew. Then he swallowed and looked straight at her. "You don't want to know."

"If I didn't want to know, I wouldn't have asked."

"Maybe you shouldn't have asked."

"Was it that bad?"

"*Ya*," he said, without hesitation. "It was bad. And it's a place you don't want to *geh*."

She nodded, matching her mood to his. "I never intend to."

"*Gut*."

"Was it hard to get off drugs?"

He grimaced. "What's with the third degree, Elisabeth?"

"It's not a third degree. I'm just making conversation."

"That's not what it feels like."

"I didn't mean it to feel that way. I'm genuinely curious." She set her fork down. "But if you don't want to talk about it, we don't have to. I'm sorry I brought it up."

They sat in silence for a long moment. The murmurs of the other conversations in the room surrounded them, and she wished Aaron would say something. Just as she thought they were having a good time—okay, a decent time—she had to say something to grind everything to a stop.

"Elisabeth?"

She looked up to see her sister, Ruth, standing by the table. "What is it?"

"We need your help in the kitchen. Carol's *mami* and a few other women haven't had a chance to eat yet." She looked at Aaron for a moment, then back at Elisabeth, a puzzled expression on her face.

"All right." She rose from her chair and moved to pick up her plate. Aaron stood up.

"I'll see you later?" She met his eyes, searching to see if he was still upset with her. If he was, she couldn't tell, as his usual passive mask was firmly in place.

He gave her a brief nod, then walked away. She followed him with her gaze and saw him walk out the door. With a sigh, she picked up their plates and headed to the kitchen with Ruth.

"What's going on with you and Aaron?" Ruth asked as they entered the Mullets' crowded kitchen. In addition to two women washing and drying dishes, two others were stirring pots on the stove while others were preparing dessert.

Elisabeth took the plates to the sink and handed them to one of the washers. "Nothing. We were just eating together."

"By yourselves." Ruth lifted her brow, a sly smile on her face.

"Only for a short while. We were eating with the Mullets, but they'd finished their meal and left."

"Mm hmm." Ruth gave her a knowing look, then went to the kitchen table where their mother was slicing pies and cakes.

"We're just friends!"

Several of the women, including her mother, stopped and looked at her.

Elisabeth ignored their stares, irritated with Ruth for bringing the subject up in the first place. She found an apron and put it over her dress, then busied herself with the work in the kitchen.

But she couldn't put Aaron out of her mind. Were they friends? She wasn't sure. One moment they were getting along and the next they were irritated with each other. That didn't seem like a friendship to her.

She had no idea where they stood with each other, and for some reason that really bothered her.

Anna glanced at Lukas sitting beside her, enjoying a plate piled high with creamy celery casserole, crispy fried chicken, warm buttery rolls, and steaming cabbage and noodles. In between bites he visited with Tobias and Rachel, who were seated across from them. She took note of how the brothers were a contrast not only physically but in temperament as well. Tall and lean, with wavy blond hair and blue eyes, Tobias was quick with a joke and enjoyed teasing everyone in sight. Lukas's dark hair and complexion seemed to match his usual no-nonsense mood. While he could be lighthearted, he approached nearly everything with absolute seriousness, a quality she appreciated and one of the many things she liked about him.

She glanced at her own plate, which was almost empty. Happiness that she hadn't felt in a long time flowed through her. When he had asked to take her to the wedding a couple of days ago, she wasn't completely sure she wanted to go, but she had agreed to anyway. It was getting harder and harder to tell Lukas no to anything.

The anxiety she thought she'd feel during the

wedding service never materialized. She also hadn't thought about Daniel much at all lately, as Lukas continued to move into her thoughts and into her heart. She remembered what he'd said to her a couple of months ago, when he had first told her he liked her. *What you see is what you get.* He had been right about that. Unselfish, honest, and loyal, he turned out to be everything Daniel wasn't.

"Anna?"

She turned at the sound of Lukas's voice. His dark brows furrowed slightly as he looked at her. "You're awful quiet all of the sudden. Everything okay?"

She looked up to see that Tobias and Rachel were gone. "Oh, I'm sorry. I didn't even see them get up. I hope they didn't think I was rude."

"*Nee*, I'm sure they didn't. You seemed to be in deep thought."

"I was."

"About what?"

Facing him, she said, "Daniel."

"Oh." He picked up his fork and turned it back and forth in his fingers. "I was afraid of that."

"What?"

"I almost didn't ask you to come today. I thought it might bring back bad memories." He set down the fork and pushed back the chair. "We can leave if you want."

She put her hand on his forearm. "*Nee*. I've

had a great time, Lukas. I'm glad I got to talk to your brother and sister-in-law. And the food has been *sehr gut*."

He looked at her hand on his arm, then back at her. His lips curved in a smile. "I'm glad you're enjoying yourself. I want you to be happy, Anna."

She lost herself in the warmth of his gaze. "Oh, I am, Lukas."

Chapter 7

"*C*'mon, Elisabeth. I promise, it will be fun."

Elisabeth stood outside Gabe's blacksmith shop, talking to her friend Deborah, who had stopped by after her morning shift at Mary Yoder's Amish Kitchen, where she was a waitress. Elisabeth had known Deborah for years, since they were in school together, but Elisabeth hadn't seen her much since they had both started working. She was surprised to see Deborah pull up in the Miller's driveway, and even more surprised by her invitation.

"I don't know, Deborah. Who's all going to be at the party?"

"Some people from work."

"So it's a work party?"

"*Nee*, not just people from work. Other friends. Amish friends." Deborah tugged on the wristband of her knitted navy blue gloves. "This isn't like you, Elisabeth. I've never known you to turn down an opportunity to *geh* out."

"This is different." Elisabeth had restricted her social life to mostly Amish gatherings, and she liked it that way. Up until a few months ago, Deborah had been a part of the same group of friends, but she hadn't been at any of the singings this fall. "I've never been to one of these parties."

"I have, and trust me, you'll have a *gut* time. It's at James Schrock's house, back in his barn. You know how huge that thing is. It can hold over two hundred people."

Elisabeth frowned. She'd heard through the grapevine that James was a shady character. He was eighteen, and since they'd all left school, he'd turned wild, cutting his hair short and even getting a car. His parents did little to curb his bad behavior. "I heard one of his parties got broken up by the police."

"*Nee*, that was just a rumor. Look, I really want you to come. You can meet some of my new friends."

"New friends?"

"*Ya*. One of them just moved into Middlefield. He's really nice. We can all just hang out for a while."

"I don't know," Elisabeth said, biting her lower lip.

"If you don't like it, you don't have to come

back. Someone can even take you home early if you want." She moved to stand next to Elisabeth and linked her arm through hers. "I miss you. We haven't done anything together in a long time."

Elisabeth had to admit that she'd also missed her friend. "There's a barn raising at the Bontragers' on Saturday. Why don't you come to that?"

"I can't make it Saturday."

"Why not?"

"I have to work."

"Then stop by after work."

"I can't." She released Elisabeth and stepped away. "You know, you're being a little snobby about this."

"Snobby?"

"Yeah." Deborah rubbed her finger under her nose. "Like you're too *gut* to *geh* to the Schrocks'."

Elisabeth shook her head, appalled her friend would think that. "That's not it at all. I don't think I'm too *gut* for anything."

Deborah shrugged. "I'm just saying that's how it seems to me."

"All right. I'll think about it."

"That's all I'm asking." She tugged on the bow of her black bonnet before climbing into her buggy. "Chase and I will be by to pick you up around eight tomorrow."

"Chase?"

114

"*Ya.* He's the one I want you to meet. Just started working at the restaurant. We've been hanging out. And he has the sweetest car you've ever seen. I have no idea what kind it is, but it's so cool!"

Elisabeth took a step toward her friend. "Wait, I haven't said I'd *geh.*"

Deborah merely grinned and grabbed the horse's reins. "See you tomorrow night!"

Elisabeth half waved to Deborah as she pulled her buggy out of the driveway, wondering at the change in her friend. *Sweetest car? So cool?* Since when did Deborah talk like that?

She turned around to head inside, only to see Aaron standing there. Her heart leaped to her throat, and she put her hand over her chest. "*Gut* grief! You scared me! I didn't know you were standing there."

His blue eyes, normally void of emotion, were chips of ice, and his mouth was set in a thin line. "You're not seriously thinking about going to that party, are you?"

"You were eavesdropping?"

He leaned forward, ignoring her question. "Are you?"

She'd spent half a year wishing she could elicit some kind of reaction from Aaron Detweiler, but overbearing disapproval wasn't it.

He didn't wait for her to answer. "Doesn't matter. You can't *geh.*"

115

Her hackles rose. "Excuse me? Since when do you tell me what I can or cannot do?"

"Since you're considering doing something stupid, that's when."

She put her hands on her hips. "Number one, you shouldn't have been eavesdropping on a private conversation—"

"It's not private when you're standing out here two feet from the Dumpster. Anyone could have heard you. What if Moriah had come outside? Do you think she'd be happy to know you were going to a Yankee party?"

"It's not a Yankee party. It's at the Schrocks'."

"I guarantee there'll be more Yanks than Amish there."

"So?" Elisabeth was starting to see why Deborah thought her snobby. Aaron was coming across the same way. "You act like being around Yankees will give me a disease or something."

"Don't be so dramatic. That's not what I mean. You know what goes on at those parties."

Elisabeth crossed her arms over her chest. She wore a navy blue sweater over her dress, but it did little to ward off the early spring chill in the air. "Since I've never been to one, I don't." She didn't mention that she'd heard what happened at some of those parties, especially about the drinking. "And since when do you have the right to act like my big *bruder*? Or worse, my *daed*?"

"In this case I have every right."

"*Nee*, you don't." She brushed past him and went back inside the shop, straight to her office. When she tried to shut the door, he grabbed it, stopping her. "Will you just let it *geh*?"

He stepped inside the office and closed the door behind him. "*Nee*. I won't. Not until you tell me you aren't going to the Schrocks'."

"I don't know why you're making such a big deal about this." She went to her desk and sat down, then picked up the accounts ledger. Maybe if she ignored him he would go away.

"Because unlike you, I've been to these types of parties. And I know what goes on there." When she didn't respond, he went and stood beside her, not speaking.

She finally looked up at him. "Deborah's my friend, Aaron. She wouldn't invite me if there was going to be trouble. And you haven't attended every party in Middlefield. I'm sure this one will be fine."

"And what if it isn't? What if there's drinking? People using drugs? Girls and guys pairing off to go into cars or up in the hayloft? Because that's what these kids do, Elisabeth. They get drunk and high. I'm sure I don't have to tell you what else they're doing."

Her face heated, and she turned away. "I wouldn't do something like that."

"When you're under the influence of alcohol or drugs—or both—you're capable of anything."

He took a deep breath and let it out. "I've done a lot of things I'm not proud of, and I've paid for them. With jail time, remember?"

She turned and looked up at him, fully expecting to see his hardened expression. Instead, she saw regret.

"You don't want to get caught up in that, Elisabeth. Because I know how tempting all of that freedom is. All of the things we've been told not to do. Then once drugs and drink get ahold of you, it's almost impossible to break free."

"You did it."

"*Ya*, and it was the hardest thing I ever had to do in my life. I went to rehab while I was in jail. And when I got out I had to fight the temptation to go back to my former life. To start drinking and using again. I'm still paying the consequences of those choices."

Under any other circumstances she would have appreciated that he had finally revealed something so important, but she couldn't help but feel talked down to. "That's you. I don't drink, and I've never even seen a drug. And I can't believe you think I'd go off with some guy and . . . and . . ." Anger took the words from her mouth. She gripped the ledger book until the sides bent. "I have work to do."

"Promise me you won't *geh* to that party, Elisabeth."

The lowness of his voice, along with the intensity and a touch of pleading in his words, almost made her look at him again. But she held her ground and thrust open the account book, tapping random numbers on the calculator as if she were deeply involved in balancing the books. Only when she heard him leave, loudly shutting the door behind him, did she look up. Through the small window on the office door, she saw him storm off toward the forge.

Hurt coursed through her. She couldn't believe how little he thought of her. After all this time of working together, he thought she had so little character . . . so little *common sense*. Even when she had explained and defended herself, he still didn't trust her enough to let the subject drop.

And since when did he actually care what she did? He'd never expressed any interest in what she did outside of work, and he had done nothing but refuse the gestures of friendship she'd extended his way, their miniscule conversation at Carol and Christian's wedding the one exception. What right did he have to tell her what to do?

Well, she'd prove him wrong. She'd go to the party with Deborah tomorrow night, she'd have a good time, and she'd stay out of trouble. She'd show him she wasn't as weak and stupid as he thought she was.

"This is useless, Aaron." Gabe picked up a warped horseshoe, the second of a pair of shoes

Aaron had made a little over an hour ago, just after he had talked to Elisabeth. He had a feeling everything he said went right through her ears without sinking into that stubborn brain of hers.

"Sorry." He grabbed the shoe and its ruined match and tossed them into a pile of scrap. He'd recycle the shoes later, but he hated doing poor work. He had always taken pride in producing quality work for Gabe and his father. He never wanted to let them down.

Gabe looked at him, his expression concerned. "You seem to have something on your mind. Anything you want to talk about?"

Aaron shook his head. He didn't want to worry Gabe about Elisabeth, and he held on to a thin reed of hope that what he'd said to her would make her change her mind. "I don't want to get behind on that order for that farm down in Ravenna."

"All right." Gabe touched Aaron's shoulder. "But if you need anything, let me know. The work's important, but not as important as *family*."

He nodded, touched by Gabe's words. "*Danki*."

Gabe patted him on the arm and walked away.

For the rest of the day, Aaron tried not to think about Elisabeth going to the Schrocks', but it took every ounce of his concentration to put her out of his mind. He'd never been so relieved when quitting time drew near.

A few minutes after five o'clock, he saw Elisabeth walk out of the back office and exit the shop. Shoving his work gloves in his pockets, he went out after her. She might fight with him again, or even ignore him, but he had to give it one last shot. "Elisabeth. Wait."

She didn't turn around, so he continued to go after her. When she finally stopped at the bottom of the Millers' driveway, he moved to stand in front of her. The only way she could avoid him now was to turn her back on him and walk away. Fortunately she didn't. "We need to finish our talk. I wanted—"

"There's nothing else to say."

Dusk had descended, and the sky was clear, turning the day's brisk air downright cold. Not that the temperature would have an effect on certain social plans. For some of the kids, it was never too cold, too hot, or too much of anything to have a party. "I disagree. Let me take you home and we can discuss it."

"Stephen's on his way to pick me up, so I already have a ride. I'll see you on Monday."

"Elisabeth, listen to me. I'm asking you—"

"If you say 'don't *geh* to the party' one more time, I'll scream." She glared at him. "It's not up to you what I do."

"*Nee*, it's not."

"Finally we agree on something."

"But in this case, I'm right."

"You only think you're right."

Her words, laced with derision, bruised his ego, but he continued. "I don't know what I can say to convince you—"

"There's nothing you can say. I'm not like you, Aaron Detweiler. I'm nothing like you. And on Monday morning I'll be more than happy to tell you what a *gut* time I had at the party." Elisabeth turned her head in the direction of the Bylers' buggy as it pulled into the driveway. "There's Stephen."

Aaron squinted, watching her dark figure disappear as she walked toward her brother. He had half a mind to go after her again, but he knew it would be a lost cause. He could repeat himself until his voice gave out, but she'd made up her mind.

As Stephen and Elisabeth drove away, he suddenly realized that his insistent stance had probably spurred her to attend. A couple of years ago, if someone had badgered him the same way, he would have thumbed his nose too.

Chapter 8

Deborah was right. Chase did have a "sweet" car. Elisabeth didn't know very much about automobiles, but she liked the cherry color of Chase's vehicle, including all the silvery chrome on the wheels and the front of the hood. Yet despite her appreciation for the car's looks, she felt awkward climbing into the backseat.

Deborah turned around in the front seat. "Chase," she said, pointing to the driver. "This is my friend, Elisabeth. Elisabeth, meet Chase."

Chase glanced over his shoulder and grinned, revealing perfectly straight and impossibly white teeth.

"Nice to meetcha," he said.

The overhead light in the car dimmed after Deborah shut the door, but in her quick assessment of him, she saw that his hair was cut short over his ears, with blond spiked tips dotting the crown of his head. He wore a hooded red sweatshirt.

Deborah whirled around in the seat and looked at her. "I'm so glad you changed your mind and decided to come with us." She pulled the bobby pins from her prayer *kapp*. "You're going to have so much fun!"

Elisabeth leaned forward. Keeping her voice low, she asked, "What are you doing?"

"Taking this thing off." She pulled the last of the pins out of the *kapp* and yanked it off, dropping it on the seat beside Chase. Then she took the pins and rubber band out of her long brown hair and let it flow down her back, shaking it out. "There. That feels much better."

"You shouldn't do that," Elisabeth said. "What if someone from church sees you?"

"I don't care. I haven't joined the church yet, remember? Besides, there will be kids from church at the party, and I guarantee you I won't be the only one without a *kapp* on. You should take yours off too."

"*Nee.*" Elisabeth didn't care if she was the only one there with a *kapp* on, she wouldn't be without it. She hadn't joined the church either, but she planned to soon, and if word got back to the elders that she'd been out in public without her head covered, she would hear about it. She had gotten her fill of lectures today, thanks to Aaron.

"You need to chill out, Elisabeth." Deborah leaned her head back against the white leather upholstery. "Don't be so uptight."

Elisabeth sat back in her seat, bewildered by her friend's shift in attitude. Chase turned on the radio, and the thumping of the bass reverberated in her ears. She thought to tell him to turn it down, but she changed her mind. Even though she didn't care for the music, she didn't want to come off as a whiner. That would earn her a few more words from Deborah, and right now she'd rather her friend stay silent.

Besides, when did Deborah get so wild? Elisabeth remembered when they both had turned sixteen, they and their group of friends had said they wouldn't go crazy like a few other Amish teens did. Now Deborah seemed to have forgotten all about that discussion. Or maybe she didn't care anymore.

Aaron's warnings came to mind, but she shoved them away. She wasn't Deborah and she wasn't him. If someone offered her a drink, she'd refuse. If they wanted her to try drugs, she'd say no. She wasn't tempted by those things. There was no reason why she couldn't attend this party, hang out with people, and have a good time without getting sucked into all that.

When they showed up at the Schrocks', Chase bypassed the driveway and maneuvered his car through the side yard, then back to the barn where other cars and buggies were parked on the grass. Elisabeth peered out of the backseat window. Someone had started a bonfire, and she could see several kids standing around it, talking and laughing as tendrils of smoke stretched up toward the sky. The kids were a mix of Amish and Yankee, and all had cups or bottles in their hands.

Chase killed the engine. He turned to Deborah, then to Elisabeth. The flickering light of the fire shone through the car window and reflected on his face. "Ready to party?"

"*Ya.*" Deborah flung open the door and scrambled out of the car.

Elisabeth slowly got out of the car, all her confidence disintegrating. A weird sensation came over her, as if she were itching from the inside out. As she looked around, she didn't recognize anyone. She saw a couple of girls who, like Deborah, had removed their *kapps*. They stood next to three other young women who had kept their head coverings on. At first glance she noticed more guys than girls, more Yankees than Amish. The more she surveyed the scene in front of her, she realized the males outnumbered the females by a long shot.

"C'mon," Deborah said, taking Elisabeth's arm and interlocking their elbows together. "I'll introduce you to some of the gang."

Gang? How long had Deborah been hanging out with these people?

Deborah dragged Elisabeth to the group of kids hanging by the fire. Elisabeth crossed her arms as she was introduced to everyone. The heat from the fire felt good on her chilly body but did little to relieve the anxiety churning inside her. Right after the introductions, Deborah pulled Elisabeth over to two Yankee couples leaning against a dark-colored car. The air surrounding them reeked of smoke, and not from the smoke of the bonfire. Deborah's introductions were so hasty, Elisabeth didn't remember anyone. She let her friend lead her around like a lost puppy, then straight to the barn.

A gas-powered light hissed inside, illuminating the massive barn. The scent of hay overpowered everything, but she didn't detect a single sign of animals. Apparently, the barn was for storage only. Deborah took her to the left side of the barn, where bits of straw and hay littered the floor. She saw several coolers with open lids packed with ice and beverages.

"Take your pick." Deborah pointed to a large blue plastic cooler. "That one holds the beer and wine coolers. The green one has the harder stuff. You know, tequila, rum, vodka."

"Is that all there is to drink?"

Deborah gave her an incredulous look. "What else do you need?"

Elisabeth pulled Deborah to the side. "When did you start drinking?" she whispered.

"Elisabeth, don't be such a prude." Deborah's tone was cutting. "There's nothing wrong with having a beer or a wine cooler every once in a while."

"*Ya*, there is. And I'm not touching any of that stuff. What about pop? Or bottled water, at least?" If there wasn't anything nonalcoholic, she wouldn't drink at all.

"Over there." Deborah waved to a small red cooler, then walked toward it. She flipped open the lid. "I think there's some diet in here," she said bending over. Her brown hair fell around her face like a curtain. She stood up and handed Elisabeth a generic diet soda. "Here you go."

"Aren't you going to have some?"

"*Nee*, I'm getting a beer. Oh, look. Standing over there by Chase. That's Randy."

Elisabeth followed Deborah's gaze. A young man wearing a plain white Amish shirt, black coat, and broadfall pants was in deep conversation with Chase. Although he dressed Amish, he had a Yankee haircut, and he held an amber bottle in his hand. Both guys looked up at Elisabeth and Deborah. Randy lifted his hand in a small wave.

"Who's Randy?"

"Only the cutest guy in Middlefield. Isn't he gorgeous? Oh, and he's waving us over. Come on, I'll introduce you to him."

Elisabeth shook her head, a sudden attack of nerves hitting her. She'd never been shy, but she wasn't eager to meet Randy either. "I'm okay. You go on. I'll sit over there and drink my soda."

Deborah put her hands on her hips. "I didn't bring you out here to be a wallflower, Elisabeth."

"I won't be a wallflower, I promise. Just let me ease into the party slowly."

"Okay. Fair enough. Do you mind if I *geh* see Randy? I'm dying to know what he wants."

Elisabeth nodded, relieved her friend bought her excuse. "Have fun."

Deborah grinned. "I'm sure I will."

After Deborah flounced away, Elisabeth scanned the barn, looking for a place to sit down. Most everyone seemed content to hang out by the bonfire or the coolers, but she wasn't eager to join either group. She spied a couple of small stacks of square hay bales in the corner. No one was around, so she sat down, unnoticed by the partygoers, who didn't seem to care whether she was there or not.

She definitely wasn't having fun.

Not that she would have admitted it to anyone, and especially not Aaron, but she should have heeded his advice. Next time Deborah invited her to a party, she would refuse. Her friend could drag someone else next time.

She slowly sipped her soda, feeling more out of place and uncomfortable with each passing minute. Teens and young adults came in and out of the barn, most of the guys grabbing beers, while the girls took wine coolers. After about twenty minutes a few guys broke into the "hard stuff" and started pouring bottles of different colored liquids into red and blue plastic cups. She had no idea which drink was which. She'd never been around alcohol; no one drank at her house. She didn't understand why anyone wanted to drink liquor anyway—the couple of guys who took a sip made funny faces afterward, sometimes even yelling out loud, as if the liquid hurt going down their throats.

She set her can down on the hay bale next to her. Although it was cold outside, the barn was fairly warm, and she removed her coat then crossed her arms over her dark blue sweater. Deborah had disappeared from the barn with Randy, leaving her alone. Aaron's warning about the hayloft entered her mind, and she didn't want to think about what Deborah and Randy were doing. What she wanted was to go home. The Schrocks lived several miles from her house, but if she couldn't find someone to take her home, she'd walk.

She moved to get up when she saw Chase approach, two cups in his hand.

"Having fun?" he asked, sitting down next to her.

"Not really. I was actually thinking about going home."

"Already?"

She glanced at him, finally able to see his face in the full light of the barn. He was nice looking, with a square jaw, close-set green eyes, and a full mouth. When she breathed in, she caught the scent of his cologne, which actually smelled really good.

"Here," he said, holding out a blue cup to her. "I thought you might want something better than a diet pop."

She shook her head, not reaching for the cup. "I appreciate the offer, but I don't drink. Diet soda is *gut* enough for me."

"I understand. But I'd like to change your mind. This is my special lemonade. For people who don't drink. Don't worry, there's not enough alcohol in here to get a flea drunk." He grinned. "Trust me. You'll like it. Money back guarantee if you don't."

She looked at the cup, doubtful. "I don't think so."

He leaned forward and scooted close against her. "Just one sip? If you don't like it, you don't have to finish it."

"I said *nee*."

He frowned. "Suit yourself. But if you change your mind, let me know." He set the cup down on the ground.

"I'm going to find Deborah." Elisabeth moved to stand up, but Chase put his hand on her arm.

"She's busy with Randy." He gazed at her with hazy eyes. "I don't think she'd want you to interrupt them."

"Maybe I should interrupt them. I don't want her to get into trouble."

Chase laughed. "Don't worry, she won't. They'll be fine. I'm sure Randy will be the perfect gentleman." He moved closer to her. "Sure you don't want to try this lemonade?"

"Positive." His cologne suddenly went from nice to cloying. It made her stomach flip and not in a good way. She moved farther from him, the hay rustling beneath her dress.

"All right, I can respect a teetotaler." He held up his cup. "Cheers?"

Reluctantly she touched her can of diet cola to his drink, whatever it was.

"You don't know what you're missing." He took a long swig from his cup.

"Oh, I think I do." She had thought to ask him to take her home, but now that he was drinking, she wouldn't get into a car with him. The prospect of walking tonight loomed before her. But she'd rather spend an hour or so footing it than risking her life riding with him.

"So are you planning to sit here all night?"

She turned to look at him. Somehow he had managed to get closer to her without her realizing it. If she scooted any farther on the hay bale, she would fall off. "Only until I find a ride home."

"You just got here."

"This really isn't my type of party."

"Oh? Then what is?"

"The kind where there's less drinking and more singing."

"Like rapping and stuff?"

She shook her head, and for the first time since she'd climbed into Chase's car, she almost smiled. "You're not from here, are you?"

"Nope. Moved here from Cincinnati a few months ago. How long have you been friends with Deborah?"

"Years. Since we were little girls."

"Then how come we've never met before?"

"Deborah and I don't hang out much anymore." *And now I know why.*

"I didn't think I'd seen you at any parties." He lowered his voice. "Because I would have remembered if I had. I'm glad you decided to come tonight. It would have been a shame if I'd missed meeting you."

Elisabeth looked away from him but noticed that he glanced around the barn. "There are a lot of people in here," he said.

"I only see five."

"My point exactly. I know a place that's more private. We can talk more there."

"*Danki*, but I'm fine right here. This hay bale is actually very comfortable."

"But this place is more comfortable. Warmer too."

She gave him what she hoped was an annoyed look, and she was gratified when he leaned back, putting some distance between them. He didn't say anything for a moment, as if he was in deep thought, and she hoped he would get up and leave. His next words dashed those hopes.

"How about I get you a refill?"

Her can was only half empty. "I really don't want any—"

Before she could finish the sentence, he covered her hand with his and plucked the can from her grip. "Be right back." Chase jumped up from the hay bale and walked over to one of the coolers.

Elisabeth looked around the barn for an escape, less than impressed with Chase's blatant flirting and more than a little creeped out. The Amish boys she knew were much more subtle about letting a girl know they liked her, and she preferred their approach to Chase's over-the-top style. Not that she would consider going out with a Yankee anyway. Especially any of the boys she'd met tonight.

"Here you go." He sat back down beside her.

If he were any closer he would be parked in her lap. Not wanting to appear completely rude, she accepted the fresh can of pop. "*Danki.*"

"That means thanks, right?"

"*Ya.*"

"*Ya,*" he mimicked. "I like how you said that."

She fought the urge to roll her eyes, hiding her annoyance with Chase by taking a drink. A bitter, burning taste coated her tongue, and she spit the soda out. "What is this?"

"Rum. Thought your drink needed some sweetening up."

"That wasn't sweet, that was terrible." She wiped her mouth with the back of her hand.

He grimaced. "Good grief, chill. It's not that bad. It'll warm you up."

"I don't appreciate you putting alcohol in my drink!" She dropped the can beside her and shot up from the hay bale.

"Whoa." Chase stood up. "Hang on a minute."

"I will not hang on a minute. That was a rotten thing to do."

"I know, and I'm sorry." He touched her shoulder but she shook him off.

"Leave me alone." She took a step away from

him, intending to leave the barn, but he skidded in front of her, blocking her escape.

"Please, wait. Look, I'm really sorry." He dipped his head so he could look her straight in the eye. "You're right. That was a low thing to do."

Her face pinched at the smell of alcohol wafting from his mouth. Her breath probably reeked, too, thanks to him.

"I shouldn't have spiked your drink." He threaded his hand through his hair, actually looking distraught. The blond-tipped spikes stood up straight. "It's just that, well, I want to know you better, and I thought it would be a good way to loosen you up."

"I don't need any loosening up." She tugged her sweater closer around her body, bending her toes inside her black tennis shoes. "And I don't think we need to know each other better."

"Why? You have a boyfriend?"

Elisabeth couldn't figure out if Chase was simply dense or being stubborn, and she didn't care. All she cared about was getting out of that barn and away from him. "I'm going home."

"C'mon, give me another chance." He stood in front of her, between her and the entrance of the barn. When she looked around, she noticed everyone had suddenly disappeared. Dread pooled in her belly.

Chase slid his arm around her shoulders, pulling her tight against him, then half-guiding half-shoving her behind a tall stack of hay bales.

"What are you doing?"

He put his mouth close to her ear. "I know we can have a lot of fun together."

She tried to shove him away but he wouldn't move. "Let me go!"

"I like when girls play hard to get." He bent down and pressed his mouth to hers.

Yuck. He reeked of alcohol and his lips were clammy. She tried to push him away again, but he kept kissing her. Finally she clamped her teeth on his bottom lip.

"Yow!" He jumped back, touching his lip. He pulled his fingers away, but she hadn't drawn blood. "You bit me."

Her heart slammed against her ribcage, but she wouldn't back down. "I'll do worse than that if you don't leave me alone."

He smirked. "Right. Like what?"

Before he said the last word, she kicked him in the shin.

His eyebrows shot up in surprise. Then he limped away from her, muttering several curse words that made her ears burn.

When he disappeared, she leaned against one of the stacks, fighting to regain her composure.

Chapter 9

*A*aron pulled his buggy up to the Schrocks' barn, yanking hard on the reins. He had fought with himself for the whole evening before coming out here, changing his mind over and over. Elisabeth was an adult, and she had been right about one thing, she didn't have to listen to him or do what he told her. But it was that stubbornness, along with her naiveté, that ultimately convinced him he had to find her again.

Just seeing the barn, hearing the raucous laughter coming from drunk and high kids, inhaling the mixture of wood, cigarette, and marijuana smoke, brought back memories he'd fought to purge. He'd promised himself and God that he would never be in this situation again, face-to-face with temptation. Yet he knew if he hadn't taken the risk and come to the party, he'd never forgive himself if something happened to Elisabeth.

He jumped out of the buggy and hurried toward the folks gathered outside the barn, looking for a familiar face, or at least someone he thought might know Elisabeth. The party wasn't all that well attended, probably due to the coldness of the night. A few kids stood around a bonfire, and he saw the exhaust pumping into the air from a couple cars. No doubt a few of the partygoers had decided to huddle inside for warmth, among other things. He headed closer to the barn. An Amish kid stopped him, drink in hand, his gait wobbly. No possible way was he old enough to drink.

"Wanna beer?" he said, holding out a dark brown bottle to him.

Aaron's gaze landed on the bottle, and a familiar craving came back. He had never gotten hooked on the drink, but his downward spiral had started with one beer. "*Nee.*"

"You sure?" The kid tilted the bottle back and forth. "It's *gut* stuff."

"*Nee*, it's not, and you shouldn't be drinking it either."

"*Ach*, what's your problem? It's just beer."

He needed to get the youth's attention, and his own, off the beer. "Do you know Elisabeth Byler?"

The boy shrugged. Puffs of cold air came out of his mouth as he spoke. "Never heard of her."

"What about another *maedel* . . . Deborah something?"

"Nope. Don't know either one." The kid took a swig from the bottle, then strode back to the bonfire.

Aaron pressed on to the barn, where a small group of partygoers stood around several different colored coolers. He approached, glancing at the interior of one of the coolers. It was completely empty, save for a pool of melting ice on the bottom. He noticed the cooler next to it held a few beers, and from experience, he knew the third cooler probably held the hard stuff. He'd never attended a party where there was only beer.

From what he'd witnessed so far, he could see they had all consumed plenty of alcohol. His hope that Elisabeth had stuck to pop or water diminished. Peer pressure was strong at these parties, another thing he had plenty of experience with.

He turned and looked at the opposite side of the barn. He spotted a couple coming from behind one of the numerous stacks of bales. The boy leaned down and kissed the girl, zigzagging as they walked. Although she wore an Amish dress, she didn't have on a *kapp*. Her long brown hair flowed to her waist. The boy wore Amish clothing but had a Yankee haircut. As Aaron walked toward them, he recognized Deborah.

"Where's Elisabeth?"

"How should I know?" Deborah kept her arms around the young man's waist. Her eyes were red-rimmed. "I'm not her babysitter."

"You brought her to the party," Aaron gritted out.

"Correction," she said, holding up one finger. "Chase brought her to the party. I only invited her along."

"Who's Chase?"

"This guy I know. And from what I saw a little while ago, she was getting to know him too." Deborah giggled and leaned her head on her companion's shoulder.

Aaron clenched his fists. He scanned the barn and considered tearing apart every hay stack to search for Elisabeth.

"Hey."

Aaron turned. The kid with Deborah jerked his head, gesturing toward some hay bales on the far side of the barn.

"I saw your friend. With Chase. They went over there."

"When?"

"Just a couple of minutes ago."

"*Danki.*" Aaron glanced at Deborah, then back at him. "Did you drive?"

"*Nee.* Don't have a car, just the buggy."

"You been drinking?"

"*Ya.* A bit."

Aaron scrubbed his hand over his face. "Is anyone here sober?"

"Doubt it."

"Got a cell phone on you?"

He nodded, but seemed embarrassed to admit it.

"Call a cab and go home," Aaron said as he hurried toward the far side of the barn. Hopefully the young man would take his advice, but he wasn't counting on it. He didn't listen to common sense advice when he was that age either.

"Elisabeth!" He called out as he made his way across the barn. He heard muffled voices coming from behind one of the stacks near the back of the barn.

As he made his way toward the sound, a guy with spiked hair appeared. Aaron noticed he was limping and moving as quickly toward the exit as possible.

Aaron shot his hand out and caught the guy by the arm. He looked him up and down and noticed his red hoodie and jeans. "You Chase?"

"Let go of me, backwoods jerk!"

Aaron held on to him and could smell the alcohol on his breath. "Only after you tell me if you've seen a girl—she's got blonde hair and blue eyes. Short, thin. Amish. Someone said she came back here with a guy named Chase."

Scowling, he yanked his arm out of Aaron's grip and took off.

"Elisabeth!" The musty smell of hay filled his nose. He called out her name again, fear overcoming him the longer it took for her to answer him.

"Aaron?"

He welcomed the relief of hearing her voice, even though it came from the same direction as the red hoodie guy.

"What are you doing here?" Her blue eyes were wide, her complexion pale.

"Are you okay?"

141

"I'm fine."

But she didn't look fine. Her lower lip trembled, and her arms were wrapped tight around her. When he moved closer to her, she backed away.

"What happened?"

"*Nix*. Can you take me home?"

Her small voice tugged at his heart. "*Ya*. I'll take you home."

She started walking toward the exit of the barn, her arms still crossed, staring straight ahead.

He fell in step beside her, shoving his hands in his pockets, and cast a glance in her direction. She didn't look at him.

When they reached the outside, he pointed to the left. "My buggy's over here."

She nodded, and they headed that way.

"Aaron? Aaron Detweiler?"

Aaron nearly tripped over his feet at the sound of the familiar voice. He turned to see a girl swaying slightly as she moved toward him. Even in the low light he could tell who she was. As if he could ever forget. *Kacey*.

"I can't believe it's you." She stood in front of him, her black curly hair spilling over her shoulders. Her jeans clung to her body like they had been plastered on, and she had on a tight V-necked sweater. She held a cigarette in one hand and a bottle of beer in the other. "Never thought I'd see you at one of these again."

For a moment he didn't know what to do, his

mind transported back to when he and Kacey were dating, hazy memories flooding over him. His feet wouldn't move.

"Don't say you don't know who I am." She transferred the cigarette to her other hand and threaded her fingers through his. "I know better than that."

Glancing over his shoulder, he saw Elisabeth staring at him. He looked back at Kacey and pulled his hand from hers. "We're just leaving."

"We?" Kacey looked past Aaron's shoulder. "So you found yourself an Amish girlfriend, *ya*?" She giggled, then took a drag from her cigarette. "Well, if you get bored with her, you know where to find me."

Suddenly the wail of sirens pierced the air.

"*Cops!*" someone yelled.

Chaos broke out all around him as car engines roared to life. Amish kids jumped inside their buggies, and headlights flipped on, spreading blinding light everywhere. Aaron ran to Elisabeth.

"The police are here?" Alarm laced her voice.

"They will be soon," he shouted. "We have to get out of here! Now!"

Her eyes widened. "Aaron, I don't want to *geh* to jail."

"Neither do I!" But if he didn't leave before the police arrived, they might detain him. And if they ran his name through their computer system, he could be dragged back to the station. They'd throw him in a holding cell before he could explain himself. He couldn't risk that.

Anxiety crashed through him as he saw the blinking blue and red lights of a squad car pulling up to the Schrocks' property. His mind whirred. There was a chance he and Elisabeth could get inside the buggy and the police wouldn't come after them. But he had no idea how many cop cars were out there, and with the slow speed of the horse, he could be caught. He looked across the road, barely making out a large field that seemed to stretch for acres.

He grabbed Elisabeth's hand. "C'mon!"

"Where are we going?"

He didn't answer, just dragged her along. They ran across the road. The police headlights flashed on them, but he didn't slow down. Instead, he and Elisabeth ran into the field, plunging into the darkness.

"I can't see!" Elisabeth exclaimed.

"Quiet!" Legs pumping, he felt the tall winter grass brushing against his trousers. He had no idea what was in front of them, but it couldn't be as bad as what waited for them back at the Schrocks'. His toe hit a hard object and he tripped, sending him and Elisabeth flying forward.

"Umph!" He landed on his stomach, hard. Elisabeth hit the ground beside him, letting out a small cry. He flipped to his side and pulled her close to him, putting his hand over her mouth.

"Shh," he said, low into her ear. "They'll hear you."

He couldn't see her expression, but he could feel her heart pounding against his chest. He half expected her to bite down on his hand, but she didn't. Instead she remained quiet. He removed his hand from her mouth, then felt the warmth of her breath on his cheek.

He tried not to breathe in the clean scent of her hair or think about her beside him. Instead he focused on staying hidden, making sure neither one of them did anything to reveal where they were.

They lay on the cold ground for a long time, not moving, the grass providing camouflage. Aaron strained to listen to the commotion across the street, his heart hammering in his chest. He could see the red and blue lights from the car reflecting in the sky. As long as the cops were still there, they didn't dare move.

"Aaron?" Elisabeth's voice was barely audible.

"What?"

"How long do we have to stay here?"

" 'Til the cops leave."

"Do you think they'll find us?"

"Not as long as we keep quiet!"

"Oh. Sorry."

Elisabeth moved closer to him, and she almost seemed to be snuggling against him. She lay on her back, leaning her head against his chest.

Then he realized why. Her body was shaking; she'd left her coat in the barn. Automatically his arm went around her shoulders. His pulse continued to race, but not just because he was afraid of getting caught by the police.

Finally the lights disappeared, and Aaron heard the crunch of the police car's tires as it traveled down the dirt road. Only one squad car had shown up, but that didn't mean the police hadn't alerted other officers to be on the lookout for drivers under the influence.

Moments after the police left, and when the only noise he heard was the night music of crickets and frogs, he moved his arm away from Elisabeth.

"Is it safe?" she whispered, her head still lying on his shoulder.

"Let me check." She moved, and he sat up slowly. The scent from the bonfire wafted toward them, but the lights in the Schrocks' barn were out. He didn't see or hear anyone else.

"We can *geh* now."

"*Gut*, because I'm freezing." She sat up, then rose to her feet.

He jumped to his feet and stripped off his jacket. "Here." He put it around her shoulders. She slipped her arms inside the sleeves. The coat dwarfed her slim body.

He could see the remnants of the bonfire and headed in that direction, with Elisabeth trailing slightly behind him. His heartbeat finally slowed down as he realized he and Elisabeth were alone. He had no idea how many of the partygoers had been taken in by the police, if any. That the police hadn't had any backup made him think only a few of the youth had been busted. He said a silent prayer of thanks he hadn't been among them.

Aaron heard Elisabeth stumble behind him, and he slowed down his pace. He took her hand and together they navigated the dark field and crossed the road to the Yoders'. Only when they reached his buggy did he release her hand.

Aaron steered his horse to the road, then headed to Elisabeth's house. When he was several yards away from the Schrocks', he turned on the buggy lights and the small lamp inside. He snuck a look at Elisabeth. She sat on the other side of the seat, as far from him as she could, her arms hugging her body.

He reached back behind the seat and pulled out an old, clean quilt and handed it to her. She took it, but instead of wrapping it around herself, she set it on the seat and stared straight ahead. He'd never known Elisabeth to be anything but a chatterbox, but she hadn't spoken since they'd left the Schrocks'.

After a few moments, her silence unnerved him so much he had to speak. "Are you all right?"

She nodded.

"Are you sure?"

"I'm fine, Aaron." Her tone was flat and life-less.

"You don't sound fine." He gripped the reins, the leather digging into the palm of his hand. "Did something happen back there?"

"*Nee.*" She shifted in her seat, angling her body away from him.

"Because if somebody was messing with you—"

"I said nothing happened." She looked down on the floor. "Take me home, Aaron. I just want to go home."

It took nearly forty-five minutes to get to her house. By the time they arrived, he figured it was close to midnight. All the lights were out at the Byler home when he pulled into the driveway. As soon as the horse came to a stop, Elisabeth opened the door and jumped out. She started to shut the door, then hesitated.

"You were right. I shouldn't have gone." Then she shut the door and ran to the house.

He considered following her, then thought better of it. He didn't want to risk waking up her parents, which would surely happen if he fol-lowed her inside the house.

It wasn't until he'd made it almost home that he remembered Kacey. He hadn't seen her since he'd gone to jail. She was the last person he thought he'd run into at this party. Two years since his arrest and she was still drinking and smoking. Her ultra-thin frame made him suspect she was still using drugs too. It saddened him to think that at twenty-one she was still hanging out with younger kids and getting high.

Aaron shook his head and turned into his driveway. Despite his thoughts about Kacey, he couldn't get Elisabeth out of his mind, or their narrow escape from the police. The memory of lying next to her ran through his mind, but he forced it away. He didn't want to think about how good it felt to hold her for those brief moments.

He pondered what had happened before he found Elisabeth coming from behind the haystack. Something went on, and he had no idea what, but he had a strong suspicion Chase was involved.

"Elisabeth. Elisabeth!"

Elisabeth opened her eyes at the muffled sound of her mother's voice. She squinted against the sunlight that streamed through her bedroom window. A bitter, sour taste coated her mouth. She licked her dry lips and tried to wake up.

A knock sounded at her door. "Elisabeth? Are you sick? It's past seven."

She bolted upright out of bed. Seven? Normally she was up before five-thirty. "Just a minute." She rose from her bed, walked to the door, and opened it.

Emma Byler stood in the doorway, a puzzled look crossing her face. "Why are you wearing one of your brother's coats?"

Elisabeth glanced down at Aaron's coat, surprised. She hadn't realized she'd slept in it. After Aaron dropped her off she went straight upstairs and right to bed, trying to put the party behind her. But she tossed and turned most of the night, which probably explained why she'd overslept. "I'm cold," she explained.

"I've never known you to go to bed with a coat before. Or sleep in your *kapp*." She peered at Elisabeth. "Are you sure you're all right?"

No, she wasn't all right, but Elisabeth wasn't about to admit that to her mother. Or explain that the coat she wore belonged to Aaron. "I don't think I'm feeling so *gut*."

"Oh dear, I hope you haven't caught Stephen's cold. It took him two weeks to get over it. Well, there's still some breakfast left over downstairs. Biscuits and gravy, scrambled eggs, and a few pancakes. I don't think your brother ate them all."

"I'm not hungry."

Emma frowned. "You must not be feeling well. You've never turned down breakfast." She put the back of her hand to Elisabeth's forehead. "You don't feel warm."

"I think I'm mostly tired."

Emma gave her a pointed look. "Maybe you stayed up too late. How was your outing last night?"

Elisabeth's face flushed. "Fine," she said quickly, then backed away from the door.

"I'm glad you had a nice time. Oh, there's some grass on your coat." Her mother reached over and plucked two blades off her shoulder. "Some over here too. Where did it all come from?"

"I, um, don't know."

"There's probably grass on your bed. Make sure you shake out your quilt. Don't worry about the chores. Ruth can help me with them this morning. Why don't you get some rest, and if you feel better, you can come downstairs later."

"*Danki, Mami.*"

When her mother walked away, Elisabeth closed the door, then leaned against it, thankful she didn't have to go downstairs, and even more thankful her mother hadn't questioned her any further. What she told her *mami* wasn't a complete lie—she really didn't feel very good. But it had little to do with catching germs.

Her eyes closed as the memories flooded back. Deborah leaving with a guy and abandoning her. Taking a sip of the drink Chase had spiked. And worst of all, him practically dragging her behind the haystack. Opening her eyes, she wiped her mouth with the back of her hand, as if she could erase the fact that he kissed her. She should have gone home the minute he had started talking to her.

Regret filled her. She'd always wondered what her first kiss would be like and had always imagined it would be with the man she loved,

151

the man she would marry. Instead it had been at a party with a slobbery, drunk Yankee. And she could never take it back.

Taking off Aaron's coat, she shook it out, a few more blades of grass floating to the floor. Then she walked over to her bed and plopped down, ignoring her mother's advice about shaking out the quilt. She hugged Aaron's coat to her body. Why hadn't she listened to him? She knew the answer to that. Because her desire to prove him wrong had overridden her common sense.

A tingling sensation traveled through her body as she thought of their narrow escape from the police. She'd probably be sitting in the pokey if he hadn't shown up. Why had he come anyway? Certainly not to attend the party. Maybe he wanted to rub her mistake in her face. But if that was his reason, then why didn't he? He'd had the opportunity on the ride home. Instead he gave her his coat, handed her a quilt in case she was cold, and asked her what was wrong with genuine concern. More important, he didn't press her when she didn't want to talk about what had happened. If she didn't know any better, she would have thought he actually cared.

Then there were the tense moments waiting for the police to arrive, when she was in the cradle of his embrace. She'd never been that close to a man, save for Chase, and he didn't count. But lying there, holding her breath as she waited to see if

152

they would be discovered, the weirdest thing happened—she found herself enjoying their closeness. She liked the feel of his arm around her, the scent of his clean shirt, the thump of his heartbeat in her ear as she rested her cheek on his chest.

Not that it mattered how she felt. Aaron had been protecting them both from the cops. She doubted he would give the episode—or her—much thought. That was Aaron's way. But she knew she wouldn't stop thinking about it for a long time.

Elisabeth pulled her bobby pins and *kapp* off and laid them on the small nightstand. Then she lay down on the bed and pulled her legs to her chest, her head resting on the coarse fabric of Aaron's coat. The sunbeams soon faded, replaced with dark clouds. Droplets plinked against her windowpane. Within moments she had fallen asleep, still thinking about Aaron.

When she awoke a couple of hours later, she felt physically better but no less troubled inside. Still, she had to put everything behind her and face the rest of the day. According to her growling stomach, her appetite had returned.

She walked to her bureau and adjusted the angle of her small mirror. Looking at her reflection, she scowled. No wonder her mother didn't question her when she said she didn't feel good. She brushed out her long hair, pinned it up, then put on her *kapp*. After changing into a fresh dress, she felt better. But before going downstairs, she brushed the grass off her quilt, running her palm over the blue and white basket design. Later she'd bring a broom upstairs and sweep the floor, but right now she wanted to eat.

Crossing the room, she went to the door and opened it, only to see Ruth standing there, her fist poised to knock.

Elisabeth's hand went to her chest. "Don't do that, Ruth. You startled me."

"How was I supposed to know you were going to open the door?" Ruth tilted her head to the side, her dishwater-blonde eyebrows raised. She peered over the rims of her glasses. "You don't look sick to me."

"I'm not sick." Elisabeth stumbled over her words. "I . . . wasn't feeling well. But now I'm better."

"Just as we finished all the chores, naturally."

Elisabeth rolled her eyes. "What do you need, Ruth?"

Ruth cleared her throat. Out of all Elisabeth's siblings, Ruth was the most serious, with Lukas taking a close second. Stephen was contemplative and quiet, but Ruth took the prize when it came to having a staid demeanor. It was as if she'd been born a miniature adult. "Aaron Detweiler came to see you."

Elisabeth stood still. Aaron had been here? Probably to pick up his coat. That he hadn't had it on a cold day added another layer of guilt. "When was he here?"

"A couple hours ago. I told him you were sleeping, and he said not to wake you. He did want me to give you this, though." She held out a small folded piece of paper.

Elisabeth took it from her. "Is that all he said?"

"*Ya*. Then he left." Ruth took a step back from her. "You really need to brush your teeth."

Elisabeth scowled. Ruth was nothing if not blunt. "*Danki* for the hygiene tip."

Ruth headed down the hall. "Are you coming downstairs?"

"*Ya*. In a minute."

"Hmph. If I'd known that, I would have left the bathroom for you to do."

Elisabeth closed her door and ran her tongue across her teeth. Ugh. Her sister was right, she did need to brush them. A few swigs of mouthwash were probably in order too.

She unfolded the scrap of paper, noticing that it was a receipt for a candy bar from the local pharmacy in Middlefield. A few words were scribbled on the back.

Stopped by to see if you're okay. Aaron.

Wow. Now this was unexpected. He'd probably used up his lunch hour to get to her house. He didn't have to do that, or even leave a note. Maybe he did care, at least a little. Folding the slip of paper into a small square, she put it under her pillow and smiled.

Chapter 10

*E*arly Monday morning, Aaron inserted his key into the lock at the blacksmith shop. But when he twisted the key, he realized it was already unlocked. The light in the main shop was off, but he saw a faint glow coming from the office. He set his blue lunch cooler on one of the work tables and crossed the room. Peeking through the small window on the door, he saw Elisabeth sitting at her desk, a stack of invoices in front of her as she wrote in the account ledger. What time had she come in? It was just past six thirty in the morning, but she looked like she had been there for a while.

Aaron knocked lightly on the door. She jumped, then motioned for him to come inside.

"Sorry." He stepped inside the room. "I didn't mean to scare you."

"It's okay. I wasn't expecting anyone here until seven."

"I wanted to get a head start on the day. Saturday was really busy, and I still have a few things to catch up on." He leaned back against the door and thrust his hands into his coat pockets. "We did have a break midday, and I stopped by your house."

"I know. Ruth told me." She turned and removed his coat from the back of her chair. "Here. *Danki* for letting me wear it. I'm sorry you had to go without a coat over the weekend."

He took it from her. "No problem. My *daed* has several coats and jackets he's collected over the years." He touched his chest. "He won't even miss this one."

"Still, I should have given it back to you when you dropped me off."

"I think you needed it more than I did." He started to hang his coat on the rack of pegs on the wall, but she intervened.

"Let me do that—"

"It's okay—"

Both of them held the coat, and he looked down at her, touched by the vulnerability and uncertainty in her eyes. It was as if at any moment she expected him to tear into her or give her a lecture about what happened. But he would never do that. He gently took the coat from her and hung it on the peg. "Are you okay?" It was a safe question, vague enough for her to answer but not so invasive that she would clam up.

"*Nee.*" She looked down at her feet.

Unlike her disarrayed appearance the night they were escaping the police, this morning she was perfectly pulled together, her light blonde hair neatly combed and parted, her *kapp* pinned on straight, the white ribbons tucked into the front of her dress. After a moment, she glanced up. "I feel really stupid."

"You shouldn't."

"I can't help it. You tried to warn me. You told me what would happen and I didn't believe you. I owe you an apology."

"Elisabeth." He took a step toward her, an unexpected urge to comfort her entering his thoughts. "This is me you're talking to. Aaron Detweiler, former jailbird. The *mann* with a record, remember?" The lights went on in the shop.

"Gabe's here, so I need to get to work. I'll talk to you later." He turned to leave.

"Aaron, you don't have to do this."

He faced her. "Do what?"

"Make me feel better."

His lips lifted in a partial smile. "I know. But I want to try."

Business had finally picked up at Esh's Amish Goods during the Christmas season. The shop was doing so well that Anna had hired Ruth, who was on vacation from school, to help with the holiday rush. Christmas was in less than a week, and Anna had been spending extra time at the store in the evenings, straightening merchandise and restocking shelves. She prayed the success would continue, and she was already planning ways to keep customers returning after the holidays. Things were also busy at home, as her mother had decided to invite a couple of families to the house Christmas evening.

With everything that was going on, she didn't have time to deal with the doctor. But earlier this month the pain had become more frequent, and at times, unbearable. She'd had no choice but to visit the gynecologist, and he had just finished giving her a physical exam.

Anna pulled the blue and white hospital gown closer to her body, fighting her embarrassment. Her stomach churned as the tall doctor sat down on a wheeled stool and opened a medical folder. His expression inscrutable, he pulled an ink pen out of the pocket of his white lab coat and pointed to various places in Anna's records as he scanned the papers.

Dr. Caxson removed his reading glasses and looked at her, compassion in his eyes. "Ms. Esh, according to your symptoms, I suspect you have endometriosis."

She frowned, unfamiliar with the medical terminology. "Endometriosis?"

"It's when the endometrial cells growing inside your uterus grow outside of it. That's what's causing your pain. But the only way to be sure is for me to do a laparoscopy."

"Isn't that surgery?"

"Yes, but it's something I can do in the office and won't take very long. What I'll do is make a tiny incision below your belly button and insert a lighted tube which will let me see how far the endometriosis has progressed outside your uterus. If the tissue hasn't grown too much, I'll prescribe medication for the pain."

"And if it has?"

"I'll remove the implanted tissue during the lap procedure."

She chewed her bottom lip as she mulled over his words. "How long is the recovery time?"

"Most patients have the most pain the day after the procedure, but you should feel back to your normal self within a week."

"I see. And what will happen if I don't have the surgery?"

"I can't be sure unless you have the laparoscopy, but I predict your pain will increase, and to be honest, there's a very real possibility you won't be able to have children, since endometriosis interferes with conception. But once the tissue is removed, your pain will decrease and you should have no problem getting pregnant." He picked up her medical records and flipped through them. "Are you married?"

"*Nee.*" Lukas' image passed through her mind.

He closed the file. "I don't recommend putting off the surgery for very long, or your problems will likely increase." He rose from his wheeled stool and held out his hand. "Once you've decided about the surgery, call my office and we'll make an appointment." After shaking Anna's hand, he turned and left the room, his brown loafers squeaking against the linoleum.

Anna's legs dangled over the side of the examining table as she tried to soak in what the doctor had said. It had never dawned on her that she couldn't have children. But that had been her most fervent desire once—to get married and have a large family. And while she had stifled those desires for so long after Daniel, Lukas had reawakened them. Even though they hadn't officially started courting, she had been thinking more and more often about telling him that friendship wasn't enough for her anymore.

But now, everything had changed.

She sat up straight and took a deep breath. The doctor hadn't said that she was infertile; he only said that there was a possibility, if she didn't have the laparoscopy done. The surgery would only take a day, and according to Dr. Caxson, the recovery would be quick. Having the surgery would solve the issue; she had to believe that. Encouraged, she quickly dressed, left the examining room, and found one of the nurses.

"I was just coming in to talk to you," the woman said. Her hair, the color of carrots and cut in a straight bob against her chin, swayed as she talked. "Dr. Caxson has some pain medication for you to try."

"All right," Anna said, impatience coloring her tone. "How soon can I have the surgery?"

"You can ask at the front desk. They'll schedule it for you." She handed Anna a prescription slip. "Good luck, sweetie."

"Thanks." Nerves strung tight, she made her way to the receptionist, who scheduled the procedure for the third week of January. At least she could focus on the Christmas rush at the store without having to deal with surgery too.

"You're gonna burn the house down with all these stinky candles." Zeb took his hat off and waved it over one of the cinnamon-scented candles on the coffee table in the living room.

"Zeb!" Edna went to him, snatching away his hat. "You're the one who's going to catch on fire if you keep doing that."

Anna laughed as she set a platter of butter cookies next to the candles.

"I don't see why we have to have all this stuff around here anyway." He gestured to the fragrant pine bows hanging on the mantle of the fireplace, filling the room with their fresh scent. Bright red apples were interspersed in the pine branches, adding a festive punch of color. He shuffled across the room and plopped down on his old rocking chair. "Fancy stuff we don't need."

Anna looked at him, unwilling to let her crotchety uncle spoil her good mood. She was also determined not to think about the surgery. No, tonight she would focus on celebrating the birth of their Savior and enjoy visiting with the Bylers and Detweilers. Edna, Emma, and Sarah had become fast friends over the past few months.

"Where's your Christmas spirit, *Onkel* Zeb?"

"Here." He dug into his pocket and pulled out a red-and-white-striped candy cane. A faint smile played on his lips, causing Anna to giggle.

"Give me that." Edna held out her hand to Zeb. "Those are for the *kinner*."

"And people say I'm mean," Zeb grumbled, but he handed the sweet to Edna, who put it in a basket on a small table near the front door.

"Now, behave yourself, Zeb. Company will be here soon." Edna tucked an errant strand of hair into her *kapp* and blew out a long breath.

"*Mami*, everything's perfect." Anna went to her. "Don't worry, we'll all have a *gut* time."

"I hope so. It's been so long since we've had so many visitors. Not since your *daed* died." She looked at Anna. "Christmas is always the hardest."

"I know." She walked over and put her arm around her *mami's* shoulders.

Edna leaned into the half hug, then stepped away. "All right, they'll be here any minute. I'm going to check on the chicken and noodles."

When her mother had left, Anna went to the window and looked out into the darkness. It had started snowing earlier that day, and when she squinted, she could see a faint layer of white on the ground.

Moments later she saw the lights and reflective tape from three buggies as they came up their road. She stepped away from the window and went into the kitchen. "They're here."

Edna pulled a large pan of bubbling chicken and noodles out of the oven and put it on top of the stove. She shut the oven door and yanked off her red-and-green quilted oven mitts. "Go ahead and let them in."

Anna went to open the front door, as Zeb hadn't budged from his chair. Emmanuel and Sarah Detweiler arrived first, followed by Joseph and Emma, Elisabeth, Stephen, and Ruth Byler. Moriah and Gabe, along with their two daughters, Velda and Ester, came in next.

The women and children went to the kitchen while the men settled in the living room and immediately engaged in conversation. But Anna tuned out their voices as she looked out the window again. Where was Lukas? Surely he was coming. The entire Byler family had been invited.

"Lookin' for someone?"

Anna let the curtain fall and turned around to see Zeb staring at her, his hands folded over his belly. "*Nee.*" She moved away from the window.

"Sure looked like it to me."

"Just watching the snow fall." She didn't want to admit anything to Zeb or to the other men in the room. Although she didn't need to worry

164

about them, as they were discussing whether they were all in store for a hard winter this year.

"Hmph." He started rocking back and forth in the chair. "You're a terrible liar, Anna. Which is *gut*, because lying is a terrible thing."

Guilt jabbed at her. "I'm going to see if *Mami* needs help in the kitchen."

"You do that."

Anna left to go to the kitchen, which was abuzz with activity and lively conversation. But her good spirits had taken a dive in Lukas' absence. Where was he? Was he spending Christmas with someone else? Had his feelings for her changed?

Maybe she had waited too long to tell him how she felt. Correction, she had made him wait too long.

"Anna?" Elisabeth came up to her. "Will you help me spread the tablecloth?"

"*Ya.*" She took one end of the white cloth while Emma took the other. As they opened it and put it on the table, she couldn't resist asking, "Is Lukas coming tonight?"

"I thought he was. He said something about it a few days ago. Then again, I don't always know his comings and goings. He rarely tells me anything, except that I'm too nosy."

"Oh."

"But I've never known him to miss a family gathering." Elisabeth smiled. "So he'll probably be here."

For the next couple hours Anna tried not to look at the clock and resisted the urge to check the window. She tried to enjoy the meal and the company, but her thoughts were filled with Lukas. Until that moment she hadn't realized how much she had wanted to spend Christmas with him. Or how much she missed him now that he wasn't here.

Over the din of the conversation in the kitchen, she heard a knock at the door. Jumping up from her chair, she said, "I'll get it." Then she dashed out of the room, trying to hide her smile. Finally, he was here.

But when she opened the door her excitement vanished. It wasn't Lukas standing on her uncle's front porch.

It was Aaron Detweiler.

By the disappointed look on Anna Esh's face, Aaron knew he'd made a mistake by coming. He was already a couple of hours late, having gone back and forth about whether to join everyone for Christmas. His mother had wanted him to come, but he hadn't made up his mind when they left. After spending part of the evening alone, he'd decided to go. This was family after all, and they wanted him here.

Except for Anna, apparently.

"Hi," she said, her tone reflecting the dejection in her features.

"Um, sorry I'm late." He stood there, the moment filled with awkwardness. "Maybe I should *geh*."

"What?" She gave her head a small shake, then looked at him. "Aaron, I'm so sorry." Stepping aside, she motioned for him to come inside.

"Are you sure?"

"Of course I am. I'm glad you could come."

"Okay, because I wasn't sure for a minute there."

Her face reddened. "I had something on my mind when I opened the door, that's all. You're always welcome here."

He walked inside, giving her enough room to shut the door.

"Let me take your things. Then you can *geh* in the kitchen and get something to eat."

As he removed his hat a few flakes fell off. The ride to the Eshes' hadn't been bad since there was only a thin coating of snow on the roads. But the flakes were coming down heavier now, so there was no telling what condition the roads would be in by the time he left.

He handed Anna his things and moved farther into the living room. He met his father's gaze. The old man's look of approval settled Aaron's nerves. He greeted the rest of the men in the room before going to the kitchen, inhaling the lingering aromas of pine and cinnamon that always reminded him of Christmas.

He entered the kitchen, surprised to see it empty. But Anna had said he could get something to eat, and he was starving. Seeing an empty plate near the stove, he picked it up and dished up a healthy serving of chicken and noodles, added a spoonful of mashed potatoes, then smothered all of it in gravy before sitting down at the table.

He had finished his prayer and picked up his fork when the opposite door of the kitchen opened. Looking up, he saw Elisabeth standing there.

"Aaron!" She grinned, then went to him. "I was hoping you'd be here."

Aaron couldn't help but smile in return. He was glad to see Elisabeth had returned to her normal, bubbly self. After spending a couple of days brooding at work, she had shown up one morning with a plate of chocolate chunk oatmeal cookies and a bright smile. She hadn't spoken about what had happened at the party, and he didn't ask. It must not have been as bad as he'd assumed, and he didn't want to do anything to spoil her good mood. He liked seeing her happy.

She put her hands on her hips. "Why are you so late?"

"I had things to do."

"Oh."

Her bright expression weakened, and he knew he was the cause of it. Suddenly he didn't want to give her excuses anymore. "Actually, that's not true."

Curiosity entered her blue eyes. Perhaps it was because of the muted gas lighting in the Eshes' kitchen, but he'd never noticed how pretty her eyes were before. Round and clear, with long, light blonde lashes that rested on the top of her cheeks when she blinked. She sat down next to him. "So what kept you?"

He looked down at his plate. "*Nix.*"

"What do you mean *nix*?"

"*Nix.* I didn't have anything to do tonight. In fact, I spent the past two hours doing nothing."

"You came here out of boredom?"

"*Nee*, Elisabeth. I came here because I didn't want to be alone on Christmas."

Her gaze grew soft and she put her hand on his arm. "Aaron, you don't ever have to be alone."

Her tender touch seeped through the fabric of his shirt, sparking something inside him. "*Danki.* I really needed to hear that."

She smiled, giving his arm a squeeze. Then she leapt from her chair. "I'll be right back. Enjoy your food."

"Where is everyone else?"

"Upstairs, looking at quilt patterns. Bor-ing."

"I thought you *maed* liked that kind of stuff."

"Not all *maed* are alike, Aaron." With that she left the room.

Aaron thought she was absolutely right. He didn't know anyone quite like Elisabeth Byler.

Chapter 11

*E*lisabeth went to Edna's room in the back of the house. She had hoped Aaron would show up tonight, and when he hadn't, she had been disappointed but not surprised. Now that he was here she could give him his Christmas present.

She searched for her tote bag, finding it under a pile of coats on Edna's bed. Her mother had made the bag a couple of years ago out of scraps from dresses Elisabeth had outgrown, and it was one of Elisabeth's favorite possessions. She reached in and pulled out a medium-sized square box, white and unadorned. Grinning, she dropped the bag back on the bed and went to the kitchen.

Aaron was drinking a glass of pop when she walked back in. She held the gift behind her back, relieved to see the kitchen was still empty. While she wasn't embarrassed about giving Aaron a gift, she was glad she could give it to him when they were alone.

Sitting down next to him, she handed him the box. "Merry Christmas."

Shock registered on his face, and he didn't accept the gift. He just stared at it.

His reaction poked a hole in her bubble of

happiness. "There's nothing alive in it. Or poisonous. I promise it's 100 percent safe."

"I'm sure it is." Finally he took it from her. "I'm surprised, that's all."

"*Geh* on, open it." She leaned her chin on the heels of her hands. "I hope you like it."

He slid his finger underneath the strip of tape fastening the lid closed, then opened the box. His eyebrows lifted as he pulled out a navy blue scarf. "Did you make this?"

"*Ya.* I knitted it myself." As he examined it, she hoped he wouldn't notice how many stitches she'd dropped, or that it was a bit uneven on the ends. She'd never been a great knitter, but she had tried.

"It's nice. Very soft." He put the scarf back in the box and looked at her. "*Danki*, Elisabeth. I'm sorry. I don't have anything for you."

She sat back in her chair. "That's okay. I didn't think you would. Not because I think you're a scrooge or anything, although maybe you are, I don't know."

"Huh?"

"Never mind. I just want you to know that I didn't make it because I expected you to give me something back. I made it because I wanted to give you something for Christmas, and to say *danki*."

"For what?" he asked. "I haven't done anything."

"Sure you have. You always seem to be there

171

when I need you, and I appreciate it. If you hadn't shown up when you did at that party . . . I don't want to think about what might have happened."

"I'm glad I was there too."

"I also appreciate that you didn't rub it in my face about how wrong I was. Believe me, I learned my lesson. I'm sticking to singings and frolics from now on."

"*Gut* idea." He fingered the scarf again. "This was really nice of you, Elisabeth." He grinned.

There was that smile again. She was amazed by the way it transformed his face and warmed her heart. "Wow, you really have a gorgeous smile."

Did she just say that out loud?

His face turned pink and he glanced away.

"Uh, I mean it's nice. In a good-looking way." She just kept digging that hole deeper and deeper. "I mean—"

"*Danki*, Elisabeth." He picked up the scarf and his plate, taking the plate to the sink. Tucking the box under his arm, he went into the living room to join the other men.

Elisabeth laid her head on the table. Why oh why had she said that out loud? He must think she's *ab im kopp*, or worse, that she had a crush on him. Which, of course, she didn't.

"Something wrong, Elisabeth?"

She lifted her head to see Anna standing beside her. "*Nee*. Unless you count making an idiot out of myself as something wrong."

Anna sat down beside her. "I'm sure whatever you did, you didn't make an idiot of yourself."

"Oh, I'm sure I did." She told Anna what she said to Aaron. "Now he probably thinks I like him."

"Do you?"

"Of course I do. We work together, and he's helped me out." More than she cared to admit.

"I don't mean as a coworker or a friend. You knitted him a scarf, after all."

"For Christmas. There's nothing wrong with that."

"*Nee*, there isn't." Anna brushed a few crumbs off the tablecloth with the side of her hand. "It was a nice thing to do."

"That's because I'm a nice person." She smiled, feeling less like a fool. "Speaking of liking people, what's going on with you and Lukas?"

Anna's smile faded. "*Nix*. He's not here."

"I know, and that's strange. I can't imagine where he'd be."

"It doesn't matter. I'm sure wherever he is he's having a *gut* time." Anna stood up and went to the sink, turning on the water.

"Do you need some help with the dishes?"

She shook her head. "There's only a few left. We washed most of them earlier." Facing Elisabeth, she said, "Why don't you *geh* upstairs?"

"Are they still talking about quilts?"

"Probably."

Elisabeth let out a sigh. "Thrilling."

She pushed back from the table. There wasn't anything else for her to do, so she might as well go back upstairs. She was tempted to go in the living room and sit with the men, but knowing them, they would be talking about work, and she wasn't in the mood to listen about the intricacies of cabinet building or the pros and cons of using coal or carbon in the forge. What she really wanted to do was go out and catch snowflakes on her tongue, like she used to do as a child. But she wasn't a child anymore, and she needed to put those things behind her. If discussing textile designs helped do that, then she'd participate.

Yet she couldn't resist stepping out the back door and watching the snow float to the ground for just a minute. Looking around, she stuck her tongue out to taste the flakes, then went back inside.

"I forgot how tiring having company could be." Edna wiped the top of the stove with a wet rag. "I'm exhausted. But it was a nice time, *ya*?"

"*Ya*, it was." Despite her disappointment about Lukas not showing up, Anna liked visiting with everyone. She especially enjoyed talking to Elisabeth, whom she suspected was in a bit of denial about her feelings for Aaron. Then again, if anyone was an expert on denying their feelings, it was Anna.

She walked over and took the rag from her mother's hand. "Let me finish this, *Mami*. You *geh* ahead to bed."

"Are you sure?"

Anna nodded. "There's not much else to do. I'll finish up in here and put out the candles in the living room."

"Zeb is in there."

"Still?"

"*Ya.*" Edna shook her head. "He fell asleep about an hour ago. Don't worry about him. He'll wake up and go upstairs in a little while."

"All right."

"*Gut nacht*, Anna." She kissed her daughter's cheek. "*Hallicher Grischtdaag.*"

"Merry Christmas. Night, *Mami*."

Anna wiped down the last dish and put it in the cabinet. She turned off the gas light in the kitchen and went into the living room. Sure enough, Uncle Zeb was snoring away in his rocker. She took the quilt off the back of the couch and laid it over him, then turned to blow out the candles. Just as she was about to extinguish the last one, she heard a knock on the door.

Startled, she paused for a moment. Who would be coming here this late at night? It was still snowing out, so maybe someone was stranded on the side of the road and needed help. She went to the door and opened it.

"Merry Christmas."

Anna's mouth dropped open at seeing Lukas standing in front of her. Snow covered his black hat and the shoulders of his coat. He held a box in his hand.

"All right if I come in?"

She didn't say anything for a moment, unable to comprehend that he was here. She just gripped the door and stared.

"Anna?" He tilted his head, a puzzled look crossing his face.

"*Ya?*"

He hesitated, as if waiting for her to respond. When she didn't, he frowned. "Can I come in?"

"What? *Ya.* Come in." She moved so he could walk past her, then shut the door and turned around, still surprised to see him. "I didn't mean to make you stand out there in the cold."

"I'm really late, and I'm sorry."

"I didn't think you were coming."

Lukas nodded. "I didn't think I'd ever get here myself. I was on the way but a buddy of mine stopped by and he needed help with one of his cows. Seemed she decided Christmas was a *gut* day to have a calf, but the calf had other ideas."

"Are they both okay?"

"*Ya.* The calf finally came out. *Mudder* and *sohn* are doing fine. But by the time it was over I was a mess and had to get a shower. I got here as fast as I could after that."

She should have known he'd been helping

176

someone. That was typical Lukas. "You didn't have to come. I would have understood."

"I know, but I wanted to be here so I could give you this." He reached in his pocket and pulled out a small box wrapped in plain brown paper.

"Lukas, *danki*." Surprised and touched, she took the box from him.

He laid his coat and hat on the closest chair.

"Are you hungry? I can fix you something to eat."

"*Nee*. I'm fine."

"We can sit down here." She gestured to the sofa on the opposite side of the room.

Lukas looked at Zeb sleeping in the chair. "Sure we won't wake him up?"

"I doubt it. He fell asleep while everyone else was still here, so I think he's gone for the night."

They sat down and Anna held the box in her hands, anticipating the gift inside. "Can I open it?"

"I insist."

She tore off the paper and lifted the lid. Nestled on a small square of white cotton was a silver watch pin. "It's beautiful, Lukas." She looked up. "I love it."

He let out a breath and grinned. "*Gut*, because I can't take it back."

She touched the glass covering the face of the watch. It was a lovely gift, and the nicest one she'd ever received. It made hers pale in comparison. "I have something for you too. But it's not as nice as this."

"You got me something?" He seemed genuinely surprised.

"*Ya.*" She got up and went to her bedroom, coming back with his present. "Like I said, it's not much."

"It's great!" He took the brand new straw hat from her. "How did you know I needed a new one?"

"I noticed the other one was starting to fray, so I thought you might like a replacement."

"Well, I need it now because last week I set it on a table in the woodshop and Stephen knocked over a can of stain. Ran all over the brim."

Anna smiled, pleased that he liked her gift. She sat next to him, a little closer than she had before.

He put the hat in his lap and looked at her. "*Danki*, it's a *gut* hat." He leaned over and kissed her cheek. "Hope that was all right," he whispered in her ear before pulling away.

Her heart flipped, her cheek still tingling from the warmth of his lips. "*Ya.*"

He reached for her hand, then entwined his fingers in hers. "And is this all right too?"

Her mouth went dry as he tightened his grip on her hand. At this point she couldn't even speak; she could only nod.

His lips tipped up in a grin. "What about going

out—and I'm not talking about as friends? Are you ready for that now?"

She swallowed, every part of her tingling at the tender look in his eyes. "*Ya*, Lukas. I am."

"About time."

Both she and Lukas looked over at Zeb, who was wide awake in the chair. He tossed the quilt off his body and slowly stood up, his bones cracking as he straightened. "Took you two long enough to figure this out. You should have been courtin' a long time ago. I'm going to bed. Let me know when you're havin' the wedding."

Anna's mouth dropped open as her face flamed. "He was awake the whole time?" She turned to Lukas, who was chuckling.

"Guess so," he said.

"Then he saw you kiss me!"

Lukas leaned forward. "I don't think he's going to tell anyone. And you know what?" He kissed her cheek again, his lips lingering. "I don't care if he does."

January arrived, bringing its crisp temperatures and blankets of snow. It had been a little over a month since the Schrocks' party, and Elisabeth had put the incident out of her mind. She had better and more important things to think about, like her job and her growing friendship with Aaron.

He had shown up to work the day after

Christmas wearing the scarf she'd made for him, and she noticed he'd worn it every day since. He had also joined her for lunch twice. If her remark about his smile had bothered him, he didn't show it. Instead they talked about all kinds of things, and she found out that he liked ice skating, something she'd only done once. They decided to meet on a Sunday afternoon at his parents' house, which had a small pond in the back that had frozen over.

"You sure we won't fall through?" Elisabeth peered at the cloudy ice from the safety of the bank.

"Positive. I already tested it." He finished tying his black skates and stood up. "You ready?"

She had her skates on, a pair of white ones borrowed from one of her friends. Suddenly she wasn't all that eager to step out onto the pond.

"What's the matter, Elisabeth?"

Looking at the ice again, she said, "I don't know about this."

"Are you scared?"

She looked at him. His voice and expression weren't taunting. Glad that he wasn't making fun of her, she said, "*Ya.* I think I am."

"You think?"

"I'm indecisive sometimes. I can't help it."

He held out his hand, which was covered in a thick woolen glove. "Trust me. Nothing's going to happen."

Her gaze landed on his hand, which was steady

and sure. Slipping her gloved hand in his, she let him lead her out on the ice.

Still holding her hand, he turned to face her, then grasped her other hand. Skating backward, he pulled her toward him. "See? It's solid."

Pushing one wobbly leg forward, she tried to match his strides but soon gave up and let him drag her around the pond. It wasn't long before he noticed.

"You're not skating."

"I'm not? I thought I was."

"Standing still doesn't equal skating." His nose and cheeks glowed red from the cold.

"I beg to differ. I'm moving."

"Because I'm pulling you." He released her hands and skated away from her.

"Aaron, what are you doing?" Her arms flailed as she tried to regain her balance. She couldn't do this without holding on to him.

"Teaching you to skate." He glided up beside her and put his hand at her waist, then took her right hand in his.

"How about you teach me how to stop first."

"I thought you said you'd been skating before." He guided her slowly around the perimeter of the pond.

"Once. When I was five."

"Then you have some catching up to do."

She cast him a sidelong glance. "You're enjoying this, aren't you?"

He flashed his rare and still gorgeous smile. "Very much."

"I'm glad I can entertain you." Her left foot shot out in front of her, and for a moment she thought for sure she'd land right on her backside. But Aaron caught her, saving her from disgrace.

"I think we need to start with the basics," he said.

The next hour passed quickly as she tried to get the hang of moving around on thin blades. She spent most of the time staring at her feet, which seemed to have a mind of their own. After a few spins around the pond, the ice became grooved and pocked, and she had trouble balancing. Still, she wasn't about to pack it in, not until she could at least let go of Aaron's arm.

When she was finally able to skate a few steps by herself, Aaron took off and circled the pond at an amazing rate of speed. He flew around her once, then skidded to a stop about ten feet from her, sending shards of ice flying from his blades.

"I'm impressed." She tilted forward for a minute, then managed to right herself without falling. Maybe she'd get the hang of this after all. "Where did you learn to skate like that?"

"Older brothers and their friends. We'd play broom hockey out here all the time when I was a *kinn*. At first they told me I couldn't play until I learned how to skate, so I'd spend hours on the ice until I could. Then they got mad because I skated better than they did. But they always wanted me on their team."

"I don't think I could ever skate that well."

"Just takes practice. Lots of practice."

"And some skates that fit. My feet hurt."

"You want to stop?"

She nodded. She was also freezing. Skating was fun, but now it was just painful.

"Okay."

They moved off the ice and to the wooden bench on the edge of the pond. She sat down and lifted up her feet, glad to be off the ice.

He bent down and started untying his skates. He had them off and his boots on before she could finish untangling the laces of even one of her skates. Then she realized they were in a knot. After she fumbled with them for a moment, she heard Aaron say, "Here. Let me try."

She looked at him, then held up her foot, rearranging her skirt for modesty. He scooted closer to her, balanced her skate on his knee, and took off his gloves.

A few minutes later he gave up. "This is some knot." He looked at her. "I can't undo it."

That wasn't good. "I can't walk around wearing one ice skate for the rest of my life."

"That would be a sight to see."

"Not funny, Aaron."

"I know, I know. Here, let me see if I can pull

it off." He put one hand on her ankle, then grasped the blade and pulled.

"Yow! Not so hard. I want to keep my foot."

"Sorry." He pushed back the brim of his hat, his brows furrowing. "Let me try something different." He cupped the heel of the skate and started to tug on it, then wiggled it back and forth. He did that several times until her foot started to slip. "Okay, now I think I can pull it out." Gripping the blade, he gave it a hard yank, sending the skate and him flying backward off the bench and into the snow.

"Are you all right?" She moved to the edge of the bench and looked at him lying flat on his back.

"*Ya.*" He sat up, then burst into laughter.

She couldn't help but laugh too. When she caught her breath she asked, "Where's my skate?"

"Over there." He smiled and pointed to the skate, sticking blade up in the snow. Grabbing his hat off the ground, he shook the snow from it and put it back on his head, then scrambled up and retrieved her skate. "Here you go. Tell me you can get the other one off by yourself?"

She giggled. "I think I can manage." And she did, since she hadn't tied a knot in the laces.

He sat down beside her as she slipped on her snow boots. When she looked at him, he was still smiling. His happiness warmed her heart.

"You know," he said after a long moment, "I haven't had this much fun in a long time."

"Then it was worth embarrassing myself on the ice."

"You didn't embarrass yourself." His expression grew serious. "Some *maed* wouldn't have gotten out there, not unless they could skate perfectly."

"*Perfection* isn't a word I'm familiar with." She checked to see if her black bonnet was still tied beneath her chin, glad to discover it had remained in place.

"Neither am I."

"Right, because none of us is perfect. Thank goodness we have a heavenly Father who doesn't care and is very forgiving."

He leaned forward and put his elbows on his knees, staring at the pond. "Something I've experienced firsthand."

"Then why do you keep punishing yourself?"

He sat up and looked at her. "I'm not doing that."

"*Ya*, you are. You had fun today, Aaron. There's nothing wrong with that."

"I never said there was."

"But you act like there is."

He frowned. "Because I'm not smiling and laughing every moment of the day?"

She shook her head. "Because you cut yourself off from people."

He didn't say anything for a long moment, just stared at the snow covering the tops of his boots.

"There's a reason for that, Elisabeth. Having fun and hanging out with friends was all I ever cared about. I lived for the next party, the next high. Then it all came crashing down." He turned to her, his breath frosty in the cold air. "Life is serious now. I learned there are more important things than having a *gut* time."

"I know that. But don't you think there should be a balance? Why does it have to be one way or another?"

"I don't know. I guess I haven't figured that out yet." He looked out at the pond again. "How did you?"

"Oh, I don't have anything figured out."

"You seem to."

His response surprised her, because she felt just as lost as ever. "I don't, Aaron." She sighed. "Half the time I don't know what I'm doing, or what God wants me to do."

He let out a flat chuckle. "Join the club."

"At least you can ice skate."

He smiled. "A few more times out there and you will too."

"Maybe, but not today because I'm still freezing. Let's *geh* inside."

As they walked toward the Detweiler's house, Aaron took Elisabeth's skates from her and carried both pairs to the house. By the time they got to the back porch, she was cold and craving some hot chocolate.

Aaron's mother met them at the back door. "Elisabeth, someone's here for you."

"For me?"

"*Ya*. She said her name is Deborah. She said she had to talk to you right away. I was going to send her to the pond, but then I saw you coming back. She's in the living room." Sarah leaned forward, lowering her voice. "She seems *sehr* upset."

Elisabeth looked at Aaron and shrugged. "I don't know what's going on."

"*Geh* and talk to her," he said.

As she walked into Aaron's living room, she saw Deborah in front of the big picture window, looking outside.

"Deborah?"

When her friend turned around, the first thing Elisabeth noticed were her red-rimmed eyes. Alarmed, she asked, "What's wrong?"

"Oh, Elisabeth." Deborah went to her and grabbed her hands. "I'm in trouble. Big trouble." Tears pooled in her eyes. "I think I'm pregnant."

Chapter 12

"*A*aron, will you get me the cocoa powder from that cabinet?"

Aaron followed his mother's instructions and handed her the cocoa as she stirred milk in a pot over the stove. He moved to sit at the kitchen table, wondering what Deborah was doing here. She'd probably stopped by Elisabeth's house and found out she was here. But what could be so important that she couldn't wait to talk to Elisabeth later?

"Do you know Deborah?"

He looked at his mother, who was adding cocoa to the milk. "*Nee.* We only met once." He doubted Deborah remembered that encounter.

Sarah adjusted the gas flame underneath the pot. "I hope that poor *maedel* will be all right. She was distraught when she got here."

Aaron tapped his fingers against the table, wondering the same thing. He also thought back to his conversation with Elisabeth at the pond. He'd been surprised to learn that she felt she was mixed up too. He would have never guessed that about her. Yes, she could be impulsive and at times forgetful, and her inclination for poking her nose where it didn't belong could be annoying. But there were so many other things about her he found fascinating. Her optimism. Her sheer joy for life. Her ability to laugh off her failings and press on no matter what. Those were qualities he wished he possessed, qualities he found extremely appealing. It didn't hurt that her terrific personality was wrapped up in a pretty package either.

He stilled his hand, realizing that wasn't the

first time he'd been thinking about how attractive he thought she was. He'd been thinking about that a lot, since Christmas when she'd given him the scarf. A month later and he was still touched by her thoughtfulness. He'd wracked his brain trying to think of something suitable to get her in return, but he didn't think she'd want a pair of horseshoes or a handmade sconce. It just drove the point home that he had little to offer her.

"The cocoa's almost done." His mother glanced at him over her shoulder. "I wonder if I should take some to them or let them speak privately?"

"I'll take it." Aaron took two of the mugs his mother had filled and left the kitchen, heading down the hallway. As he neared the living room, he could hear them talking, but he couldn't make out who was speaking or even exactly what they were saying, their voices were so low. A few words jumped out at him. *Trouble. Parents. Help.*

He practically stomped into the room, warning them of his arrival. "Anyone thirsty?"

Both girls looked at him, and he could see why his mother had been concerned. Tears streaked down Deborah's face, and Elisabeth looked like she wanted to throw up.

Elisabeth went to him. "*Nee*, Aaron. Tell your *mami danki*, but Deborah and I have to *geh*."

"All right, let me get my coat and I'll drive you home."

"Deborah brought her buggy. I'll go with her."

189

She motioned for her friend to follow her. "I'll see you at work tomorrow." They rushed out of the front door.

Through the window, Aaron watched them leave in the buggy, the horse trotting at a swift pace. He frowned, genuinely worried now, and headed back to the kitchen. He set the mugs of cocoa on the table.

His mother looked at the still-full mugs. "They didn't want any hot chocolate?"

"They left."

"Already?"

He nodded.

"That's strange, isn't it?"

"*Ya*," he said, glancing at his mother. "Very strange." So strange, he didn't know what to think.

"I can't be pregnant, Elisabeth. I just can't be."

Elisabeth gripped the reins of Deborah's horse with one hand and reached out for her friend's hand. "Maybe you're not."

"But I checked the date on my calendar this morning. I've never been late."

"Are you sure you haven't made a mistake?" She tried to wrap her head around what Deborah was saying. Her friend was pregnant and unmarried. She had never personally known anyone who had gotten pregnant outside of wedlock.

Her stomach rolled. How could Deborah have

done this? How could she have given herself to anyone but her husband?

Taking a deep breath, she forced herself to stay calm. Deborah was already a wreck; she didn't need to make her friend feel worse.

"What am I going to do?"

Elisabeth squeezed Deborah's hand, then let it go. "First thing is to find out for sure. Have you taken a pregnancy test?"

"*Nee.*"

"Then we need to get one." She had gone to the pharmacy with Moriah when her sister had been pregnant with Ester, so she knew exactly where to find them.

Twenty minutes later, they pulled into the pharmacy parking lot. The snow plows had cleared the lot, heaping high piles of dirty snow on the perimeter. Elisabeth steered the horse to the hitching post, then started to climb out of the buggy.

"I don't know about this, Elisabeth. " Deborah sniffed, wiping her nose on a damp handkerchief.

"About what?"

"What if someone from church sees me? You know how people talk."

You should have thought of that before. "I'll *geh* in there with you."

"Then they might think you're pregnant too."

"I don't care what they think, Deborah. Right now I'm worried about you."

Deborah looked at her, tears dangling on her lashes. "You're such a *gut* friend, Elisabeth. I was awful to you the night of that party. I'm sorry."

"It's all right. Let's get this over with."

They got out of the buggy and Elisabeth tied the horse to the hitching post. They hurried inside and went straight to the aisle where the pregnancy tests were.

"Which one should I get?" Deborah scanned the shelves.

"This one," Elisabeth said, grabbing the one she remembered Moriah using. She thrust it at Deborah. "Now, let's go check out."

On the way to the check-out counter, Elisabeth grabbed a couple of candy bars.

"What are those for?" Deborah asked.

"You can't just buy a pregnancy test by itself."

"Oh." Deborah took the candy bars and put them on the counter along with the test. The cashier came over and checked them out.

"You want these in the bag?" The cashier drawled, holding up the candy.

Deborah's head bobbed up and down.

After the cashier put the merchandise in the bag, Deborah took it and immediately walked to the front door. Elisabeth started to follow.

"You want your receipt?" the cashier asked, holding a piece of paper.

Elisabeth snatched the receipt out of her hand and went back to the buggy. She climbed in beside her friend and shoved the receipt into her bag before starting out for Deborah's house.

Half an hour later, Elisabeth paced the length of Deborah's bedroom. Her friend was in the downstairs bathroom, taking the test. *Please Lord, let it be negative.*

She turned at the sound of Deborah entering the room, her face ashen. Elisabeth's stomach lurched. She knew without asking what the result was.

Instead of panicking as she had before, Deborah sat down on the bed, a faraway look on her face. "What am I going to do?"

"You have to tell the father."

Deborah looked up at Elisabeth. "I can't tell Chase about the *boppli.*"

Elisabeth's eyes widened. "Chase?"

"*Ya.* Chase is the father."

"Stephen, help me load these up in the buggy," Lukas said, pointing to three small child-sized hickory chairs and a box of other wooden toys lying next to it. "I told Anna I'd have these at the store for her today."

Stephen slapped his palms together to get rid of the sawdust that had accumulated on them, then grabbed two of the chairs without saying anything. The whir of a hydraulic wood saw followed them out the door as they headed for Lukas' buggy. His horse stretched back his ears as the men approached. When they finished loading up, Lukas said, "You want to come out to the store with me?"

"*Nee*. I've got plenty of stuff here to do."

Lukas pushed his hat back on his head. "Not so much that you can't take a little time off to come with me. I know Anna would like to see you."

"Maybe another time."

"All right." Lukas looked at him. At sixteen, Stephen was three years younger than Lukas, but had already passed him in height. He wouldn't be surprised if he grew right past Tobias, who was five feet ten inches tall. Lukas was two inches shorter.

Stephen gave him a nod, then turned around and went back inside.

Lukas shoved his hat lower on his head and climbed into the buggy. The January air was crisp, but the sun shone at full strength.

A short time later, Lukas pulled into the parking lot of Esh's Amish Goods. He tied his horse to the hitching post, then walked to the back of the wagon and pulled out two of the three rocking chairs. He'd come back for the box in a bit. When he entered, he saw Anna behind the counter. "Hello."

She looked surprised to see him. "What are you doing here?"

His smile faded. "The rockers? I said I'd bring them, remember?"

"Oh, *ya*. That's right." The confused look on her face disappeared. "I can't believe I forgot about that."

"Snow, sleet, rain, not even heavy traffic on 87 will keep your delivery *mann* from his mission."

She laughed. "You're more than a delivery *mann*, Lukas."

"Flattery will get you everywhere." Grinning, he held up the rocking chairs. "Where do you want these?"

"Just put them in the back."

He did as she asked, then returned to the front. "Be right back."

After he'd unloaded all the rockers, he went to Anna. "I wish I could stay longer, but I need to get back."

"That's all right. I'm really busy this morning." She glanced away.

There weren't any customers in the store, but maybe she meant she was busy with paperwork. Looking to see if anyone was around, he leaned over and kissed her cheek. "See you later."

"Bye." Her cheeks rosy, she waved as he walked out the door.

Anna watched Lukas as he left. She had forgotten he'd mentioned he was delivering the rockers today. Where was her mind this morning? But she knew the answer to that. She'd been on edge since she'd gotten up.

"Anna?" Her mother emerged from the back room. Today was Thursday, or as her *mami* teasingly called it, her "Zeb-free" day. Each Thursday she helped Anna in the store from open to close while Zeb spent Thursdays with his Yankee friend Charlie, who took him to the flea market in Bloomfield. It was the one day of the week they didn't have to worry about Zeb getting into trouble.

"What do you need, *Mami*?"

"What is this about?"

She looked at her mother, surprised at the tightness in her voice. Then she saw the pink paper in her hand, torn from a message pad, with her doctor's appointment and the word *surgery* written on it. Anna thought she had put the paper inside her purse, but she must have neglected to do it.

"Who's having surgery?"

Anna's first reaction was to lie. She hadn't wanted anyone to know about the surgery. But she couldn't do that, not to her mother's face. If only she had paid more attention. But she'd been so distracted this week.

She sighed. "I am."

"What?" Edna went to her. "Why? When?" She gripped Anna's arm, forcing her to face her. "What's going on?"

"I was going to tell you tonight."

"When's the surgery?"

"Today."

"And you weren't going to tell me until tonight?" She let go of Anna's arm and tossed the paper on the counter, hurt and dismay evident in her features. "How could you keep this from me?"

"It's an outpatient procedure, and I'll be home by the afternoon. I'll be fine by tomorrow."

"And what exactly are you having done?"

"A laparoscopy." She explained to her mother about her visit to Dr. Caxson. "So you see, there's nothing to worry about."

Edna leaned against the counter, distress contorting her features. "I wish you would have told me. I could have helped."

"There's nothing you can do, *Mami*."

Edna didn't look convinced. "At least I can go with you. We'll close the shop for the day."

"I won't do that. Thursday is one of our busiest days of the week. Besides, Ruth is coming in to help out today after school."

"Then call the doctor and reschedule the appointment for when I can be there with you."

"I can't."

"Can't . . . or won't?"

Anna didn't respond. Her mother wouldn't understand. She hadn't come to this decision lightly.

"Anna? Are you listening to me?"

Clearing her thoughts and focusing back on her mother, she said, "*Ya*. And I told you I can't cancel. Susan's coming to pick me up in a few minutes."

"Anna, I don't understand why you want to go through this by yourself. Does Lukas know?"

"*Nee*, and I don't plan on telling him." They'd only been courting for a couple of weeks, and even though they had been friends much longer, she couldn't imagine talking to him about something as personal as this.

"But what if the surgery doesn't work?"

"It will." She heard a honk from the parking lot and grabbed her purse off the desk.

"Anna, wait."

"I can't, *Mami*. Susan's here." She headed for the door, glancing over her shoulder before opening it.

Edna stood behind the counter, her head bent slightly. She could hear her mother whispering, no doubt saying a prayer on her behalf. Despite their argument, she was grateful to be blessed with a praying mother.

She stepped outside the store, a cold blast of air hitting her full force, despite most of her face being obscured by her bonnet. A few flakes of snow had started to fall, and a sharp wind swirled around the hem of her sage green dress. Her black knee socks did little to keep her legs warm.

Susan waved from the driver's side of her Buick sedan. Anna waved back and opened the door, climbing quickly inside, thankful for the warmth of the car's heater. Although Susan knew about the doctor's appointment, she didn't know the specifics.

"Ready to go?" Susan said, pulling the gearshift down.

"*Ya.*" Anna looked out of the passenger window, a fresh wave of nerves assaulting her. A shiver passed through her body, one unrelated to the wintery cold. "God willing, I'm ready."

Later that morning, Anna moved to sit up from the examination table, still groggy from the anesthetic the doctor had given her an hour or so ago. A sharp, burning pain stabbed her below her belly button. She winced. Both Dr. Caxson and his nurse assisted her to a sitting position, then he wheeled his stool to the table and sat down in front of her. "How are you feeling?"

"All right. Was the surgery a success?"

Compassion entered his eyes. "The endometriosis was more extensive than we thought. I ablated as much of the implanted tissue as I could."

She struggled to comprehend his words. The medical jargon was unfamiliar to her. "That's good, isn't it?"

"It is. You should be experiencing less pain now with your next cycle. But I have to be honest with you—there's still a possibility you won't be able to conceive."

Without thinking, Anna's hand went directly to her abdomen. It was sore from the laparoscopy, but she barely felt any pain. Numbness flowed over her until she sensed almost nothing. "Why?"

"In my experience, patients who had similar problems with endometriosis had a low chance of getting pregnant—about twenty percent."

His answer gave her hope. "But there's still a chance."

"A small one. There's a greater chance of the endometriosis recurring, which would require more surgery." He rose from his seat. "I wish I had better news, Ms. Esh. If you start experiencing pain again, come see me right away. Don't ignore it or think it's going to get better. Make an appointment immediately."

Once the doctor left, Anna sat, motionless. Any grogginess she'd felt from the anesthesia had disappeared. She saw everything with painful clarity.

She might not ever be able to have children.

"You okay, sweetie?" The nurse came over and put her arm around Anna's shoulder.

Anna looked at her, fighting her despair. "Do you have children?"

The nurse nodded slowly. "Three."

"Then you are very blessed."

She gave Anna a small smile that was meant to be encouraging, but had the opposite effect. "I am indeed." She squeezed Anna's shoulder. "You should have a couple of refills of that pain medication Dr. Caxson gave you on your last visit. Take two of them when you go home, and sleep for the rest of the night. No heavy lifting for the next few days, okay?"

Anna dipped her chin in a half nod. When the nurse left, and she began to dress, Anna realized what she had to do. She couldn't accept the doctor's diagnosis, not yet. Not until she had spent a long time on her knees in prayer. Miracles happened all the time, she truly believed that. Story after story from the Bible filtered through her mind. Displays of God's divine power. And before she would let Dr. Caxson cut her again, she would seek the Lord first, and ask him for healing.

She met Susan at her car, ignoring the pain from the small incision.

"How did it go?" Susan asked, revealing a row of shining braces on her bottom teeth.

"Fine," Anna said. "Everything is going to be fine." And Anna knew that if she told herself that enough times, she would eventually come to believe it.

"Beautiful work, *sohn*."

Lukas stood next to his father as they surveyed the hope chest on the table in front of them, in the very back of Byler and Sons' woodshop. Made completely of fragrant cedar, it was large enough to hold at least five full-sized quilts, if not more. He'd spent many late nights over the past couple of weeks crafting the chest, hand sanding it to perfect smoothness then applying cherry stain. He had just finished putting the fourth and final coat of clear lacquer on the chest when his father came in.

Joseph Byler tugged on his dark brown beard, the hair streaked with silver. "Cold tonight."

"Work's keeping me warm." The temperature in the shop was barely warm enough to dry the lacquer, but he had wanted to finish the chest tonight.

"You never said who the chest was for," Jacob commented. "Care to let me know? Or is it a secret?"

"*Nee*, not a secret." He hadn't wanted to reveal the recipient to anyone, not until he was finished. "It's for Anna."

Joseph raised a brow. "I didn't realize she sold such large pieces in her store. Did she ask you to make it?"

"*Nee*. It's a *gschenk*." Lukas bent down and looked at the bottom edge of the chest, making sure none of the drying varnish had dripped. Several lamps hung from the ceiling, and like the small heater in the corner of the room, they were all powered by gas.

"That's quite a *gschenk*. Is it her birthday?"

"Nope." He straightened and looked at his *daed*. Surprise registered on Joseph's face as he caught on to Lukas' unspoken meaning. "I suspected you two were courting. You've been spending a lot of time helping out over at Zeb's place. But marriage? You two haven't known each other that long."

"Since August."

"And now it's January. Only five months."

"I think that's plenty of time." He noticed the concern in his father's eyes. He hadn't thought to discuss his wedding plans with him or anyone else, as was typically the Amish way. Usually no one in the community knew of the impending nuptials until the couple made an announcement in church a couple of weeks before the wedding. But his father's concerned expression changed Lukas' mind. "I thought you might be a little happier for me, *Daed*."

"Oh, I am, I am. It's just that . . . well, you're young, Lukas."

"I'll be twenty next month."

"She's a few years older than you, *ya*?"

"It's not an issue. Besides, Tobias was the same age as me when he married Rachel."

"*Ya*, but Tobias and Rachel knew each other since they were *kinner*. Besides, if they hadn't married, they would have driven each other and the rest of us *ab im kopp*." Joseph grinned.

Lukas smiled back. From what he could tell, his brother and Rachel had a great marriage, but they still engaged in friendly verbal sparring every once in a while. Both of them seemed to get a kick out of pushing each other's buttons. Lukas preferred a less volatile relationship and appreciated Anna's calmness. He turned and inspected the chest once more, making his way slowly around the table. "I don't see any reason to wait to get married when I'm ready now."

"What about Anna? She's also sure?"

"I hope so."

"You don't sound convinced."

Lukas paused. In his heart he knew Anna loved him, even though she'd never spoken the words. He had seen it in her eyes Christmas night, and he knew she would have never agreed to date him unless she completely trusted him. Anna didn't give her affection lightly, and he treasured it.

He planned to bring her here Saturday night to present the chest to her as a wedding gift. He imagined their future together, filled with love, faith, and family. A huge family, he hoped. Nothing would make him happier than to have a house full of children to come home to after a long day at work. Well, he could think of one thing better—coming home to his beautiful Anna.

"Seems you have your mind made up. Then I guess this is as *gut* a time as any to talk about the business."

Lukas walked back over to him, alarm shooting through him as he took in his father's stern face. "What about the business?"

"I've been thinking about the future. About retirement, actually."

Lukas frowned. He couldn't imagine his father ever retiring from carpentry. Joseph Byler had worked as a carpenter, then as a master woodworker, for over thirty years. For the past ten years Lukas had worked in the shop with his *daed* and Tobias. Stephen, now at age sixteen, had just joined the business full-time this year. Everyone expected the three of them would continue on with Byler and Sons—eventually. Their father still had a lot of years left in him. "Retirement?"

"Not now," Joseph assured. "But in a few years. After all you *kinner* are married."

Lukas did some mental calculations. His three younger siblings—Elisabeth, Stephen, and Ruth —were still in their teens. Ruth, the youngest, was only thirteen, and in her next-to-last year of school. Stephen was far too young to think about marriage. And eighteen-year-old Elisabeth . . . only the good Lord knew what would happen to Elisabeth. She never seemed serious about anything.

"I thought I'd start laying the groundwork now, though, to be fair to you *buwe*." Joseph clapped his large, calloused hand on Lukas' shoulder, his expression as solemn as Lukas had ever seen it. "I'd like you to take over the shop for me."

Lukas' mouth dropped open. That was the last thing he'd expected his father to say. "But *Daed*, what about Tobias? He's your oldest *sohn*. Shouldn't he be in charge?"

Joseph shook his head. "I love Tobias, I really do. And he's grown into a fine *mann*. But he doesn't have the passion you do for the work. He sees it as just a job, something to do to make money so he can support his *familye*. And while he does *gut* work, he doesn't have your drive or your head for business."

Although he warmed to this father's compliments, Lukas still remained uncertain. "What do you think Tobias will say?"

"I've already discussed it with him, and he's perfectly fine with you being in charge—as long as you don't boss him around *too* much."

Lukas smiled sheepishly. "He mentioned that to me once."

"A lot more than once." Joseph laughed. "But we all know he needs some redirection from time to time. So what say you? Do you want the business? When I retire, of course."

Lukas grinned and held out his hand. "*Ya, Daed*. I do."

Joseph grabbed his son's hand and shook it, then clapped him on the back. "I'm proud of you, *sohn*. I know you'll take *gut* care of this business. You've shown me you love it as much as I do."

"*Danki*." His father's words were true. He loved being a carpenter, and he loved working for his father and with his brothers.

He looked back at the finished chest, pleased. Everything was falling into place. Not only could he offer Anna the chest, he could promise her a comfortable life. Byler and Sons had turned a profit for more than a decade, and despite the spiraling economy, Lukas saw no reason why it wouldn't continue to do so. God had blessed their family and rewarded their hard work.

Better yet, Anna wouldn't have to worry about finances at Esh's Amish Goods, which he knew were constantly on her mind. Or about Zeb and her mother. He could take care of her and her family and would be honored to do it.

"I'm glad we got that settled. Been weighing on my mind." Joseph tugged on his beard again. "I'm going inside. You coming along?"

"In a bit. I want to do some more finish work on the chest."

"All right." Joseph walked toward the door, then stopped and turned around. "Lukas?"

"*Ya?*"

"You prayed about you and Anna, *ya*?"

Lukas nodded. He'd prayed about the two of them from almost the day they'd met.

"*Gut, gut.* Then if this is what you want—what you both want—then I'm happy for you."

Lukas grinned. "*Danki, Daed.* That means a lot to me."

A short while later, Lukas reached the limit on what he could do to the chest. It was as perfect as he could make it, and considering the late hour, he needed to stop. He walked the short distance across the driveway to his home.

In his bedroom, Lukas undressed, then slipped beneath the sheets of his twin bed, exhaustion overcoming him. For the past four months he'd been working a lot of hours, but the fatigue was worth it. Sleep proved elusive, though, as Anna ran through his mind. He thought about his plans to ask her to marry him. What if she said no? What if he'd been wrong about her feelings for him all along?

He pushed those thoughts aside. Anna Esh would be his wife. He couldn't imagine living without her.

Chapter 13

"Lukas, where are you taking me?"

"Shhh. I said no questions."

Anna gripped Lukas' arm with both hands. He had picked her up from work half an hour ago, and she was glad for the change of scenery. Today had been a busy day, even for a Saturday. Despite being wrapped up in her work, she said several prayers that day for healing. She was determined to go to God every chance she had, laying her worry and burden at his feet. Still, she didn't feel completely at peace. But that wouldn't deter her from her prayers.

Lukas' good mood was infectious. It wasn't long before Anna shed her worries and relaxed on the buggy ride to his house. Assuming he had brought her over for supper, she looked forward to spending time with his family. But once they had arrived at the Bylers', he had caught her off guard by asking her to close her eyes before helping her out of his buggy. Now he was guiding her somewhere. She felt a tiny thrill move through her as Lukas took her hand and threaded his fingers through her own. She loved the feel of his rough skin against her palm, knowing that his calluses were the result of long hours of hard work.

She heard the sound of a door opening, then smelled fresh wood. Warmth enveloped her. "We're in your *daed's* shop."

"*Ya*, but don't open your eyes." He squeezed her hand and led her forward, guiding her steps until he released his grip. She heard him move to stand behind her, then felt the light touch of his hands on her shoulders. "Okay, you can open them."

Her eyelids parted and she drew in a deep breath as she took in a gorgeous hope chest. "It's beautiful, Lukas." A true work of art. The cherry-stained wood gleamed in the fading sunlight coming through the windows of the shop. Before she realized it, she had reached out her hand to touch the glossy wood, only to pull back at the last minute.

"It's okay," Lukas said softly. He took her hand in his and placed it on the top of the chest.

She ran her fingertips along the smooth lid, marveling at the perfect shape of the rectangular chest. There were no visible flaws anywhere—not in the grain, the stain, or the shiny finish.

"Open it up."

Anna hesitated. She knew cedar was more expensive than the typical pine or oak used to make most Amish hope chests. Usually the pricey chests were special ordered by Yankees. She didn't want to damage the piece in any way since he had obviously spent a lot of time and effort in making it. She glanced over her shoulder and looked up at him. "Are you sure?"

Lukas smiled. She loved how the cleft in his chin widened a bit when he grinned, and for the moment she forgot about everything but him. Sometime between the ride home and when he led her to the shop, he had removed his black hat, and she marveled at the deep black color of his hair. His skin tanned in the summers, but his hair never lightened, and the darkness was a gorgeous contrast to his hazel eyes.

"Anna, I want you to open the chest."

She could see the anticipation in his eyes, and it both confused and excited her. He moved to stand next to her as she carefully lifted the lid.

The smoky-sweet scent of cedar filled her senses. "Mmm," she said, unable to keep her pleasure to herself. "I love the smell of cedar."

"I know."

She glanced at him and smiled at the twinkle in his eye. Peering inside, she could see the interior of the chest was as perfect as the outside, although free of stain and lacquer. Deep and wide, she could tell right away the chest would hold several quilts and bed linens. "You do such beautiful work, Lukas. I would be happy to sell this in my shop."

But before she could close the lid he stopped her. "That's not why I showed it to you. Did you notice anything else inside? Look carefully." He stepped close to her, his hip touching hers.

She looked inside the chest again, this time scanning the interior more thoroughly. Then she saw it, in the bottom right hand corner. Two plain letters had been carved deep into the wood. *AB*.

AB?

He put his arm around her shoulders and gently turned her to face him, then dropped his arms and took her hands. "Anna . . . I made this chest for you."

Her breath caught. "You did?"

"*Ya.*" He rubbed his thumbs over the top her hands. "A wedding gift. To put at the foot of our bed."

Tears sprang to her eyes. "Oh, Lukas."

"Anna, I love you. You would make me the happiest *mann* in the world if you would be *mei frau*."

Tears sprang to her eyes.

He grinned, stroking her cheek with the back of his hand. "Don't cry, *lieb*. I never want to make you sad."

"I'm not sad," she said, her voice growing thick. "You make me so happy, Lukas. I'm so lucky to have you in my life."

"*Nee*, I'm the lucky one." He gazed at her intently. "We'll have a wonderful life together, Anna. God has blessed me—blessed us—with a *gut* livelihood. I'll be able to provide for you and our children."

She swallowed and forced a smile. "How many children?"

He smiled. "About a dozen or so."

"Oh."

His grin faded. "Anna, I'm kidding. If you don't want that many *kinner*, we won't have that many."

"*Nee*, it's not that."

"Then what's wrong?" He touched her face. "Don't you want to marry me?"

She could barely contain her emotions. She wanted to marry Lukas more than anything. He had healed her broken heart, made her believe in love again. She couldn't think of anything better than spending the rest of her life with him.

But would that life include children? And what if it didn't? Would he still love her?

"Anna?"

She gazed into his eyes, unable to look away.

"I know what you're thinking. And I promise you I'll never abandon you. We will be married, Anna Esh. Next week, if you want to."

He thought she was worried about him doing the same thing Daniel had? If he only knew how wrong he was. But she didn't dare tell him. Instead, she said, "I don't think we can do it that soon."

"Then when? Church is this Sunday. We can announce it at the service."

"We should wait a few more weeks."

"Then the end of February, but not longer than that. I love you Anna, and I don't want to wait to marry you."

She swallowed the lump that formed in her throat. His words strengthened her resolve, and her faith. God would heal her. He wouldn't deny children to a good man like Lukas. "I love you, Lukas, and I can't wait to be your *frau*." She wrapped her arms around him and held him tight, never wanting to let go.

Elisabeth plopped her bag on top of her desk and rummaged for the key to the safe. She could never find anything in this purse, mostly because she couldn't keep things organized. She dumped out the contents and searched through a variety of receipts, pens, a few sticks of gum, her wallet, a pad of paper, three unopened Band-Aids, six paper clips, and a book with a pink pig and a green purse on the front. She shook her head. Ruth must have stuck the book in there. She was always trying to get Elisabeth to read.

"Looking for something?"

Elisabeth glanced up to see Aaron standing in the doorway. "*Ya*. My sanity."

"Think you'll find it in that mess?"

"I doubt it. But . . . aha!" She picked up the key, which had been lying underneath the Band-Aids. "This is what I needed." She set the key to the side, then opened her bag and held it below the edge of the table so she could slide everything back inside. She'd sort it out later. Right now she needed to put some insurance papers in the safe. She dropped her bag inside the bottom desk drawer and shut the door. Turning in her chair, she looked at Aaron. "Did you need something?"

"Just wanted to know how your friend was doing. She was pretty upset the other day when she came to the *haus*."

She's pregnant and won't tell the baby's father, who is a Yankee and a jerk, but otherwise she's peachy. Elisabeth certainly couldn't tell Aaron that. She couldn't tell anyone that, as Deborah had begged her not to say anything about the pregnancy. Elisabeth had agreed, but she had urged her friend to at least tell her parents. When she had spoken to Deborah last night, she still hadn't broken the news to them.

"She's doing better." Which was half of the truth. At least she wasn't sobbing uncontrollably anymore, although Elisabeth chalked up her extreme reactions to being pregnant, remembering how drastic her sister's mood swings had been recently. Her niece or nephew was due in April, but sometimes she wondered if Moriah would make it until then. No wonder Gabe came dragging into work a couple mornings a week.

"Glad to hear it. I wanted to tell you . . ." He glanced down at the ground, crossing one foot over the other. "If she needs any help, let me know."

Touched by his generous and unexpected offer, she nodded. "*Danki*, Aaron. I'll tell her." Not that he could do anything, but just knowing he was willing meant so much.

Gabe came up behind Aaron and poked his head through the doorway. "Elisabeth, would you mind watching Velda and Ester for a little while? We're going into town. I have to take Moriah to the doctor."

Elisabeth jerked up from her chair. "Is she all right? Is there something wrong with the *boppli*?"

He shook his head. "She's got a sinus infection, I think. Or the flu, I'm not sure which. All I know is she's miserable."

"I'm glad to hear that. Not that she's sick. I mean I'm glad it's nothing serious."

Gabe smiled. "Me too. We're leaving in a few minutes, so I'll need you to come over soon."

"Be right there." She picked up the key off the desk, along with the insurance papers, and handed them to Aaron. "Could you put these in the safe for me?"

"Sure." He took the key and papers from her, then stepped to the side.

"Oh, and don't be surprised if I need your help with the *kinner* again. Remember what happened last time."

Aaron's look was dead serious. "You won't need any help, Elisabeth. You can handle them."

She smiled, appreciating his support. As she walked to the house, she had no misgivings about babysitting her nieces. Aaron had confidence in her, and because of that, she had confidence in herself.

Aaron knelt down in front of the safe on the opposite side of the file cabinet. As he inserted the key into the lock, he remembered when Gabe had picked it up from the discount store in West Farmington. It wasn't fancy, Gabe had said, but it was fireproof and theft proof, and they kept the cash and the important papers inside. Gabe and John used to have a small cash box they stored in the desk, but as the business grew, so had the need for a safe. He lifted the heavy lid, put the insurance forms inside, and locked it back up.

As he moved to stand, he noticed a paper on the floor by the desk. He picked it up and realized it was a receipt. Knowing Elisabeth would want to file it, he started to place it on her desk, but then noticed it was from the local pharmacy. A personal receipt. It must have fallen out of her bag when she was searching for the key.

He glanced at it for a moment, noticing she'd bought two candy bars. The third item she purchased stopped him cold.

A pregnancy test.

Elisabeth thought she was pregnant? He crumpled the receipt in his hand and fell back into the chair. His mind went back to the Yoder's party, when that Yankee Chase had come out from behind the haystacks. He'd been back there with Elisabeth. When she had appeared, he had suspected something was wrong, but she'd refused to talk about it. Then later, she said she was confused and didn't know what to do. Now he could see why.

His head fell into his hands. Elisabeth, pregnant? He couldn't believe it was possible. Except for a couple days after the party, she had seemed fine. Yet why else would she buy a pregnancy test?

"Aon!"

He turned to see Velda run into the office, a

sweet smile on her round, chubby face. Shoving the receipt in his pocket, he scooped her up and sat her on his lap, still trying to make sense of what he'd discovered.

Elisabeth appeared a few seconds later, holding Ester in her arms. She stood in the office doorway, the baby contentedly resting on Elisabeth's hip while she sucked her thumb.

In that moment he could picture Elisabeth as a mother. She would be a good one. But she didn't deserve to go through motherhood alone. If Chase was the father of her child, she would have to. He couldn't imagine her leaving the Amish faith to marry him.

"Aon." Velda reached up and tugged on his hair.

He pulled on one of the strings of her tiny black *kapp*. "What are you doing out here?"

"She wanted to see you," Elisabeth said.

"Is everything okay?"

"*Ya*. I've got everything under control."

But Aaron wondered if she really did.

"*Danki* for coming with me, Elisabeth." Deborah reached across the buggy seat and squeezed Elisabeth's hand. "I don't know how I could get through this without you."

They were sitting in her buggy at the far end of Mary Yoder's parking lot, waiting for Chase to get off work. Deborah had quit the restaurant shortly after discovering she was pregnant.

Elisabeth rubbed her hands together. At least he was working the morning shift, which meant he got off before three o'clock. Despite the cloudless, sunny sky, the air was still cold. She wished she would have brought a blanket to keep both her and Deborah warm while they waited.

She looked at her friend, who stared out of the side of the buggy into the lot. "How are you feeling?"

"Nauseated. I threw up twice this morning."

"Moriah had the same problem. It goes away after a few months though."

"I hope so. I can't keep anything down." Deborah looked at Elisabeth. "What do you think he's going to say?"

"Hopefully the right thing."

"What if he wants me to marry him?"

Elisabeth couldn't imagine marrying a Yankee man. She wouldn't be able to leave her faith or her family. But what if she were in Deborah's shoes? She didn't know what she would do. "Do you love him?"

She looked down at her lap. "*Nee.*"

"Then why were you with him?"

"Randy and I only had a couple of dates after the party, then he didn't want to see me anymore. He told me at the restaurant, and I was upset. Chase noticed, and he started paying attention to me. He said I was pretty, and that he liked me. That he wanted to be with me. Elisabeth, I was so stupid, I should have never believed him. It only happened one time, and then he barely talked to me after that." She sighed. "You know why I can't tell my parents about the *boppli*?"

Elisabeth shook her head.

"It's not because I'm afraid of what they'll do. I'm afraid they won't do anything."

"I don't understand."

"You're so lucky, Elisabeth. Your parents care about you. Mine don't."

"That's not true."

"*Ya*, it is. They've been like this since I turned sixteen. I don't know what I did to make them stop caring, but they did."

Deborah's revelations shocked Elisabeth. "How do you know that?"

"One time I was gone for a whole weekend. I missed church and everything. I was staying with one of my Yankee friends. I didn't let them know where I was going or where I was. And when I showed up back home, they acted like I'd never been gone."

"Did you tell them where you were?"

"Like that would matter. My mother just told me to go do the wash because it was Monday." Deborah looked at Elisabeth. "Mondays are laundry days," she said with evident bitterness in her voice.

Deborah looked back into the parking lot again. "Chase should have been off work by now."

"He'll be out in a minute." Elisabeth thought about what her friend had said. She couldn't imagine how parents could just stop caring for their child. Elisabeth's parents had always wanted to know what their *kinner* were doing. She thought it was annoying sometimes, especially when she finished school and didn't want to be treated like a kid anymore. But now she understood the reason why they were so diligent. They loved her. Deborah was right, she was lucky. Lucky and blessed.

"There he is." Deborah gripped the edge of the buggy seat. "I don't even know what I'm going to say to him."

"Tell him the truth. That's the only thing you can say."

"Come with me. I can't do this by myself."

Elisabeth shook her head. "Deborah, I can't—"

"Please?"

She looked at her friend's terrified face, and she found herself nodding. How did she get so deeply involved in this? All she wanted to do was support her friend. Now she would be face-to-face with the guy who had tried to force himself on her. She had never wanted to see him again.

But she would never tell Deborah what had happened in the Shrocks' barn. No need to toss a match on the haystack. "All right. I'll *geh* with you."

"*Danki*, Elisabeth. He's going to his car, so we need to catch him before he leaves."

They exited the buggy and rushed across the parking lot to Chase's car. He had just opened the door when he looked up. He quickly looked away and ducked inside.

"He's ignoring us," Deborah said, sounding much stronger than she had a few minutes ago. "Chase!" she called out. "Wait!"

They reached the car just as he turned on the engine. Elisabeth knocked on the window and saw the color drain from Chase's face. He pressed a button and the window slid open.

Chase looked from her to Deborah. "Uh, hi."

Now that they had his attention, she waited for Deborah to speak. When her friend didn't say anything, Elisabeth elbowed her arm.

"I need to talk to you," Deborah finally said.

He rubbed the back of his neck. "I'm kinda busy now. Maybe we can meet somewhere later."

"This won't take long."

His gaze narrowed as he looked at Elisabeth. "Why is she here?"

The guy sitting in front of her was far removed from the confident, smooth man she'd met at the party. Looking at him now through the clear light of day, she saw he was just a normal guy with a weird haircut. She'd never liked the way Yankee guys cut the back of their hair so short.

"She's my friend, and I want her here," Deborah explained.

He gave Deborah an impatient, expectant

look. "Can you hurry this up? I have to be somewhere."

"I'm pregnant."

The color drained from his face. "You're . . . *what?*"

"Pregnant. I'm going to have a baby."

"Why are you telling me?"

Deborah leaned closer to him. "Because you're the father."

"Oh no." He shook his head, his eyes sparking. "You're not pinning that on me."

"But we were together last month."

"How do I know you haven't been with some other guy?"

"Because I'm not like that!" Hurt laced Deborah's voice.

Elisabeth's heart went out to her friend. From the angry look on Deborah's face, she could see Deborah hadn't expected Chase's reaction. She hadn't expected it either.

"You could have fooled me. You started coming on to me the moment I met you."

"That's not true! And you know it, Chase."

He ran his hands through his blond-tipped hair. "I don't know what kind of game this is, but I won't be a part of it. You're not trapping me."

"This isn't a trap. I told you because I thought you had the right to know." She exhaled. "Right now, I don't know what I'm going to do."

"You're thinking of having an abortion?"

"*Nee*, I would never do that."

"Whoa. You weren't thinking I'd actually marry you?" he sneered. "No way. Look, I don't care what you do. Have an abortion, raise it yourself, marry some backwards Amish guy, it doesn't matter to me. Just leave me alone. "

"But your baby—"

"That's not my baby. We were both drunk. I don't even remember what happened that night."

"You're lying."

He leaned forward until he was inches away from her, his gaze narrowing with ire. "If you say that baby's mine, I'll say you were with three other guys that night. You'll have to take me to court to prove me wrong."

Elisabeth had vowed not to say anything during this conversation, but Chase had pushed her over the edge. "How can you be so cruel? She's carrying your baby."

"Since when is any of this your business?" He turned on the car. "We're done here." He rolled up the window, then pealed out of the parking lot.

Elisabeth stood there for a moment, feeling as if she'd been physically assaulted. She could only imagine how Deborah felt. She looked at her friend, stunned to see the calm look on her face. "Are you okay?"

"*Ya*." She turned and looked at Elisabeth. "Strangely enough, I am."

"I'm so sorry he did that to you. What a creep."

"He's a creep all right. And I'm glad to be rid of him." Deborah turned to her. "Could you take me home?"

"Sure."

When they reached Deborah's house, Elisabeth leaned over and hugged her. Deborah pulled away, her eyes filled with tears.

Elisabeth had to fight her own urge to cry. "What are you going to do?"

"I'm not sure. But I'm glad I told him. And this probably sounds crazy, but I'm glad he doesn't want anything to do with me or the *boppli*."

"*Nee*, it doesn't sound crazy at all. He's an awful person, Deborah."

"I see that now." She let out a bitter chuckle. "Believe it or not, Randy said we couldn't go out because he wants to join the church. I told him I wasn't ready to do that. He said he had to make a choice, and he chose being Amish over staying with me."

"So you two never . . . ?"

"Never." She sighed. "I don't know how I can face him. Or my parents. Or the church."

"Are you thinking about joining?"

"I don't know. I have a lot of thinking to do." She gave Elisabeth a weary smile. "And praying. God and I haven't been on speaking terms for a long time."

"I'll pray too."

She watched Deborah go inside her house,

saying a silent prayer for her friend, wishing she didn't have to go through this. She hoped God would use this to bring Deborah back to him.

As she drove home, her thoughts went to Aaron. Although his and Deborah's situations weren't the same, there were some similarities. Both of them had turned their back on their faith and made bad choices. They had to pay the consequences of those choices—Aaron with jail time and Deborah with an unexpected pregnancy. Seeing Deborah's turmoil firsthand made her understand Aaron more. How hard it must have been for him to return to the Amish, to face the church and God and ask for forgiveness, only to be unsure whether he'd truly received it.

She spent the rest of the trip home praying for both of them. When she arrived, she steered the buggy into the barn. She unhitched Daisy and led her into her stall, then gave her fresh feed and water. Still consumed with thoughts about Aaron and Deborah, she stroked the horse's nose, watching her eat.

A few moments later she heard footsteps behind her. Probably Ruth, wanting to know why she was late for supper. Elisabeth doubted Ruth was ever late to anything in her life. Although she was only fourteen, she had always gone by a precise schedule and had expected everyone else to as well. "Tell *Mami* I'll be right there, Ruth." She gave the horse a light a pat on the nose, then turned around. But it wasn't Ruth she saw standing in the middle of the barn. It was Aaron.

"Hi," he said.

"Hi."

He stood there for a moment, then shifted from one foot to the other, his eyes darting from right to left without directly looking at her. He'd never seemed so ill at ease in her company before.

"Is everything okay, Aaron?" She hoped it was, because she didn't think she could take another trauma tonight.

He finally looked at her. "I was about to ask you the same thing."

"I'm fine." She wasn't, of course, but she didn't need to tell him that. A chill hung in the air, and she was eager to get inside. "There's nothing wrong." She bit her bottom lip on the lie.

"*Gut*." But the look in his eyes told her he didn't believe her.

Tired and cold, she didn't want to stay in the barn anymore. "Did you want to come in the house? I think I missed supper, but I can heat something up."

He shook his head. "I'm not hungry."

"Then how about coffee?" She rubbed her cold hands together and stood with her feet close together. Hot coffee sounded heavenly right now.

"Maybe. In a minute." He took off his hat and started bending the brim back and forth. His blond hair was matted down against his head. "I need to talk to you about something first."

Elisabeth frowned. "We can't talk inside?"

"Nope. Not about this."

Panic struck her. "Aaron, now you have me worried."

He blanched. "I'm sorry. That's the last thing I wanted to do."

"Then maybe you should tell me what's going on."

He nodded, then reached into the pocket of his coat. He took out a wrinkled, folded slip of paper and handed it to her.

Her brows furrowed as she took it from him. She opened it, then gasped. "Where did you get this?"

"On the floor in the office. It must have fallen out of your bag."

She looked away, acutely embarrassed that he had found out about Deborah. Somehow she'd have to explain to her friend that she didn't betray her confidence. Her messy purse had.

His mouth was set in a straight line, but his gaze held no judgment. Instead he seemed genuinely concerned. "Does the father know?"

"*Ya.* He doesn't want to have anything to do with the *boppli.*"

"It's the guy from the party, right?"

She nodded.

"I knew it had to be. So he's refusing to take responsibility?"

"He's a total jerk, Aaron."

He put his hat back on and took a step closer to her. To her surprise, he took her hand in his. "Marry me, Elisabeth."

Chapter 14

"What?" She pulled away, shocked and positive she must have heard him wrong.

"Marry me. We can tell everyone the *boppli* is mine."

"Aaron! Do you realize what you're saying?"

"*Ya*, I do."

"Aaron—"

"I've thought about this, Elisabeth, and it makes sense. We work together, so it wouldn't be that much of a surprise to our families. We can marry quickly, just a small ceremony. I'll take care of you and the *boppli*."

Elisabeth was so shocked she couldn't speak. He thought she was pregnant? And because of that he was offering to marry her, to claim a baby that wasn't his to help her save face? Tears sprang to her eyes. Never mind that she wasn't pregnant. Just knowing he was willing to make such a sacrifice for her made her want to weep.

"Elisabeth, don't cry. It will be okay." He moved closer to her. "I'll make sure of it."

"Aaron." She blinked back the tears. "You don't have to do this."

"I know I don't. But I want to."

"*Nee*, I mean you really don't." She let out a deep breath. "I'm not pregnant."

Confusion crossed his features. "You're not? Then why did you get a pregnancy test?"

"It's not for me. For someone else."

He paused, clearly deep in thought. "Deborah."

Elisabeth nodded.

"That's why she was so upset last week."

"*Ya*. But you can't say a word. She asked me to keep it a secret."

"I won't." He crossed the barn and sat on one of the square hay bales in the corner. She could hear him sigh with relief. Walking over, she joined him. "I can't believe you thought I was pregnant."

He glanced at her. "I saw you and Chase coming out from behind the bales. You were upset that night."

"I remember."

"You wouldn't tell me why, and I didn't want to pry. Then I saw the receipt for the test." He grimaced. "I'm sorry. I shouldn't have jumped to conclusions."

"I'm not mad. I can see why you would have thought that." She untied the black strings of her bonnet and pulled it off. "And you were partly right about Chase. He took me behind the hay bales. Then he kissed me."

"He did?"

Elisabeth noticed Aaron had practically folded the brim of his hat in half, his knuckles white from the strain. She reached over and took the hat from him before he destroyed it. "More like he tried. I bit his lip and then kicked him in the shin so he stopped."

Aaron's brows lifted. "That's why he was limping when I saw him."

"Yep. And that's why I was upset. Not only did I have a terrible time, but he put alcohol in my drink and then kissed me." She scowled at the memory. "It was gross."

Aaron grinned. "Really?"

"Really. Now don't get me wrong. I don't think kissing itself is gross."

His brows lifted higher, but his eyes were filled with mirth.

"But kissing Chase?" She shivered. "Ugh. What's so funny?"

He laughed. "You." He smiled. "I can't believe you're talking to me about kissing."

"Well, you did just ask me to marry you. Which is just as ridiculous."

His expression suddenly sobered. "I meant it. I would have married you, Elisabeth. I wouldn't have let you *geh* through that alone."

Her heart swelled. "I can't believe you would have done that for me."

"Why not?"

"Because it wouldn't have been fair to you."

"It was my idea, remember?"

"But what about you? You don't love me, do you?"

His eyes widened with surprise. "Do I love you?" He looked away for a moment, and she had her answer before he even spoke.

"See. That's why I would have never married you. I wouldn't let you be stuck in a loveless marriage. You deserve more than that. Much more."

"I care about you, Elisabeth. That would be enough for me."

Their gazes met, and a shiver coursed through her body. Daisy nickered in her stall, and the scent of hay and animals surrounded them. But she barely noticed, her mind replaying his words. He cared for her, and she realized she cared for him. A few months ago she would have never believed that Aaron Detweiler would become her best friend. But he was. Today had proved that.

He cleared his throat and looked down at the ground. "I'm sorry about your friend. What's she going to do?"

Elisabeth shrugged. "I'm not sure. But something happened when she told Chase about the *boppli*. He was horrible to her, but after he left she seemed really calm. She told me she has a lot of praying to do. I'm hoping she'll lean on the Lord."

"Me too. He got me through my time in jail and rehab. I wouldn't have been able to make it without him."

"Then maybe that's why you had to *geh* through it."

He picked up a piece of hay and twirled it in his fingers. "Makes sense. Reminds me of when I'm working at the forge. That's probably why I enjoy my work so much. With the heat and pressure, I can turn a plain rod of iron into something useful. I think God does that with us." He looked up at her. "Obviously I'm still a work in progress."

"I think you've turned out pretty *gut*."

"*Danki*. You're not so bad yourself."

"God's still working on me too." She looked down at her hands, which still held his black hat. She ran her finger across the brim.

Aaron put the hay in between his teeth and stood up, then turned around. He held out his hand to her.

Realizing he wanted his hat back, she handed it to him. He put it on his head, pushing the brim back the way he liked to wear it. A smile played on his lips, and he held out his hand to her again. "Want to *geh* skating?"

"Now? It's almost dark."

"We have some time. I'll teach you how to skate backward."

She slipped her hand in his. "Don't you think I should figure out frontwards first?"

• • •

Lukas tugged his black coat closer to his body as he unhitched his horse from the post next to the woodshop. Another busy but satisfying day. Yes, he was tired, but it was a good kind of tired, one that came from doing hard work. He looked forward to going over to the Eshes' for supper tonight. Anna had invited him yesterday after he'd dropped her off at home after work. He couldn't wait to see her. He also couldn't wait until he could see her every day as his wife. They had planned to announce their engagement in church this Sunday. A few weeks later, they would be married.

He moved to climb in his buggy, then saw Elisabeth and Aaron coming out of the barn laughing. He looked at them for a moment. They had grown pretty close since she'd started working at Gabe's shop. Still, he couldn't imagine them as a couple. Their personalities were so different. Then again, it wasn't as if you could plan to fall in love. He hadn't expected to fall for Anna so quickly.

The sun hovered just above the horizon by the time he reached the Eshes'. Although he and Zeb had done a lot of work on the place over the past couple months, he could still see things that needed repair. The house wasn't only old, it was big, with several out buildings scattered on the acreage. Inside the house was neat and tidy, but the kitchen cabinets were outdated, the railing on the stairs was warped, and the wood flooring needed to be redone. Much like Esh's Amish Goods, the house needed a face-lift. Because of this, it made sense for him to move in with the Eshes after they married. He had been over there so much lately he'd already started to think of it as home.

The scent of pork roast and potatoes hit him when he walked inside. He found Edna in the kitchen, adding a couple shakes of pepper to the stew pot.

"*Guten owed*, Lukas." Edna turned to him and smiled, then pushed up her silver wire-rimmed glasses. "I'm glad you could join us tonight. Did you have a *gut* day?"

"*Ya*. Busy, but *gut*. Where's Anna?"

Edna's brows furrowed, but only for a moment. She smiled briefly and turned back to the stew. "She's lying down upstairs."

He frowned. "Is she feeling all right?"

"Oh, *ya*. She's feeling fine. Just a little tired this afternoon. I'll *geh* get her."

Lukas sat down at the kitchen table and crossed his leg over his knee. A few moments later Anna appeared. He noticed the faint shadows underneath her eyes, along with the fatigue lining her face. He'd never seen her so tired. "Anna, is everything okay?"

"*Ya*," she said quickly, coming into the kitchen.

She smiled, then went to the stove to check on the stew. "Everything's fine."

"Are you sure?"

"Of course I am. Why would you think I wouldn't be?"

"I've never known you to take naps in the afternoon before."

She looked at him and smirked. "You don't know everything about me, Lukas."

He rose from the table. "Not yet. But I intend to." He smiled before moving to stand beside her. He leaned over and breathed in the delicious aroma from the stew. He looked at her profile, realizing she seemed pale. Putting his hand on her shoulder, he said, "Anna, you would tell me if there was something wrong, wouldn't you?"

She nodded, her eyes steadily meeting his. "Of course. But there's nothing to tell. I had a long day at work. That's all."

"Maybe you should hire someone to help now that Ruth has gone back to school."

"I can't really afford it right now. We had a *gut* day today, but business has gone down since the holidays." She moved from the stove to the cabinet and pulled out a glass. She walked to the sink to fill it with water.

Lukas followed her. "You don't have to worry about money anymore. Once we're married, you'll be able to hire someone full-time to take your place."

"You want me to quit working?"

"Eventually. *Ya*. It's what Amish do, Anna. You know that."

"But what about my business? You can't expect me to abandon it?"

Lukas could hear the panic and frustration in her voice. "*Nee*, not at all. You'll still own the business but hire others to work for you. Like my sister Ruth. There are many young women in Middlefield who would be happy to have a job."

"But Lukas . . . what if I don't want to leave?"

He frowned, not expecting her answer. As was the Amish way, young women worked outside the home until they married, or at least until their first child was born. Then they stayed home and focused on raising the children and taking care of the house and family. While they might have an income-producing job—such as making homemade goods like jams, baked items, and handicrafts—the sale of the items would also be done from the home so that the mothers would be free to tend to the work at home.

"I don't see how you could stay. Who would watch the *boppli*? Your *mudder* has her hands full with Zeb, and you couldn't take the *kinn* to work with you. And when the next *boppli* comes, can't you see how impossible that would be?"

She turned her back to him, preventing him from seeing her reaction. "You're right," she said, her voice barely audible.

He put his hands on her shoulders and guided her to face him. "We don't have to talk about this now. And I don't want to fight, or see you upset."

She nodded, then suddenly let out a light gasp, causing her to reach out and grip his arm.

"Anna," he said, bewildered and concerned.

"It's . . . nothing." She straightened. But it had taken several seconds for her to do so.

"You're in pain. I can see it."

"Just a twinge. You know, like a muscle spasm. Everyone gets those." She held out her arms and stepped back. Then she picked up her water and took a sip. "See? I'm fine." She smiled at him. "Now, let's go get something to eat before the food gets cold. Besides, you know *Onkel* Zeb. He's likely to start without us."

"He's not one to wait to eat, is he?" Lukas chuckled, but he was still a little worried, despite her reassurances that she was all right.

"*Nee*. He never has been. Part of being a bachelor all his life, I guess. He's used to only thinking of himself." Anna frowned. "I didn't mean that the way it sounded. You know *Onkel* Zeb isn't a selfish man."

"I know exactly what you meant." Lukas gave her a reassuring smile.

But as he sat down to the meal with Anna and her family, he couldn't focus much on supper. Her reaction had been severe for a small muscle twinge. And yet, what did he know? Not much about medicine and medical stuff. And while he had done well in school, he had forgotten most of what he'd learned other than what directly applied to his job and life. Maybe it was normal for women to have those kinds of spasms.

Later that evening, after Lukas went home and her mother and Uncle Zeb had gone to bed, Anna took one of the pills Dr. Caxson had given her for pain. She was down to just two pills. She read the side of the bottle. No refills. She'd have to visit him again before he would write her another prescription.

She took the pill with a sip of water, then went to the window of her bedroom and looked outside. A full moon illuminated the barn and shed, spreading its silvery light over the large field behind the two buildings. Placing a hand over her abdomen, she thought about Lukas. She had told him she was fine. But that hadn't been the truth.

Her body was betraying her, and she didn't know what to do. The pain had returned, and although Dr. Caxson had told her to call him right away, she was afraid he might tell her the one thing she never wanted to hear—that she couldn't have children. She wasn't ready to face that diagnosis yet.

She also refused to give up on God. She would continue to pray, continue to be patient while she waited on his healing. Wiping the tear that had dripped down her cheek, she stared into the night and steeled her emotions. Even though she was tired, she wouldn't let Lukas or her mother see it. She would hide her fatigue, just as she would hide her despair. Her mother would only give her a lecture, tell her to go back to the doctor and apprise Lukas of the diagnosis. Lukas would only worry, or worse, decide he didn't want to marry her.

"Dear Lord," she whispered. "Hear my prayer. Please heal me. After Lukas and I marry, I want to have a *boppli*. Just one *boppli*, that's all I ask." Perhaps if she didn't ask for too much, God would honor her request.

A week later, on a Zeb-free day, Anna and Edna were making a St. Patrick's Day display in the front window of Esh's Amish Goods. She and Lukas had announced their engagement in church the previous Sunday, which surprised no one.

In all the excitement of preparing for the nuptials, Anna felt more tired than usual. Her pain had also returned, and she was managing on Tylenol and taking early naps. As she set a bright green shamrock in the middle of the display, she couldn't stifle a yawn.

"Why don't you go home and rest," Edna said, coming up behind her.

The snow covered the ground in a thin layer, and the sun had been hidden behind thick, flat clouds for the past two weeks. This was the time of year she liked the least, when the winter days seemed interminably long and stretched out for eternity. She couldn't wait until spring and the warmer weather when she could start her garden and do some landscaping around the house. *Onkel* Zeb had said she and her mother could do anything they wanted to the house, and that courtesy had extended to Lukas as well, who had already started refurbishing the cabinets in the kitchen.

"Take the buggy. I can run things here by myself."

"I know, *Mami*." But Anna didn't want to go home. Work helped keep her mind off of her pain and fatigue. "I can't go home, at least not yet. I still need to work on the books. And count the inventory."

Edna placed two small faceless dolls into an adorable crib Lukas had made a few months ago. It was the last of several cribs he had made. They sold so quickly that Anna and Edna didn't think this one would make it to the end of the week.

Over the last few months, Anna realized that her mother liked to rearrange things, and she especially was comfortable making new displays, along with visiting with the customers. It gave Anna more time to spend behind the scenes, balancing the accounts and counting and ordering inventory. Managing the business aspect of the shop was something she enjoyed doing.

When her mother had finished with the display,

she turned to Anna. "Why don't you wait to do that paperwork tomorrow? It's not urgent, is it?"

Anna looked at her mother, wishing she could bring herself to confide in her more. "That's a *gut* idea. Tomorrow we'll do the inventory. But I still have to look at the books."

Edna said, "That can't wait either? Or maybe you can take them home."

"*Nee*, I'd rather keep them here. I don't want to lose anything."

Edna walked toward her, concern etched on her face. "Anna, I'm worried about you. I know you said everything is okay, but you've seemed overly tired lately, and a little pale. Maybe you should go back and see the doctor one more time."

Anna was about to tell her that another doctor's visit wasn't necessary when the cell phone in the back of the store rang. The *Ordnung* permitted telephone use for business purposes only, and neither the Eshes nor the Bylers owned a cell phone or had one at their house. It had taken a while for Anna to get used to having one at the store.

"Excuse me," she said to her mother, then went to the storeroom to answer the phone sitting on her desk.

"Esh's Amish Goods."

"May I speak to Anna Esh, please?"

"Speaking. How can I help you?"

"Ms. Esh, this is Dr. Caxson's nurse. I was looking over your records and noticed your prescription has run out. I was calling to see how you've been doing since the laparoscopy."

Anna looked at the doorway, then sat down and lowered her voice. "Fine. Everything is going well."

"You're not having pain?"

"Um . . ."

"Ms. Esh, if your pain has returned, you need to see Dr. Caxson right away. Would you like to make an appointment now?"

"I don't have my calendar handy." She shoved her small planning calendar to the side. "And I'm not really having much pain. Just a twinge every once and while." Guilt over the lie assaulted her. *Lord, forgive me.*

"Ms. Esh, normally I wouldn't press you to make an appointment. But if you're having any complications, you need to be seen. Your endometriosis could have worsened, which could cause significant health problems."

Alarm replaced Anna's upset at the nurse's words. Was her situation that dire? The nurse seemed to think so, but Anna couldn't accept that. Still, to get the woman off the phone, she said, "Like I told you, I'm fine."

The nurse paused. "If anything changes, don't hesitate to call the office. We'll get you in as soon as possible."

"Thank you. I'll keep that in mind."

After the call, Anna dropped her head into her

243

hands. Fatigue washed over her, making her want to crawl in a hole and close her eyes for the next two days. She should be thinking about her wedding, about becoming Anna Byler, not worrying about hiding her pain.

"Who was that?"

Anna lifted her head and sat up straight at the sound of her mother's voice. "No one," she said, rearranging the already neat piles of paperwork on her desk.

"You sure spent a lot of time talking to 'No one.'" Edna came further into the room. "I overheard part of the conversation. What's going on, Anna?"

Anna didn't say anything. Her mind suddenly came up blank; she couldn't think of any excuses.

Edna reached for a nearby chair and sat down. "Was that the doctor's office?"

"What made you think that?"

"I might be advancing in years, *dochder*, but I'm not addled yet. And by the grace of God, I'll be a sharp as *Onkel* Zeb by the time I'm his age. I didn't think you were telling me everything about your last visit with Dr. Caxson, and I can see by the look on your face that I'm right." She softened her tone. "Please. Tell me what's going on?"

Anna took a deep breath. "Dr. Caxson's office was just calling to follow up on my procedure."

"That sounded like more than a follow-up call."

Tired of lying, she said, "I'm having a little bit of pain. The nurse said I should *geh* back and see the doctor."

"Then why didn't you make the appointment?"

"I don't know." She rose from her chair. "What if something's really wrong?"

"All the more reason to see the doctor."

Anna turned around and faced her mother. "*Mami*, I'm getting married in a couple of weeks. I don't have time."

"You'll have to make the time." Edna went to her. "Tell me what I need to do, and I'll do it."

"It's not that simple." She threaded her fingers through her hands. "Lukas wants a large family."

"I know you do too. Your *daed* and I also wanted lots of children, but God's ideas were different. I'm grateful he blessed me with one."

"But what if I can't give him even one? The doctor said there was a possibility I might not be able to get pregnant."

Edna brought her hand to her face. "Oh, no."

"He said I might need to have surgery again."

"Oh, Anna," Edna said, her voice cracking. She leaned forward and took Anna's hand. "This is serious. Why haven't you made that appointment?"

"Because what if he's wrong? Doctors can be wrong, *Mami*."

"Then if you think he's wrong, get a second opinion. There are plenty of doctors around here. You can go to Cleveland if you need to."

Edna paused, looking up at Anna. "But you won't, will you? You won't because you know deep down that Dr. Caxson isn't wrong."

"*Nee*. I don't. And even if he's right, that doesn't mean that God won't work a miracle." She swallowed the lump clogging her throat. "Sarah prayed for years for a child. She was in her nineties when she had Isaac. And Hannah, she prayed and had Samuel. Why can't the Lord do the same for me?"

"You want to have a child when you're ninety?"

"*Mami*, you know what I mean!"

"Does Lukas know?"

Anna shook her head. "I can't tell him."

"You have to. He's going to be your husband. He needs to know this."

"If he finds out, he might leave me. And he'd be within his rights, too, if I can't guarantee him a child."

"You're not giving him enough credit."

"Daniel left me without a reason. Lukas would have every reason to cancel our engagement." A tear escaped, and she wiped it away. "I love him so much. I don't want to be without him."

"But you're not being fair to him. You're lying to him, you're endangering your health—"

"I'm trusting God!" Anna took her mother's hands in hers. "Are you telling me not to trust him? Not to put every ounce of faith I have in his power?"

"*Nee.* I would never tell you that. But Anna, what about Lukas? Wouldn't it make sense for both of you to pray? Together?"

Anna released Edna's hands, then turned her back to her. "I can't tell Lukas. Not yet."

"Then when?"

"After the wedding."

"Anna, look at me."

She hesitated, then turned, her heart rending at the pain she saw in her mother's eyes. "I remember how distraught I was when I found out I couldn't have any more children after you were born. But as difficult as that was, I can't imagine the pain you're going through right now. But please, for your sake, and for Lukas', you have to tell him about the diagnosis."

"And dash his dreams of a big family? Look at his sister, Moriah. She's expecting her third child. Tobias and Rachel have Josiah. You should see how Lukas is with his nieces and nephew, *Mami.* He adores them. All he can talk about is when he has children of his own. How can I tell him that he won't, because of me?"

"God will give you the strength to do so. If you believe he has the power to perform a miracle, then trust he will help you and Lukas make the right decision about this."

Anna pressed her lips together until she couldn't feel them anymore. Her mother's words were logical, but they rang hollow in Anna's heart.

Her *mami* didn't know how many sleepless nights Anna had spent thinking about how she could tell Lukas, imagining the look on his face when she did, fearing his reaction when he found out that she had kept this from him for so long.

And what about her hope? There was still a slim chance that she would get pregnant. She couldn't let go of that right now.

Wiping the tears from her face, she went to her mother and sat down on the chair in front of her. "Please, *Mami*," she said, her voice quaking. "Promise me you won't tell Lukas about this."

"Anna . . ." Edna's face turned red as she began to cry. "Don't ask this of me."

"This is my body, my relationship. I know what I'm doing. It may not seem that way to you, but it's true."

Edna ran her hand across her forehead, her face a myriad of tortured emotions. At that moment the bell at the front of the store jingled. Anna handed her mother a tissue from the box on her desk, and then grabbed one for herself. She had just finished wiping her eyes when Lukas burst into the office, carrying a plastic bag filled with food.

"I thought you two might want some lunch," he said, holding up the bag. "Sub sandwiches from Middlefield Cheese. I asked for that extra spicy mustard you like, Edna." He paused, his eyes moving from one woman to the other. He frowned, then set the bag on her desk. Concern reflected in his eyes. "Anna, have you been crying?"

Anna looked away from Lukas and took in her mother's glance, noting the uncertainty painted on her face. Her breathing stopped as she looked from her *mami* to Lukas, then back to her *mami*. They were the only ones in the store; it would be the perfect time to tell Lukas everything. He already suspected something was wrong. Edna took a step forward, and Anna's stomach churned.

"Anna?" Lukas asked, his tone more urgent.

Edna suddenly stepped between them. "*Danki*, Lukas," she said, taking the bag from him. "Anna's just fine. We were just talking about her father, and I'm afraid we both got a bit teary-eyed."

He looked at Anna, then back at Edna, compassion in his eyes. "I'm sorry."

"It's fine." Edna smiled, any trace of her earlier upset completely gone. She peeked inside the bag before pulling out a plastic container holding a sub sandwich on white bread, stacked with ham, turkey, Swiss cheese, and lettuce. "I think this one's for you. It has your favorite cheese on it." She handed Anna the sandwich, a tight smile on her face. "You're future husband is *sehr* thoughtful, Anna. You are very lucky to have him."

Breathing out a heavy sigh, she gave her mother a grateful look as she accepted the sandwich. Her *mami* would keep her secret. And despite the guilt that raged within her over asking her mother be a party to her deceit, she still felt a huge measure of relief that Lukas didn't know the situation. There would be time for that after the wedding. Until then she would keep praying that everything was all right.

Chapter 15

So is everyone ready for the big day?"

Elisabeth took a bite out of her turkey and cheese sandwich before answering Aaron. They were sitting on the front porch swing at Moriah and Gabe's, enjoying a rare warm day in March. It wasn't too warm, as they were both wearing their coats, but the sun was shining, and they were tired of eating lunch inside every day. As she chewed she tried to push the swing with the toe of her shoe, but she couldn't quite reach.

Aaron glanced down, and without saying anything, he stuck out his foot and gave it a shove. The swing gently rocked back and forth.

"It's chaos," Elisabeth said. "The wedding is still four days away, but *Mami* is making everyone crazy. Well, mainly me."

"Why?" Aaron took a swig from a bottle of pop.

"When she gets nervous about something, she cleans. Not only that, she makes everyone else clean. I remember her being like this when Moriah got married, but at least that made sense because the wedding was at our house. I don't understand why she's making me clean everything twice." Elisabeth rolled her eyes. "If you only knew how much I hate cleaning the bathroom."

"I can imagine."

They sat in comfortable silence for a few moments, Aaron keeping the swing moving, enjoying the fresh air. A buggy passed by, the driver lifting his hand in a wave. Elisabeth and Aaron waved back.

"You're coming to the wedding, right?" When Aaron didn't answer her right away, she said again, "Right?"

"Thinking about it." He popped a couple of potato chips in his mouth and chewed.

"Oh, *nee*. You're coming and that's final."

"Is that so, Your Bossiness?"

"Aaron, I can't believe you." She shoved her half-eaten sandwich in the bag and jumped out of the swing. Whirling around, she faced him, irritated. "You really aren't coming? After you've made so much progress?"

"Progress?" He looked up at her, his face the picture of calm. "What am I, your pet project?"

"Of course not. But I thought you understood that you don't have to separate yourself from people anymore."

"I do."

251

"Then why aren't you going to the wedding?"

"I never said I wasn't."

"*Ya* you did."

He leaned back in the swing, his hands behind his head. He had taken off his hat earlier that day, and a heavy lock of blond hair hung over his eyebrows. "I said I was thinking about it. And I think I'm going. Actually, I planned to all along."

"Ooh." Elisabeth took a step forward, bending toward him. "Then why didn't you say so in the first place?"

"And miss this fine display of temper? I wouldn't dream of it."

She reached out to give him a playful thump on the shoulder, but he caught her wrist, holding it lightly. "I wouldn't do that if I were you."

"Oh really. Who's going to stop me?"

"I just did." He moved his hand from her wrist to her hand, then clasped her fingers.

Suddenly the mood between them changed. His smile faded, along with the laughter in his eyes. Their blue hue darkened to nearly gray, and she saw his gaze drop to her mouth.

A tiny thrill went through her, and her pulse quickened. She wondered what it would be like to kiss him. She didn't know, but she knew in her heart that it would be wonderful.

The sound of a car approaching made them jump apart. Elisabeth stared at him, trying to get her heartbeat to slow down. But it wasn't working, because even though he had jumped out of the swing like a rock out of a sling shot, she couldn't take her eyes off him. Or stop thinking about him kissing her.

Uh oh. This isn't gut.

"Must be a customer." Aaron picked up the trash from their lunch and strode by her as if nothing had happened between them. And she figured as far as he was concerned, nothing probably had. He didn't look back as he rushed down the porch steps and over to the shop.

Elisabeth went to the edge of the steps, confusion rolling inside her. Where had those feelings come from? She liked Aaron, cared about him, but as a friend. A best friend. Yet the emotions surging through her a few minutes ago were anything but friendly. They weren't unwelcome either.

She gripped the white banister that surrounded Moriah and Gabe's porch. As the small gray compact car parked next to the blacksmith shop, she fought to get her mind and heart on the same page. Aaron was her friend. Period. That's all he would ever be. He didn't have feelings for her. Why should he? Aaron had so much to offer a woman. He was smart, a talented blacksmith and farrier, he had a great sense of humor, and no one could ice skate better than he could. No one was kinder or more unselfish either. He was gorgeous to boot, especially when he smiled.

And who was she? A part-time clerk who couldn't

cook or knit with any skill, who hated housework and was only mildly good with children. What kind of wife would she be to Aaron? To anyone?

As she fought the pain rising inside her, she saw a woman get out of the car, a thin trail of smoke rising in the air above her. She took a puff of a cigarette, then threw it on the ground and mashed it into the asphalt driveway with the ball of her tennis shoe.

The woman was thin, almost painfully so, and her curly black hair was pulled back in a pony-tail fastened at her neck. She slammed the door and turned around.

At that point Elisabeth got a good look at her face and realized she was familiar. Memories of the party at the Schrocks' filled her mind. When she and Aaron were leaving, a woman had stopped him, calling out his name. Taking his hand. Looking and speaking to him as if she knew him well. Very well.

Envy twisted inside Elisabeth as the woman walked around the car and went into the black-smith shop. She wasn't a customer; she was here for Aaron. Elisabeth knew it. But why?

Elisabeth ran down the porch steps, determined to find out.

Aaron shoved a hand through his hair, then leaned over the table, trying to get his bearings. For-tunately Gabe had run an errand and wasn't in the shop; if he had been, he would have thought Aaron had lost his mind.

He stood back up and scrubbed a hand over his face, trying to settle his emotions. He couldn't believe how close he'd come to kissing Elisabeth. On his boss's front porch of all places. What had he been thinking?

He hadn't been thinking at all. He'd been feeling. And that scared him more than anything.

When had his feelings for Elisabeth changed? When had he stopped seeing her as a friend and started viewing her as something more? And how could he put a stop to it? Because he'd have to. Elisabeth deserved more than he could give. She deserved the best, which he wasn't.

Closing his eyes, he leaned against one of the worktables, fighting the emotional war inside him. He'd never felt this way about anyone, not even Kacey. He didn't have the right to feel such an intense attraction toward Elisabeth, or to want to court her. Or to . . .

Marry her.

He'd asked her to do just that a couple weeks ago, and she had dismissed it as ridiculous. At the time he'd been relieved she hadn't been pregnant and thus didn't need to get married. But now he could look back on that conversation, remembering her reaction, and see how useless it was to think of Elisabeth as anything but a friend. Because that's all he'd be in her eyes.

The door to the shop opened and he turned around, expecting to see Elisabeth. He shoved down his feelings and schooled his expression, refusing to let her see the turmoil brewing inside him. But the woman walking into the shop wasn't Elisabeth.

"Hello, Aaron."

The scent of cigarettes surrounded her, and he remembered she'd had a pack-a-day habit that she obviously hadn't kicked. She was only a couple years older than he was, but she seemed to have aged five since the last time they were together, right before he'd gone to jail. "What are you doing here?"

"I came to see you."

His guard went up. "Why?"

She moved to the opposite end of the table and leaned against it, looking straight at him. "Can't I visit an old friend?"

"We're not friends."

"We used to be. More than friends."

He crossed his arms over his chest. "That was a long time ago."

"I know. Too long."

"What do you want, Kacey?"

Her confidence seemed to slip a bit. "You sound like you're mad at me."

"I'm not mad. I'm suspicious. I think I have a right to be."

"But you don't have to be. I'm not going to do something to you."

"That remains to be seen."

"So you're still blaming me for your problems."

He let out a breath. "Kacey, I never blamed you for them."

She stepped away from the table and walked to him. He remembered the first time he'd seen her, he'd thought she was so beautiful. Despite the obvious toll her lifestyle had taken on her, she was still pretty. And still dangerous.

"I haven't been able to stop thinking of you, Aaron. When I saw you at that party, I remembered what fun we used to have."

"That fun landed me in jail."

"But you're out now." Her brown eyes gazed at him. "You're free."

Aaron nodded, trying to figure out what she was getting at. "You're right, I'm free. I'm free of drugs."

She paused, then let out a long breath. "Me too."

Her words stunned him. "You are?"

"I got out of rehab a couple weeks ago." Her expression softened, revealing a hidden layer of vulnerability. "Hardest thing I ever had to do."

Her confession broke through the barrier he'd put up between them. She was clean? "I'm really happy for you," he said, meaning it.

"That's why I came to see you." She averted her gaze. "I needed to know something."

"What?"

"How did you put your life back together?" Her eyes went back to him. "I didn't realize it would be so hard. Everyone I know is still using or drinking. I've been offtrack for so long I don't know how to get back on."

He let his arms fall to his sides, relaxing his stance. "One day at a time, Kacey. Did they tell you that in rehab?"

She nodded.

"That's the only way to do it. I had to put that life behind me, because if I didn't, I knew I'd be right back to using again. I came back to the Amish and to my family and joined the church."

"You're lucky you had something to go back to. I don't."

"What about your mom?"

"Who do you think was the inspiration for me to go to rehab? She's in worse shape than I am."

Remembering her parents were divorced and her father wasn't in the picture, Aaron asked, "What about friends?"

"I have a couple who are helping me out. They're good people. I was also hoping we could be friends. Hang out together every once in a while. I miss how we used to do that."

He stilled. "I don't think that's a *gut* idea."

She sighed, glancing away. "You're probably right. You've made a new life for yourself here, and you seem to be doing great. I guess I'm a little jealous of that." Looking up at him, sadness filled her eyes. "It's just so hard. I feel so alone sometimes." She went to him, then put her arms around his waist.

Before he could stop himself, his arms automatically went around her.

Elisabeth couldn't take it anymore. She stood outside of the front door to the shop, straining to hear. Why did Gabe have to build the door so thick? She couldn't hear what was going on inside, and she was dying to find out. It burned her up to think about that woman and Aaron in there alone. What were they doing for so long?

Unable to stop herself, she opened the door. What she saw made her freeze in place.

He was hugging her. Even worse, she was leaning her head against his chest.

Aaron looked at Elisabeth over Kacey's shoulder, his eyes widening. "Elisabeth," he said.

The woman stepped out of his arms, gave Elisabeth a quick glance, then looked back at Aaron. "I need to be going. Thanks."

He nodded, but didn't say anything. He stared at Elisabeth with an expression that almost looked guilty.

Elisabeth moved to the side as the woman hurried past her and out the front door. The smell of her cigarettes lingered in the shop. When she heard the car backing out of the driveway, Elisabeth looked at Aaron. "Who was that?"

"An old friend." Aaron went to the peg board on the wall and picked up a long file. Grabbing a piece of metal with his other hand, he walked to the end of one of the worktables.

"Is she an old girlfriend?"

"What makes you say that?" he replied, not looking at her. He began rubbing his file against the metal in the vise.

"You two were hugging."

"She's having a hard time right now."

Elisabeth waited for him to elaborate, but all she heard were the rough scrapes of the file against metal. She moved to stand beside him.

"What's her name?"

"Kacey."

"How long have you known her?"

"A while."

"Is that all you have to say?"

"*Ya*, Elisabeth. That's it."

Frustrated, she clenched her fists. "You dated her, didn't you?"

Aaron pressed his lips together before answering. "Yep."

"How long?"

"How long what?"

"Don't be dense, Aaron. How long did you date?"

He tossed the file aside and looked at her. "Does it matter?"

"*Ya*. It matters to me."

"Why?" He looked down at her, his eyes hooded, his emotions hidden. Just as they'd been when she first started working with him.

The thought of him going back to that guarded, secretive person increased her frustration. "Because it matters."

"Not a *gut* answer."

"Neither is yours, so we're even."

"I don't know why you're getting so mad."

"I'm not mad!" She threw her hands up in the air. "Why should I care who you date? If you want to get back together with your ex-girlfriend, who am I to stop you?" Furious, she walked toward him and looked him directly in the eye. "But if you start using again, Aaron Detweiler, I'll . . . I'll . . . well, I don't know what I'll do, but you won't like it." Spinning around, she stormed to her office, slammed the door, and plopped down on the chair in front of her desk.

She fought for breath, for calm, and thinking back to what she just said to Aaron, for dignity. He was probably laughing at her right now. She couldn't even carry out a threat properly. She wiped her forehead with her hand, wishing she could take back what she said. But she couldn't.

She waited, thinking he might come to the office, if anything to point out that she needed to mind her business from now on. But he didn't. Even after she'd collected herself enough to do some paperwork, he still didn't show up. She glanced at the clock. An hour had passed since her outburst. Curiosity overriding any sense of pride, she stood up and opened the door to see Gabe standing at the forge, with Aaron nowhere in sight.

Elisabeth walked to her brother-in-law, making sure she stayed a safe distance from the forge. He looked up at her, removing his safety glasses. "What's up, Elisabeth?"

"Just wondered where Aaron was," she asked, trying to sound as nonchalant as she could.

"He left. Asked me for the rest of the day off when I came back. We're not too busy today, so I gave it to him." Gabe put his glasses back on. "Why?"

"Just curious. I'll let you get back to work."

Gabe nodded and then went back to pounding on the anvil. Elisabeth trod back to the office, bewildered, and kicking herself. She'd probably ticked him off this time. They had argued about a lot of things but never anything this personal. Maybe she'd finally crossed the line with him.

The thought made her feel sick to her stomach.

At the end of the day, Elisabeth left the shop, still thinking about Aaron and her confusing reaction to seeing him with Kacey. She'd never been jealous a day in her life. What in the world had come over her?

She was about to climb into her buggy when she heard a car pull in behind her. When she turned, she saw Kacey. What was *she* doing here? Maybe she and Aaron had made arrangements to meet after work.

Kacey got out of her car and, to her surprise, bypassed the shop and walked directly to her. "Is Aaron here?"

"*Nee*. He left for the day." So much for her theory that they were meeting after work.

Kacey looked around and slipped her hands into the back pockets of her slim jeans. "I suppose that's a good thing. Can you give him a message for me?"

Elisabeth nodded, crossing her arms over her chest. The ribbons of her *kapp* fluttered as a light breeze suddenly kicked up.

"Tell him I'm sorry. I meant to say that in person, but I didn't."

Elisabeth's heart softened a bit at the sincerity in Kacey's voice. She didn't know what Kacey was talking about, but she didn't doubt her apology was genuine. "I will."

Kacey hesitated but then suddenly blurted, "Are you two friends?"

"*Ya*, we are."

"You're lucky. He's a great guy."

"I know."

"I wish him the best. I hope he knows that." Kacey looked at her for a moment, her lips forming a tight smile. Then she got in her car and left.

Elisabeth watched her drive away, feeling like a fool. Any trace of jealousy she'd had disappeared with Kacey's words. Aaron had said she was going through a hard time, and from the sad, empty look in Kacey's eyes, Elisabeth believed it. But instead of acting with compassion, she'd acted like a child. Kacey wasn't the only one who needed to apologize.

Chapter 16

"What a beautiful day it turned out to be." Edna burst into Anna's bedroom, a beaming smile on her face. "I thought earlier it was going to rain. But God has smiled down on you and Lukas today."

Anna smiled, trying to calm the butterflies flitting around in her stomach. Her wedding day. She couldn't believe it was finally here, and she wouldn't let anything spoil it. Over the past couple of days she was actually feeling better and had been pain free. It had to be a sign from God.

"Everything is just about ready," Edna said, walking toward her. "I spoke with Emma downstairs, and the bishop said they'll start the service in a few minutes." She took in Anna's wedding dress. It was the same style as her other dresses, but the material was dark blue. "You look lovely,

Anna. I know we're not supposed to be filled with *hochmut*, even on a day like today, but I can't help it. You're beautiful."

"*Danki, Mami*. Hopefully Lukas will think so too."

"I know he will." Edna's smile dimmed. "You will talk to him after the wedding and let him know about the pain?"

"I haven't felt any pain for a couple of days." She turned around and looked at the mirror above her dresser. "I might not have to tell him anything."

"Anna, you have to. Even if you're feeling better, you have to tell him about the procedure."

She adjusted one of the pins holding her *kapp* in place. "I will, I promise. But I don't want to talk about that now." Facing her mother, she said, "I want to enjoy my wedding day."

Edna's expression softened. "Of course. I'm sorry I brought it up. I trust you know what you're doing."

"I do." Anna picked up her bonnet and put it on. "You think they're ready downstairs?"

"*Ya*. I'm sure they are."

"Then I'm ready too." She was ready to see Lukas, to become his wife. Most of all, she was ready to start their new life together.

Another day, another Amish wedding. Elisabeth sighed from her seat up front as she watched her brother and Anna marry in the Eshes' living room. While she was thrilled that Anna was becoming her sister-in-law, this was the fifth wedding she'd attended since November, and she was getting a little tired of them. Especially when she could no longer observe a wedding, or even see a couple together, without thinking of Aaron.

She'd spent the past few days helping her family get ready for the wedding, so she hadn't seen him since they'd had their fight. But just because Aaron was out of sight didn't mean he was out of her mind. In fact, he took up so much space in there, she couldn't think of anything else.

Glancing around the room, she saw a sea of familiar faces. But no Aaron. Disappointment threaded through her. He'd said he'd be here, but maybe he'd changed his mind. Hopefully not because of her. She'd hate to think she was the reason he was staying home alone.

Then again, maybe he wasn't alone. He might be with his *friend* Kacey. A fresh wave of envy flowed over her. She frowned. Why couldn't she stop feeling jealous?

Because I'm falling in love with him.

"Elisabeth, stop groaning," Ruth whispered. "People can hear you."

Mortified, Elisabeth sat up straight, determined to focus on her brother's wedding instead of being so selfish and only thinking of herself. She couldn't help but smile at the way he looked at

Anna during the ceremony. Maybe someday Aaron would look at her the same way.

Stop it!

Wedding services lasted about three hours, and when this one was over, Elisabeth was the first to welcome Anna to the family. "I'm so happy for you," she said, hugging her.

"*Danki.*" Anna beamed. Then she looked past Elisabeth's shoulder. "Oh, I'm glad Aaron decided to come."

Elisabeth swung around to see Aaron standing a few feet behind her, several people in between them. He was talking to Stephen, his profile to her. She turned back to Anna. "I should let you go. Everyone will want to give you their congratulations."

"We'll talk later."

Elisabeth smiled and nodded, then spun around to see Aaron. But he had disappeared. She walked over to Stephen. "Where did Aaron *geh?*"

Stephen shrugged. "I don't know. We only talked for a minute, then he left."

She stood on tiptoes, searching for him in the crowd of people. After several minutes she gave up. Maybe he'd gone back to his old habit of leaving as soon as the fellowship started.

Sighing, she noticed that food was being served. She should go in the kitchen and ask if anyone needed help, but she didn't feel like doing that. What she really wanted was to be alone. She

267

walked out the back door, unnoticed, then walked toward the shed on the edge of the field behind the house. The grass had started to grow, and she knew by summer it would be past her knees.

A cool breeze lifted her dress, but the air was welcome. Again they were having another unseasonably warm March day, and she didn't even need a sweater outside. A taste of spring, although it wouldn't last long. Soon enough the cold air would return and probably another snowfall or two with it. Ohio weather was always unpredictable. She leaned against the back of the shed, listening to the voices of children running and playing.

"Elisabeth."

At the sound of Aaron's voice, Elisabeth's breath caught in her throat. She rolled her head to the side and took him in. His black hat was pushed back on his forehead, revealing a thick section of blond bang. Her cheeks heating, she suddenly turned away.

"Hi, Aaron."

He moved to stand next to her. "What are you doing out here by yourself?"

"*Nix.*"

"That sounds like something I would say."

"You must be rubbing off on me."

"I hope not."

She was about to correct him when she saw the humor in his eyes. His remark made her lips lift in a half smile. "Are you still mad at me?"

"I was never mad at you, Elisabeth. I don't think I ever could be."

"I wouldn't blame you if you were. I was a bit snippy with you the other day."

He looked at her. "A bit?"

"Okay, more than a bit. I shouldn't have been upset about Kacey." Elisabeth sighed, letting her head fall back against the shed again.

He chuckled. "If I didn't know any better, I'd think you were jealous."

Her face heated. "Me, jealous?" She laughed. But it sounded a little too loud, so she stopped and cleared her throat. "I'm not jealous."

"*Gut.*" Aaron pulled a blade of grass from the ground. "Because there's nothing to be jealous of. Kacey needed someone to talk to, and she came and saw me."

"I know that. She came back after you left."

Aaron's face registered surprise. "She did?"

"*Ya.* She said to tell you that she's sorry. And that she wished you the best."

"Wow." Aaron stared straight ahead. "I wouldn't have expected that of her."

"What happened?"

"Well, as soon as I was arrested, she dropped me completely. No contact at all." He put the blade between his thumbs and blew. The vibrating blade made a high-pitched whistle.

"You're just full of hidden talents, aren't you?"

He cast a sideways look. "I like to think so."

He let the blade float to the ground, then he moved to stand in front of Elisabeth. "I just want you to know that I have no intention of getting involved with Kacey or drugs again. I'm not interested in either. And I made a commitment to God and to the church that I'm going to keep."

"But what if she drags you back into them again?"

"She won't. She says she's clean now, and hopefully she'll stay that way. Either way, one of the many things I learned in rehab is that doing drugs is a choice. *Ya*, they're addictive, and when addiction is pulling you under, you feel helpless. But eventually you have to decide how you want to live—at the mercy of drugs or at the mercy of God. I chose God." He slipped his hands in his pockets. "I don't think I realized that until a few weeks ago. Those talks we've had really set me thinking, and I don't think I would have figured it out by myself that I wasn't just running to the Amish to keep from drugs, but I was running to God."

She looked up into his eyes, a catch in her throat. She had always thought they were blue, similar to hers, but from this close up she could see they were more of a silvery gray. "I can't take credit for that, Aaron."

He rocked back and forth on his heels. "*Demut.* That's a lovely Amish quality you possess, Elisabeth, but sometimes I think you take it too far."

"What do you mean?" Amish were supposed to be humble, to think less of themselves than more. How could she possibly screw that up? "Are you saying I'm too humble?"

Shaking his head, he said, "*Nee*. Maybe humble isn't the right word. Sometimes I get the impression you think you don't measure up." When she started to protest, he lifted his hand. "The reason I know is because I feel the same way about myself."

Lukas and Anna greeted their guests and accepted their congratulations for the next hour. They barely had time to look at each other, much less say anything. But every once in a while he would glance at her in such a way that made her toes curl in her shoes. While she was enjoying visiting with the wedding guests, she couldn't wait until they were alone.

When they had a short break in meeting the well-wishers, Lukas spoke. "I need a drink. Do you want anything?"

She shook her head. "I'm fine."

"All right. I'll be right back, Mrs. Byler." He winked, then left to go to the dining room where they were serving food and beverages.

Edna came up to her, smiling. "Having a *gut* time?"

"*Ya. Danki* for everything, *Mami*. I know you worked really hard to make this day special."

"It was nothing."

She was about to speak again when an agonizing pain took her breath away. It felt like she was being slashed with a knife.

"Anna?"

Her mother's voice sounded far away. The room swirled around her. Voices buzzed in her ear. She tried to stand, but the pain was too intense.

Everything went black.

Lukas's stomach hit his feet when he saw his Anna lying in a lump on the floor. He had just emerged from the dining room when he saw her, Edna crouched down beside her. He dropped his drink and shoved his way through the crowd toward them.

"Lukas," Edna exclaimed, remaining beside her daughter.

Carefully he rolled Anna over. His gut lurched at her ghostly face. "What happened?"

"She fainted, just a second ago. Everything was fine, then she turned around and doubled over. Before I could get to her, she passed out." Worry seeped into her eyes.

He laid his hand on her chest, feeling it rise and fall beneath his palm. Thank God she was still breathing. "We need an ambulance!" When no one responded he yelled, "I know someone has to have a cell phone here!"

An elderly woman, dressed in full Old Order garb, handed him a cell phone, her head hung low. He flipped it open and punched in the emergency number.

"911. What is your emergency?"

"My wife fainted. She's passed out."

"Sir? I'm sorry, but I didn't understand you. Do you speak English?"

Lukas hadn't even realized he'd been speaking *Dietsch.* "My wife," he said more slowly, in English, "she fainted. I need an ambulance." He gave the operator the address.

"I'll send one right over."

He hung up the phone. "They're on their way." He knelt back down beside Anna and cradled her head under his arm, distressed that she hadn't woken up.

Joseph and Emma appeared. "*Gut* heavens," Emma said, her hands going to her cheeks. "What happened?"

Edna started to cry. "*Mei dochder,*" she said through her tears. "The doctor told her this would happen, that she would get worse, but she refused to believe him."

Bewildered, Lukas looked at Edna. "What are you talking about?"

"I can't tell you. She made me promise."

"Everyone outside," Joseph hollered, guiding the guests to the door. "We need room in here."

"Edna!" Lukas shouted. "She's going to be *mei frau.* If something's wrong with her, I have to know!"

273

Edna hesitated for a moment, then nodded, tears streaming down her cheeks. "She had a procedure done a few weeks ago. She'd been feeling some pain lately, and the doctor wanted her to come in, but she refused."

"What kind of procedure?"

"I forget what it's called, but it's for endometriosis."

"What?" He'd never heard of endo-whatever.

"I don't understand it, Lukas. She wouldn't tell me everything. All I know is that there was a chance this would happen."

Shock coursed through Lukas just as the paramedics came through the door, carrying various pieces of medical equipment. They immediately went to Anna and knelt down next to her. "Are you her husband?" a stocky man with a black mustache asked.

"*Ya.*"

Anna's eyelids suddenly fluttered open. "Lukas?"

"I'm here, *lieb*." He stroked her cheek, trying to ignore the confusion whirling inside of him. He had to focus on her. "What happened?"

"I don't know." She glanced around at the men who were crouched down beside her. "Who are they?"

"The paramedics. We couldn't get you to wake up."

"Mr.?"

"Byler," Lukas said.

"Mr. Byler," he said, looking first at Lukas, then at Edna. "I'll need you both to step aside so we can examine her."

Lukas nodded, but didn't move, unable to let her go.

"Mr. Byler, could you please stand over there?"

"But Anna—"

"We'll take good care of her. But we need room to do our job."

Lukas nodded numbly, then got to his feet and walked over to the couch, leaving Anna in their hands. He watched helplessly while the paramedics asked her questions. He strained to hear her answers but couldn't because she kept her voice low. The man with the mustache listened to her heart while the other paramedic put a blood pressure cuff on her arm and some sort of large, plastic clamp on her finger. Most everyone had left the house though a few people had stayed in the room. When he felt a hand on his arm, he turned and looked at Edna.

"You have to convince her to go to the hospital," Edna said. "If you don't, this will happen again. I'm sure of it."

"How long has she known about this?"

"A couple of months." Edna's tears had dried up, her stricken expression becoming stoic. "You have to make her realize how important it is that she see her doctor right away. I just know something worse will happen if she continues to ignore what her body and the doctor are telling her."

The mustached paramedic rose from the floor and came over to Lukas. "She seems fine, Mr. Byler. Blood pressure is normal, oxygen level is good. She says she's all right, that she just felt a little dizzy and that she hadn't eaten much for breakfast. Still, we want to take her to the hospital. We asked her, but she refused. I thought you might be able to convince her to agree."

Lukas looked at Anna, who was now in a seated position on the floor, her legs tucked beneath the skirt of her dark blue dress. She cast him a sideways glance, then looked away when their eyes met. He turned his attention back to the paramedic. "Did she say why she wouldn't go?"

"Said she was feeling better and promised she'd have some lunch. But we took her blood sugar and it was normal, so I'm not sure that's the reason she fainted. Has this happened to her before?"

He shook his head. "Not that I know of."

The paramedic nodded. "We can't force her to go to the hospital, but we'd like for her to see a doctor all the same." His expression turned sympathetic. "She said today was your wedding day."

"*Ya.*" The day he'd been looking forward to for so long. Now it had turned into a nightmare. He didn't understand why Anna was refusing to go to the hospital. It wasn't normal to pass out like she did. He rubbed the back of his neck, frowning. "Let me talk to her."

"We have some paperwork to fill out, so take all the time you need."

Lukas went to Anna and slowly crouched down next to her. She looked up at him. "I'm sorry," she said. "I don't know what happened. I just felt dizzy all of a sudden."

Lukas nodded, maintaining eye contact even as she was trying to break it with him. She was lying. He could tell by the way she flinched underneath his gaze, the way her hands worried her skirt. Her skin was still pale, and the dark circles he'd noticed under her eyes a couple days ago were more pronounced. Why didn't she tell him the truth?

"I'm sure if I eat something I'll feel better." When he didn't say anything, she looked at him again. "Lukas?"

"Stop lying to me, Anna. I know," he said in a low voice, not wanting the paramedics to overhear. "I know you went to see the doctor."

Anna's movements froze.

"Why didn't you tell me you had a procedure?" Hurt, compounded by anger and confusion, built inside him. "How could you keep that from me?"

Tears pooled in her eyes. "Lukas," she said thickly. "I'm so sorry. I was going to tell you—"

Suddenly she clutched at her abdomen, folding her body in half as she groaned.

"Anna?" Lukas leaned closer to her as the paramedics surrounded them and peppered her with questions.

"Where is the pain?"

"How long have you had it?"

"On a scale from one to ten, how would you rate it?"

"Is it subsiding?"

"I . . . can't . . . breathe . . ." She looked up at Lukas and started to gasp. "Hurts . . ."

"What's happening to her?" Lukas shouted.

The paramedics didn't answer. One ran out of the house and, moments later, brought in a stretcher.

"Lukas?" Edna came up behind him. "What's going on?"

"I don't know." He looked from the paramedics to Anna, who was still clutching her abdomen. "What's happening?" he asked the paramedics.

"We're taking her to the hospital," one responded. The two paramedics counted to three and lifted her onto the stretcher and started strapping her in. "You can ride with us if you want, or follow behind."

"I'm coming with you." He spun around and faced Edna. "Can you get a taxi?"

"I'll try to call Susan."

"I'll meet you there." The paramedics were already out the door, Lukas following close behind.

"Which hospital?" Lukas asked, then called out the name to Edna.

He watched as they loaded Anna into the ambulance. She wasn't clutching her side, but her face was contorted with pain. He sat down next to her and held her hand while a paramedic sat on the other side of the stretcher.

Fear consumed him as he watched her suffer. He thought of his sister Moriah, whose first husband had died a few months after they'd married. Would that happen to him? Would God take Anna away? He prayed harder than ever that he wouldn't. Even though he was still confused and hurt about her deception, Lukas couldn't bear the thought of life without her.

Chapter 17

*P*ain. Aching, burning pain. Anna opened her eyes to see bright fluorescent lights, and she inhaled an antiseptic scent that turned her stomach. She realized where she was. The hospital. She glanced down at her body and saw a white blanket that covered her from chest to toe. Her arms were snug at her sides, and she moved them as she tried to sit up, but cried out from the agony in her belly.

"Don't try to move." A nurse came over to her

and stood at her beside. "You just got out of surgery; you don't want to move too much right now. Trust me, they'll have you up moving soon enough."

Surgery? Panic flowed through her. "When?" she said, her mouth dry and sticky.

"About an hour ago."

"What . . ." she swallowed, afraid to ask the question but needing to know the answer. "What did they do?"

"A cyst burst on your ovary. That's why you were in such pain." The young nurse tucked a strand of pale blonde hair behind her ear.

"Did they do anything else?"

"The doctor will give you more details once you're out of recovery." She put her hand on Anna's. "Right now you need to rest."

But she didn't want to rest. She needed to know what was going on. "Who gave you permission to do the surgery?"

"Your husband. You must have been in bad shape if you don't remember that. Then again, I can't imagine how much pain you were experiencing. That had to be excruciating." She smiled. "Congratulations, by the way. I heard you just got married." She patted Anna's hand. "I have to check on another patient. Do you need anything?"

Anna shook her head. When the nurse left, she closed her eyes, dread filling her heart alongside the pain from her body. Her worst nightmare: Lukas knew. Not only that, but he'd found out on their wedding day, in front of everyone. Slowly she remembered what had happened. She and her mother had been talking when she had been overcome with pain. Then everything went black, and she woke to see Lukas kneeling beside her. She shut her eyes more tightly as she recalled what Lukas had said later.

He knew. Not only had her secret been exposed, but he had to be the one to agree to the surgery, and she still didn't know everything that they did to her. Did the doctor completely destroy her chances to have children? She fought to stay awake, trying to make sense of everything that had happened. But the heaviness of sleep overcame her.

Later, when she woke up, the nurse appeared again. "We're moving you into your regular room, Mrs. Byler. Your family will meet you there in a little while. Don't let any other visitors come in; you still need to rest. If you don't, you'll have to be in the hospital longer, and you know how those insurance companies are."

Anna frowned in confusion but didn't say anything. Like most Amish, she didn't have insurance. A new worry hit her. How would she and Lukas pay for the surgery? It had to be expensive. Plus the emergency room and the ambulance . . . she couldn't imagine what all that would cost.

Despair settled over her, paralyzing her so

much that she barely recognized the discomfort from the surgery. As she was wheeled down the hall, she felt the full burden of her choices and the repercussions, and it was crushing her.

Then she saw Lukas. He was standing by the doorway, his hat in his hand, still wearing his white shirt, black vest, and black pants. His wedding suit. She could only see him from the waist up, but she could detect the worry on his face. Worry and betrayal. He lifted his hand as if to touch her, then pulled it back.

She closed her eyes at his rejection. Of course he wouldn't want to touch her. He'd probably never want to be with her again. She'd lied to him. Ignored her doctor's advice and landed in the hospital. And what if she couldn't have children? How would she ever face him again?

Lukas shifted in his chair in the corner of Anna's room. He'd never been in a hospital, and he hoped he'd never have to be in one again. He looked over at his new *frau*. She had been asleep since they wheeled her in almost two hours ago. He'd tried to nap but couldn't do it, not with his thoughts and emotions so out of control.

Edna had come and had stayed for the surgery, but afterward Lukas urged her to go home and check on Zeb. She had insisted on staying but had finally relented when the nurse insisted he was the only visitor Anna was allowed to have.

If Anna's condition changed, Lukas assured her, he'd call his father at the shop and Joseph would drive over and tell Edna.

He twisted in the chair and glanced up at the clock. Almost ten o'clock at night. He crossed his feet at the ankles and stared down at his black polished dress shoes, trying to sort through what had happened over the past eight hours. During the surgery, he'd paced the waiting room, feeling at loose ends, like he was about to jump out of his own skin. Only when they had brought her into the recovery room did he allow himself to breathe again.

And now, sitting in the dim quiet of the sterile room, he battled his emotions. Why hadn't Anna told him about this? He thought back over the past months, remembering the times she'd been pale and tired, blaming it all on work. And he had believed her. Why wouldn't he? He had never thought she would lie to him before.

But she had. And while all he had cared about for the past several hours was that she would be safe and well, now all he could think about was she had kept something so important from him. He still didn't understand the kind of surgery she'd had. The doctor had only said the surgery went well, and the nurses said the doctor would return soon. Lukas didn't want people to think he was stupid, so he didn't ask questions.

"Mr. Byler?"

Lukas looked up as the slim, gray-haired doctor walked in. *Finally.* He stood.

The doctor held out his hand. "Dr. Caxson. Nice to meet you. I just wish it was under better circumstances." He plucked a pen out of the pocket of his crisp white coat. "How is she?"

"Sleeping."

"Good. She needs to rest." He looked at Lukas. "I didn't perform the surgery, but I am Anna's gynecologist. I had hoped the laparoscopy would have solved this problem, but I didn't realize she had the cyst on her ovary."

Lukas frowned, trying to follow the doctor's conversation. "A cyst?"

"Yes. It burst, and that's what caused her so much pain." He picked up the chart at the end of her bed and thumbed through it. "Looks like the surgeon resected the ovary."

"What does that mean?"

"He removed part of the tissue from her ovary." He scanned the chart further, then frowned. "That's surprising."

"What is?"

"The amount of scar tissue and adhesions."

Lukas ran his hand through his hair, tired of being in the dark. "Doctor, I'm not going to pretend I understand you. Can you tell me in plain words?"

Dr. Caxson put Anna's chart back in its place. "Mr. Byler, in plain words, Anna has severe endometriosis, which has caused scarring on her reproductive organs."

"But the surgery solved the problem, right?"

"For now. But it's possible she'll need another surgery, especially if the endometriosis is recurring. She needs to have regular check-ups to stay on top of it."

Lukas ran a hand over his face. "You said this endo-whatever affects her reproductive organs. She'll still be able to have children, won't she?"

"I'm sorry, Mr. Byler, but in my experience this type of endometriosis renders the patient infertile. In some cases there's less than a five percent chance of conception, but I can't guarantee that will be the case for you. I'm afraid your wife might not be able to have children. I thought she had discussed the possibility with you."

Numb, Lukas shook his head slowly.

Dr. Caxson put the pen back in his pocket. "I'm sorry you're finding out about it this way. I'll be back to check on her in the morning. If she needs anything, the call button is by her bed. If you have any questions, I'll be happy to answer them tomorrow."

After the doctor left, Lukas collapsed into the chair, reality slowly sinking in. Anna couldn't have children. He and Anna would never know the joy of holding their own son or daughter in their arms. He would never experience his children growing up, never know what it was like to teach his own flesh and blood how to sand a block of wood, to learn to cut and shape it into something useful. He would never see his children bear children of their own. He would never pass down his legacy.

At the sound of Anna's soft groan, he opened his eyes. Leaping from the chair, he went over to her. "Anna?"

She looked up at him briefly, then turned her head away from him.

He put his hand on her arm. "Anna? Are you all right?" He waited for a few moments, but she said nothing.

A dam of fresh hurt burst inside him. Why was she ignoring him? He knew she was awake, but she refused to acknowledge him. He stared down at his hand, his tanned skin against the light skin of her forearm. He moved his hand to grip hers, but hers lay limply in his palm. He let it slip out of his grasp.

Turning, he sat down in the chair, clueless about what to do for her, or for himself. He knew what his father would say—pray. Take it to the Lord. But right now he was too consumed with his own misery to summon a single word of prayer.

Elisabeth stared at her paperwork, trying to concentrate. Mostly her mind was on her sister-in-law. Anna had returned home from the hospital yesterday, and Elisabeth planned to stop and visit her after work. She'd heard Anna was going to be okay, but the details of the surgery were sketchy, which she found odd. She hoped to find out more when she saw Anna this evening.

"Can I come in?"

Elisabeth looked up to see Deborah standing by the door of the office. She smiled, pushing concern over Anna out of her mind and gesturing for her friend to come inside.

"I'm glad to see you," she said to Deborah. "How are you doing?" Then she rose from her chair. "Here, sit down."

Deborah shook her head. "I'm fine. I don't need to sit. You were right about the nausea; it's getting better. Plus I've learned to eat a few saltine crackers as soon as I get up in the morning."

"That's *gut*. How is everything else?"

Her friend took a deep breath. She was dressed in full Amish clothing, complete with black bonnet and a black shawl pinned around her neck. "I told my parents."

Elisabeth's eyes widened. "What did they say?"

"They surprised me. I thought they'd be angry, or worse, not even care. They were upset, especially my *mami*." Deborah rubbed her nose. "But they were understanding too. I told them how I'd been feeling the past couple of years, like it didn't matter to them what I did. They said they were sorry and said it always mattered." She paused. "They just didn't know what to do.

They'd never had a rebellious teenager before, and they thought they could just pray me back. And in a way, they did."

"So what are you going to do?"

"That's why I stopped by." She took her purse and pulled out a slip of paper. "Here's my new address."

Elisabeth read it. "You're moving to Lancaster?"

"*Ya*. I have an aunt who lives in Paradise, and she's agreed to let me move in until the *boppli's* born. She never joined the church, but we still keep in contact with her."

"But why don't you stay here?"

Deborah shook her head. "I can't. I can't face people here, Elisabeth. Not everyone is as accepting as you."

"You might be surprised."

"Maybe. But I want to save my parents the embarrassment, at least for now. Once the *boppli's* born then I might come back. Or I might stay there, I don't know." She moved to stand in front of Elisabeth. "But whatever happens, I don't want to lose our friendship. I almost threw that away, and I don't want that to happen again."

Elisabeth hugged her friend. "Don't worry, it won't." She stepped back. "Write as often as you can."

"You too." Her eyes shone with tears. "*Danki*, Elisabeth, for everything."

"God be with you," Elisabeth called out as her friend left the office. She sat down at her desk and started to cry. She was glad Deborah seemed at peace with her decision, but she would miss her friend. Plucking a tissue from the box on the desk, she blew her nose.

At the end of the day, Elisabeth locked the door behind her. Aaron and Gabe had been delivering horseshoes to various customers around Geauga County, so she hadn't seen Aaron all day. Work wasn't nearly as interesting, or as much fun, without him around.

Half an hour later she arrived at Anna's house. Actually Anna and Lukas' house, as he had moved his things into her house right before the wedding. She felt bad that her brother and Anna had to cut their wedding celebration short. But Anna would be all right, and that's what counted.

She parked the buggy, then went to the front, carrying one of Ruth's books under her arm. She knocked on the door. A few moments later it opened.

"Hello, Elisabeth," Edna said, her voice sounding weary.

"Hi. I came to visit Anna."

"That's nice of you, but she's not up to visitors today."

"Oh. Okay, then, is Lukas here? I haven't seen him since the wedding."

Edna shook her head. "He must still be at work."

Elisabeth frowned. Lukas was working? Why wouldn't he be staying with his wife? That didn't sound like him. "Will you tell her I stopped by?"

"I will. Tell your *mudder* hello for me."

Elisabeth nodded, and Edna closed the door. As she drove home, she couldn't shake the nagging feeling that even though she'd been told Anna would be all right, nothing was truly right at all.

"Now you don't worry about that, Anna." Edna came into the living room and took the needle and thread, along with *Onkel* Zeb's shirt, from Anna's grasp. "You've only been home for a week. You don't need to be doing anything other than recovering."

"*Mami*, I can sew. Dr. Caxson said not to lift anything more than ten pounds or to climb up the stairs for the next two weeks. I can surely sew a button on *Onkel* Zeb's shirt."

"*Ya*, but you don't have to." Edna plopped herself down on the chair next to the sofa where Anna was sitting. Zeb was sitting down opposite from her, his reading glasses perched on his nose, doing the daily crossword from the paper. He leaned closer to the oil lamp on the small end table as he examined the puzzle more closely.

"Four letter word for 'ponder over,'" he said.

"Mull." Edna took the needle in hand and started sewing on the button. "I know what Dr. Caxson said. I was there, remember?"

"Egyptian crosses?" Zeb said, frowning. "How am I supposed to know the word for Egyptian crosses? I ain't never been to Egypt."

"And he said to be careful. Did you call to make your follow-up appointment yet?"

"I will. Tomorrow."

Edna put down her sewing and gave Anna a stern look. "Please, Anna. Don't tell me we're going to go through all this again."

"Japanese raw fish dish. Starts with S. Oh, that's that crazy sushi stuff." He put the pencil tip to his tongue and licked it before writing the word down. "Can't understand why anyone would want to eat somethin' raw."

"Zeb, please," Edna said. "We're trying to have a serious conversation."

Zeb glanced up from his paper, his white bushy eyebrows rising. "Oh, you two ain't botherin' me none. You just keep jabberin' on."

Anna shook her head, her lips curving upward. Leave it to *Onkel* Zeb to make her smile, even though lately all she wanted to do was cry. She could barely bring herself to look at Lukas. She was glad Dr. Caxson had told her she couldn't climb stairs. She had slept on the couch since she came home, with Lukas sleeping upstairs in what would eventually be their bedroom. They rarely saw each other—he rose early in the morning and left without breakfast, then came home late at night. He was avoiding her, and she didn't blame him.

291

Eventually she would be well enough to go up the stairs, then they would share the same room. And the same bed. What was supposed to be the happiest time of her life had turned into her biggest nightmare. Would he even want to be near her?

"Lukas workin' late again?" Zeb asked from behind his crossword puzzle.

Edna dropped her sewing. "Zeb, hush!"

"Don't you hush me. I thought he'd be hoverin' around here like he used to, especially with Anna being laid up an all."

"He had some projects to catch up on," Anna said.

"I imagine spending time at the hospital put him behind."

"Zeb!"

"I didn't mean nothin' by it." He put the paper down. "Just statin' a fact. Life gets in the way of life, you know?" Zeb picked up the crossword puzzle again. "Things happen. Don't mean it's anyone's fault."

Anna fought back tears. All this was her fault.

"*Ocean's Twelve* cast name? What's an *Ocean's Twelve*?" Zeb tossed down the paper. "Last time I do one of those *dumm* newspaper crosswords." He slowly stood up, his bony knees cracking. "I'm turning in."

"But it's only six-thirty," Edna said.

"*Ya,* but these old bones think it's past ten.

292

Guden Owed, Edna. Anna. Say the same to Lukas for me, will *ya*? I hope that *bu* comes by soon, I miss having him around."

After Zeb left, Anna lifted up her feet and swung them over the couch, settling her head against the pillows. She had just closed her eyes when her mother spoke.

"That was *sehr* nice of Moriah to bring that tuna casserole by tonight."

Anna nodded. Since Anna's return home her mother hadn't had to prepare dinner, what with members of Lukas' family and other people from the church stopping by and leaving various dishes and desserts. Anna ate out of politeness, but she had little appetite. And while she appreciated the generosity of her family and neighbors, she had seen the pity in their eyes. Most of them had been at the wedding and had seen her be carried out on a stretcher. They knew she had surgery. She wondered what else they knew? Nothing was private anymore.

"Moriah said she and Elisabeth might come by tomorrow. Would that be all right?"

Anna shrugged. "If they want to."

"Of course she wants to. Moriah had wanted to stay when she came by earlier but she had to get back and take care of the . . ."

"*Kinner.* You can say it, *Mami.*"

"Okay. *Kinner.* Gabriel had a school board meeting to go to last night. Seems they've got to hire a new teacher to take *Fraulein* Schlabach's place."

"But it's only March. The school year isn't over until the middle of April."

"*Ya*, but she's getting married this fall."

"And she's telling everyone about it?" Anna was surprised. Normally dating couples didn't broadcast their relationship until closer to the wedding.

"She is. She didn't want to leave in the middle of the school year after the wedding. So now they're doing interviews for the next couple weeks or so."

"I'm sure they'll find the right person." Anna put her arm over her forehead, ignoring the dull ache from the incision in her abdomen. The slight pain was nothing compared to the agony she went through when the cyst on her ovary had burst, but she was tired of being in pain, both physically and emotionally.

"I think I'll do the same as Zeb," Edna said, setting aside the sewing. "Do you need anything, Anna?"

"I'm fine."

Edna went to her and kissed her forehead. "Don't worry about Lukas. That *bu* loves you, and he'll come around. He just needs time."

Anna didn't say anything. Her mother left, and she rolled over on her side, wincing as she did. She knew Lukas didn't need time. Their relationship was over, and she only had herself to blame.

Chapter 18

Lukas opened the back door of the house and stepped quietly inside. He slipped off his boots, not wanting to wake anyone up, especially Anna. It was well past ten o'clock, and he knew she'd be sleeping. Guilt mixed with resentment bubbled within him as he crept past her and snuck upstairs.

He walked into his bedroom, not bothering to turn on the light. He quickly undressed and got into bed, weariness seeping through every pore. He'd been putting more than his fair share of hours in at work, trying to keep his mind off his troubles. When Tobias had told him he should go home to his wife, Lukas had told him to mind his own business. Not only was he alienating his new bride, he was alienating his family.

But he couldn't help it. Anger churned within him. He was sleeping in Anna's bed, alone. She should be beside him. They should be starting their new life together, sharing their dreams for the future, sharing the intimacies of husband and wife.

And yes, trying for a child. Yet that would never happen. Nothing would be normal. How could it be? He and Anna hadn't really spoken since she'd come home. For once in his life, he didn't know what to say. Her betrayal had cut him deeply, and the wound continued to bleed. He longed for things to be the way they were before the wedding, but even then he'd been kept in the dark. He had thought he'd married an honest woman who shared the same hopes and dreams for the future. And maybe she had. But he couldn't be sure. He wasn't sure about anything anymore.

Rolling over on his side, he closed his eyes and forced himself not to think of Anna. He failed.

Anna tossed and turned on the couch. She'd heard Lukas going up the stairs, just as she had every night. She could tell he was trying to be quiet, but she could never sleep until he'd come home. Even then, it was elusive. Finally, unable to lie there any longer, she got up and went to the kitchen.

She clicked on the battery-powered lamp but didn't know what to do next. Hunger wasn't what drew her here, but she had to do something. She prepared a light snack of two small wedges of smoked Swiss cheese and a few wheat crackers, then sat down at the table and stared at the food.

She heard movement upstairs. Probably her uncle, who usually got up in the middle of the night at least once or twice to use the bathroom. Usually he was a lot louder, but perhaps he decided not to make much of a racket this time.

But it wasn't Uncle Zeb who walked into the kitchen. It was Lukas.

She glanced up at him, surprised, taking in his tousled black hair, white T-shirt, and broadfall pants that looked like he'd just yanked on a few moments ago. Without the suspenders holding up the trousers, the waistband hung low on his narrow hips.

He paused a moment, then came inside the room. She couldn't read his impassive expression.

"Couldn't sleep?" Lukas didn't look at her as he spoke. He walked over to the cabinet and pulled down two glasses.

"*Nee.*" She looked down at her plate of untouched cheese and crackers. There was no warmth in his voice. It was as if she were listening to a stranger.

"Me neither." He filled one glass, then the other, with water before turning around and striding to the table. "Mind if I join you?"

She nodded.

He placed one glass of water in front of him and the other beside her plate, then sat across from her.

"*Danki,*" she said in a low voice.

But neither of them took a drink. They didn't say anything for a long time, the silence that stretched between them further increasing the emotional chasm.

Each time Anna looked up, Lukas was staring at the glass in front of him. The awkwardness continued until she couldn't take it anymore.

She'd rather be fighting sleep on the couch than endure this silent war between them. She moved to pick up her plate.

"We need to talk about this, Anna."

He was right, of course, but she didn't know what to say. She rose from her chair and took her food to the trash can, dumping it inside. She poured the water into the sink, then set the glass on the counter next to it.

"Are you going to ignore me, Anna? Or are you going to just wish it all away and ignore everything that happened, just like you tried to do with your condition?"

"That's not fair," she mumbled, turning around.

"Not fair?" He shot up from the table, his eyes blazing. "You lied to me, and you're saying I'm not fair." He thrust his hand through his hair and started to pace. "I can't believe this. How could you not trust me and my love for you enough to tell me?"

"I didn't want to disappoint you."

"I would have been disappointed, Anna, but not in you. It's not your fault you have endo . . . endo . . ."

"Endometriosis."

He grabbed the back of the chair, his knuckles turning white. "If you'd told me—"

"You would have married me anyway?" Her voice grew shrill, derisive. "Be honest with yourself, Lukas. If I had told you before the wedding about Dr. Caxson's diagnosis, what would you have said? Would you have called off our wedding?"

He looked at her, his face contorted with pain. "You took that choice away from me."

The truth of his words slashed at her. Unable to stand the agony in his eyes, she bolted past him, but he grasped her arm and turned her around to face him. "Wait, Anna." He released her arm, but his gaze kept her planted to the ground. "What about those times we talked about having children. You made me think . . ." His voice caught. "You gave me hope."

"Don't you see? That's why I couldn't tell you. I had hope too!" Tears ran down her cheeks, and her nose started to burn. "You don't know how hard I prayed for a miracle. I thought of all the stories in the Bible, all the barren women who couldn't have children but were blessed with one." She wiped her nose with the back of her hand and turned away from him. "That's all I wanted," she said. "Just one *kinn*. Not just for myself. But for you too. Of all the men in the world, you deserved to have your own *kinn*."

"We could have prayed together. You didn't have to suffer alone." Lukas's voice sounded raspy.

"It doesn't matter. Nothing we can do or say will change anything."

She heard Lukas come up behind her, but

when she felt the touch of his hands on her shoulder, she shrugged him off. She didn't deserve his comfort, not after what she had done. "I'm tired," she said, and meant it. Her emotional well was tapped dry, and she had no idea how to fill it, or if it would ever be full again. "I'm going back to bed." She walked out of the kitchen into the darkened living room and lay down on the couch, keeping her back to him. She couldn't keep the tears from flowing, but she held her breath, not making a sound, hoping he would leave her alone in her misery.

A few moments later her prayer was answered. She heard Lukas walking past her. Closing her eyes tightly, she feigned sleep. She sensed him pause by her for a brief moment, only to turn and tread lightly up the stairs. Only when she heard the door to their bedroom shut did she move, wiping away the tears that wouldn't stop falling.

Chapter 19

Anna savored the chilly April air during her ride to work, and welcomed the milder temperatures that came by midday. Her recovery continued to go smoothly. Physically she felt well, gaining strength every day. On her first day back, she only stayed at the store for half a day.

It felt good to get out of the house. Daffodils and tulip stems had already started pushing out of cool mounds of dirt, and soon they would be lining yards and flower beds with their vibrant colors. Before long she could take the winter curtain off her buggy, something she looked forward to each spring. She enjoyed riding with the front exposed, taking in the fresh air and breathing in the scent of tilled earth and new life.

Yet for all the things that were right in her life, there was still so much wrong. She had been given the go-ahead to climb stairs, which meant moving back into the bedroom she shared with Lukas. But while they shared the space, they shared little else, even conversation. She wondered if this was how their life together would be from now on—living together more as roommates than as husband and wife. Without a family in their future, what would draw them back together?

On the first Sunday morning she could attend church, which was being held at the Detweilers, Anna and Lukas dressed in their best clothes, each staying on their designated side of the room—Anna on the left near the window, Lukas on the right near the door. Her mother had left with Uncle Zeb a little earlier, despite him complaining that his arthritis, or "Uncle Arthur" as he liked to put it, was acting up.

Anna sat on the edge of the bed, brushing out

her waist-length hair while she heard Lukas slip on his shirt behind her. The bed creaked slightly as he sat down on his side to put on his socks.

She set down her brush on the small table near the bed and braided her hair, then coiled it into a bun and secured it with several bobby pins. She reached for her white *kapp* and put it on. Standing up, she smoothed any wrinkles from her plum colored dress, one she had made before she and Lukas got married. Turning around she was surprised to see Lukas looking at her from the other side of the bed. "What?"

He cleared his throat. "*Nix*. It's just that you . . . you look beautiful, Anna."

Anna felt her face heat, much as it did when they first started courting and he would give her similar compliments. He looked very handsome in his Sunday best, the crisp white shirt a stark contrast to the black beard that had already started growing in. He had finger-combed his thick hair, brushing the bangs to the side and revealing his gorgeous dark hazel eyes, eyes she had fallen in love with an eternity ago. Those eyes had been filled with love at one time. But now they held uncertainty.

Suddenly feeling discomfort beneath his scrutinizing look, she turned away from him, smoothing out the ribbons on her *kapp*. "We should be going."

"*Ya*," he said in a flat tone. "We don't want to be late."

Lukas opened the bedroom door, and Anna walked through it ahead of him. For the rest of the morning and the ride over to the Detweilers', they didn't speak.

Nerves danced inside Anna's stomach as she approached the Detweilers. This was the first time they had been with the community since the surgery. She reminded herself that this was the Lord's day. No one would care about her and her problems. At least she hoped so.

With Lukas by her side, she walked into the house, then down to the basement where the service was being held. She immediately noticed all the Bylers were there and saw Elisabeth motioning for her to sit with her. Leaving Lukas to sit on the other side with the men, she went to her sister-in-law.

"I'm so glad to see you." Elisabeth scooted over and made room for her on the bench. "How are you?"

"Feeling better every day." The words weren't a complete lie. Physically she felt well, better than she had in months. But that was overshadowed by everything else.

When the church service started and the congregation began to sing, she tried to join in but couldn't. The last service she'd attended was her wedding. She remembered the way Lukas looked at her, with love in his eyes as they wed. How they had been filled with hope, looking forward to the future. Without warning, a tear slipped down her face. She wiped it off, hoping no one noticed.

Feeling as if someone was looking at her, she turned. Her gaze landed on Lukas. Compassion shone in his eyes. She looked straight ahead, fighting to keep the rest of her tears from falling.

"I wish there was something I could do for Anna and Lukas," Elisabeth said.

Aaron picked up a rock and skipped it across the pond in his backyard. The church service had ended an hour ago, and he and Elisabeth had slipped away to come here. Soon they were joined by a few younger boys and girls, who were on the opposite side throwing rocks in the water with far less finesse.

"Like what?" He bent down and found another smooth stone.

"They're so unhappy. There has to be a way we can help them."

He paused midthrow, looking at her. "We?"

"*Ya.* Don't you want to help them?"

His rock skimmed across the water with ease. Satisfied, he joined her on the bench. "Maybe *we* should stay out of it and let them work things out for themselves."

She rolled her eyes. "Aaron, you know me better than that."

He leaned back against the bench, crossing his

arms over his chest. "*Ya*, I do. So what do you have in mind?"

"Since they missed out on their wedding celebration, we should throw them a party."

Aaron scratched his head. "That sounds like a *gut* idea, but I don't think we should do that right now." He'd heard through the busybody vine that Anna's emergency surgery had lasting repercussions and that she wasn't able to have children. He couldn't imagine how hard that news was on both her and Lukas. When he saw them enter church, he didn't see a happy couple. Instead he saw two people deeply hurting. "A party's the last thing they need, Elisabeth."

"I happen to agree with you. So we'll wait a few weeks before throwing the surprise party."

"Surprise party?"

She jumped down from the bench. "*Ya*. It'll be more fun that way."

"Maybe you should rethink the idea, Elisabeth."

She looked at him, biting the bottom of her lip. "Maybe. But even if we don't do the party, we need to think of something to cheer them up." Leaning down, she picked up a rock and attempted to skip it. Instead of gliding across the surface, it plunked right to the bottom. Undaunted, she tried it again, then a third time.

He watched her with a mix of amusement and admiration. She wasn't one to give up. Even the kids who had been there earlier had gotten bored with the game and left. But not Elisabeth. Taking pity on her, he got off the bench and joined her at the edge of the water. "Here," he said, picking the stone out of her hand. "Like this."

Five perfect skips.

Giving him an aggravated look, she selected another rock, then cocked her arm back to throw. He touched her arm and stopped her.

"Two problems. First, you've got the wrong rock."

"There's a right and wrong rock?"

"*Ya*, believe it or not. It needs to be smooth and flat, not like that boulder you picked."

"It's the size of a pebble."

"A *round* pebble. Look, here's a *gut* one." He snatched one off the ground. "Now, you have to hold it at an angle." He handed her the stone.

"Like this?" She held it like she was a pitcher about to throw a strike.

"That's not an angle." He put his hand over hers, moving her hand to the right position. "Now you can throw it—"

"Aaron, I think I'm too close to the—"

"Like this." He pushed her hand forward, intending to assist her in the throw. But her hand wasn't the only thing that went forward. Horrified, he watched as she fell into the pond, her white *kapp* disappearing beneath the murky water.

"Elisabeth!" The pond was deep, even near the shore. Figuring she couldn't swim, he jumped in after her. His body stiffened as he hit the cold water. Immediately he popped up for air, taking in a big gulp. He was about to dive back under to look for her when he heard her laughing.

"Aaron, what are you doing?"

He spun around and saw her treading water. "You know how to swim?"

"All Bylers know how to swim. Our *mami* made sure of it. She would take us to our cousins' near Burton in the summers. They have a pond bigger and deeper than this one." She grinned, then splashed him.

He turned his head, but not before he got a face full of water. "All right, so that's how it's gonna be." Arcing out his arm, he moved to blast her with a wave, but she ducked under before he could. Suddenly he felt a tug on his leg, and he was pulled under.

They both came up at the same time, sputtering and laughing. She was only a few inches away from him, and before he could stop himself, he reached out and grabbed her around the waist with one arm, using the other to keep them both afloat. She licked the water off her lips, and he couldn't keep his eyes off her mouth. Leaning down, he brushed his lips against hers.

She gasped. Shoving away from him, she swam back to the edge.

He groaned. What had he just done?

She scrambled out of the pond, then took off

her *kapp* and squeezed out the water, keeping her back to him. He swam out and walked up beside her.

"I'm gonna be in big trouble." Her body shook, and her navy blue dress clung to her body. She kept squeezing the *kapp*, even though she had already wrung it dry.

He touched her shoulder. "Elisabeth, I'm—"

"I have to *geh*." She ran off toward the house, her wet hair falling loose from its pins.

Water dripping from his clothes, his soaking hair hanging in his eyes, he ignored the cold seeping into his body. What had his thoughtless impulse cost him? Although he couldn't really say it was thoughtless, because he had been thinking about kissing her for a while now. But had that one kiss ruined the best friendship he'd ever had?

From the way she'd reacted, he believed it did.

"Elisabeth Rose Byler, what on earth were you thinking?"

Elisabeth shrank beneath the thick towel Aaron's mother had let her borrow for the ride home. *Appalled* didn't begin to describe her mother's reaction when she had walked into the house, her clothes sopping, her *kapp* tinged brown from the pond water. Before too many people noticed that Elisabeth had spent the Lord's day in the Detweilers' pond, her mother had tossed her the towel and sent her straight to the buggy. Now they were nearly home, and only now had her mother calmed down enough to speak.

"You're going to catch your death." Emma's glasses slipped down her nose. She shoved them back up. "How did you fall into the pond?"

Elisabeth tried to keep her body from shaking, but she couldn't. The towel was too damp to keep her warm. "Aaron was showing me how to skip rocks—"

"Aaron was back there with you?" She glared at her. "Don't tell me he was in the water too."

"He thought I couldn't swim. When I fell in, he jumped in to save me." She left out the part where they were splashing around like a couple of five-year-olds—which had been fun, she had to admit—and where he'd kissed her. She touched her fingers to her mouth, still remembering his tender touch. Now that was how a kiss was supposed to be. She had thoroughly enjoyed the brief contact.

But it had scared and confused her too. Why had he kissed her? Did he like her? Or had she done something to let him think she wanted him to kiss her? Probably, but she had no idea what. And she couldn't go around letting Aaron think she wanted him to kiss her, even though she did.

The whole thing was giving her a headache.

"You and Aaron are too old to be skipping

rocks. You should have been inside helping the women with lunch." Emma looked at her again.

Elisabeth brought the edge of the towel up to her nose and peered at her mother. "I'm sorry," she said in a small voice.

Her mother sighed. Then she started to giggle. Before long she was laughing. "Oh Elisabeth, what are we going to do with you?"

"Love me?"

"We certainly will." Emma's laughter subsided. "As soon as we get home, you go straight to the bathroom and take a hot shower. Then get dressed and stay in your room."

Elisabeth dropped the towel from her face. "I'm grounded?" she asked in disbelief.

"*Ya.*"

"I'm almost eighteen!"

"You weren't acting like it today."

With a sigh, Elisabeth remained silent. Her mother was right; she had been silly. So had Aaron, but she doubted he would be grounded like she was. How humiliating.

Still, she couldn't help from smiling as they turned into their driveway. How could she not? She'd just been kissed by Aaron Detweiler.

Chapter 20

Lukas wiped the sweat off his forehead and continued to pound nails into the piece of rough oak siding, attaching it to the wall of the barn. He and his father were helping to put new siding on one of Zeb's old barns, which had needed repairing for a long while now. They had both taken the day off from the woodshop to try to complete the project in one day. It was a hot day for April, and the sun beat down on them, making sweat pour from Lukas's body.

He took another nail from his mouth and positioned it a few inches down from the one he had just hammered in, then started to pound. He struggled to focus on his task, and not on Anna, who was working in the small garden patch on the other side of the barn. Fortunately he couldn't see her from his position. But he still couldn't get her off his mind.

It had been over a month since the surgery. Anna had gone back to work full-time, and she often spent extra hours at her store. The distance remained between them, a cavernous gap he had no idea how to breach. They were cordial to each other, ate their meals together, and told each other good night before bed, but their relationship had changed from an affectionate, romantic one to a platonic, distant one. He missed her, even though she lay next to him every night. A few times he had heard her weeping, and he longed to reach out to her. But he didn't, not knowing if she would accept his comfort or not. His own heart and soul still mending, he couldn't risk the rejection.

He aimed for the head of the nail one last time, but missed and hit his thumb. Groaning with pain, he dropped the hammer to the ground and squeezed his wounded hand.

"You all right, *sohn*?" Joseph climbed down from the ladder and looked at Lukas's hand. "Ouch. That had to hurt."

"It did," Lukas gritted out.

Joseph removed his yellow straw hat and wiped his shiny forehead with the back of his hand, then put the hat back in place. "Can't remember the last time you did that. Got something on your mind?"

Lukas tossed his hat on the ground, then plopped down next to it, still holding his hand. His thumb had turned red, and he knew eventually the nail would become black. "*Ya*. You could say that." He leaned against the barn, waiting for the throbbing to subside.

Joseph lowered himself next to Lukas. He took off his hat and set it gently beside him before turning to Lukas. "Something you want to talk about?"

Lukas shook his head.

"All right. If you're not in the mood for talking, then you must be in the mood for listening. Because I've got something to say."

"What?" Lukas asked, his father's words catching him off guard.

"You heard me. I should have said it a while ago, but I thought it was none of my business. You two are adults, and you don't need your *daed* butting into your life. But I'm afraid the time has come for me to butt in."

Bewildered, Lukas looked at his father. He noticed his beard held a few more strands of gray, and there were a couple of new creases around his eyes, eyes that were looking at Lukas with a mix of compassion and irritation. "What are you talking about?"

"I'm talking about you and your wife. When are you two going to get things settled between each other? Or are you going to spend the rest of your lives going in different circles?"

"It's not that easy," Lukas said, staring straight ahead. He breathed in the earthy smells of wood, hay, and horse and cow manure that wafted between the slats of the barn.

"Who said marriage was easy?" Joseph bent his leg at an angle and set his arm on his knee. "It's the hardest thing you'll ever do. Trust me, I know what I'm talking about."

His father's platitudes suddenly rubbed Lukas

the wrong way. "In this case, you have no idea what you're talking about. Look, *Daed*, I appreciate that you care, but my marriage is my concern. I don't want to talk about this."

"Not even with Anna?"

Lukas snapped his head up and looked at Joseph. "We talk enough."

"That's not what I'm seeing."

Forgetting about the pain in his thumb, Lukas said, "What exactly is it that you see?"

"You're hurting, *sohn*. That's as plain as day to anyone, and who can blame you? You've had a loss, and you have to give yourselves time to grieve. Instead you've been putting in extra hours at the shop, and Anna's starting to do the same. When the two of you came over the other day for supper, you barely said a word to each other or anyone else."

"Look, it's not like we've lost a *boppli*." Lukas's throat tightened as he spoke. "And Anna and I both know this is God's will. If he had wanted us to have children, we would be able to have them. But for some reason, he doesn't. We've both accepted that."

"Then you're both amazing," Joseph said. "Because I know if it were me, I wouldn't be able to say the same thing. Not this soon. And I know you, *sohn*. I know how much family means to you. So I find it hard to believe you can say those words aloud and truly mean them."

Lukas swallowed, unable to look at his *daed*. Because if he did, his father would see that Lukas didn't mean any of it. He grabbed his hat and shoved it on his head. "There's work to do," he said, standing up, then reaching down for the hammer and a couple of nails. He turned to the slab of wood and finished pounding the nail he'd missed, then slammed the hammer down on another one. He felt his father's eyes on him, but he ignored it. Even though his *daed* meant well, he had no idea what Lukas as going through. Or what Anna was going through.

Yet, did Lukas even know? Especially about Anna?

Before long Joseph had put on his hat and started to shimmy up the ladder. He paused on the third rung. "I'm here if you want to talk," he said. "Just remember that."

Lukas nodded once, but didn't say anything. A few moments later he heard footsteps, the crush of gravel-filled dirt beneath a shoe. He turned, expecting, hoping to see Anna. Instead he saw Zeb shuffling toward them, a battered and frayed straw hat perched on his head.

"Here's some cold drinks," he said, holding out two cans of soda pop. "Sure is a hot one today."

"It sure is." Lukas took the cans and handed one to his father. He popped open the top and took a long pull, the beverage cooling his parched throat. "*Danki*," he said, letting out a quiet burp.

"Hey, don't thank me, thank your *fraa*. She thought you might be getting thirsty. Don't know why she didn't bring the drinks out to you herself." He looked at Lukas, his expression stern. "I used to think you two were a little . . . what's the word for it?"

"Expressive," Joseph offered as he leaned against the ladder.

"I was thinking more like mushy, but I guess that works. And it was kinda irritating, seeing you two all lovey-dovey like that. But I hafta say, I'll take the mushy stuff to what's going on now. At least you both were happy. Now you can't get the glum look off your faces." Zeb looked up at Joseph. "This is why I didn't get married. Too complicated. Much simpler being a bachelor." He turned and shuffled away.

Lukas watched as Zeb headed for the house. He expected his father to say something, but to Lukas's surprise, his dad picked up the hammer and went back to work. Lukas did the same, but his thoughts were more preoccupied than before as he mulled over what both his *daed* and Zeb had said.

Several hours later, right before sundown, Lukas and Joseph finished residing the barn. After his father left, Lukas went inside. Everyone else had already had dinner, but there was a plate wrapped in aluminum foil on the countertop, along with a smaller plate that held a piece of cherry pie covered in plastic wrap. Famished, he wolfed down a roast beef sandwich with horseradish spread and the pie, then took a quick shower before heading upstairs. He noticed in the bathroom that Anna had left a T-shirt and a pair of old but clean pants for him to change into.

He stopped at the door of the bedroom. The light was out, which meant Anna was probably asleep. She went to bed early each night, probably as a tactic to avoid him, he realized. He thought again about what his father had said, then about the late nights he'd worked, the early nights Anna turned in. They barely spoke during breakfast, then they both went their separate ways. He felt them drifting further apart, and people close to them could see it too. One of them had to put a stop to it before they were permanently separated, a marriage in name only. There were a few couples in the community he knew who lived like that, and he had never imagined that type of marriage for himself. He didn't want that kind of marriage. He wanted what he and Anna had before.

Taking a deep breath, he opened the door and entered the bedroom. The last remnants of dusk came through the window, casting a faint glow on the room, and he could make out his wife's sleeping form. She was curled up in the shape of a backwards C, her back to his side of the bed. Her usual position. And he knew she would stay that way for the rest of the night. Tonight, though, he hoped that would change.

Barefooted he walked to his side of the bed. Slowly he sat down and reached for her. "Anna," he whispered, giving her shoulder a nudge. When she didn't respond, he tried again, louder this time. "Anna."

He heard her sigh as she partially rolled over, her head looking over her shoulder. "*Ya?*"

"We can't go on like this. Not anymore."

Anna rolled back over, her eyes wide open. Not that she had been sleeping anyway. Even though she went to bed earlier than Lukas did on most nights, she never fell asleep before he did. Tonight was no exception. She had heard him enter the house and move around downstairs, had heard the faint whine of the old pipes in her uncle's house as Lukas took his shower. She had kept her body very still when she heard him enter the room, expecting him to lie down next to her and go to sleep. She hadn't expected him to want to talk.

"Anna. Don't ignore me."

His voice sounded more forceful, but she remained still. Fear flowed through her, and she gripped the edge of the pillow. As long as they weren't talking, she could pretend that every-thing was all right. She wasn't ready to let go of that fantasy just yet.

She felt him get up from the bed, and for a split moment she thought he might leave the room—leave her alone the way she wanted. Instead he turned on the light, then came over to her side of the bed and knelt in front of her.

"Anna, I am your husband." His hazel eyes reflected frustration. "You kept your doctor's appointment from me, not to mention you didn't tell me about your condition—that you might not be able to have children."

She refused to look at him. "I don't want to talk about this."

"Why not? We have to work our way through it. I want things to be the way they used to be between us."

"They can't." She looked away.

"Why not?"

"I can't believe you're asking me that. Nothing will ever be the same again."

"I'm not saying it will. We have to deal with this, Anna. We can't ignore what happened or wish it away."

"That's not what I'm trying to do."

"Isn't it?"

She put her hands to the side of her face in frustration. He didn't understand anything. "There are reminders everywhere. Every time I see a *kinn* with her *mami*, or hear a young *bu's* laugh, the emptiness inside me gets bigger. I'll never know what that's like. To hold my *dochder*

319

in my arms. To kiss my *sohn* good night. To watch my *kinn* grow and learn and live their lives according to God. I can never, ever ignore it or wish it away, Lukas. No matter how much I want to."

His expression softened. "Why didn't you share this with me before?"

"And remind you of what I did? Of what you lost?" She turned her back on him. "I don't know why you're even bothering. I'm useless. An empty vessel. I would think you'd hate me for what I did."

He sighed. "I could never hate you, Anna." He came around and faced her, putting his hands on her shoulders. "I love you. I'll always love you. Do you think I married you just so you could bear me children?"

"*Ya*, Lukas. That's all we talked about before the wedding. How many children you wanted. How big our family would be."

"I thought you had those dreams too."

"I did. But . . ."

"But you knew they wouldn't come true." He put his finger beneath her chin and lifted her head so that she could look at him. "I'm going to be honest with you, Anna. And when I'm finished talking, I want you to be honest with me. No lies, no deceptions." He licked his lips and kept his gaze on her. "I'm angry with you for not trusting me enough, not *loving* me enough to tell

320

me what was going on with you. And you know what? Up until today, I was thought it was okay that we were barely speaking to each other. Because then I wouldn't have to face the part I played in all this."

"Your part? You've done nothing wrong, Lukas. This is all my fault."

"*Nee*, it's not. I should have made you feel safe enough to tell me. I knew how Daniel hurt you and how hard it was for you to trust me. I should have noticed you were in pain, Anna."

"Don't blame yourself. I didn't tell you about the doctor visits, and I hid the pain from you. I never said a word about any of it. How could you have been able to tell?"

"I look back on it now and there were signs, little things I saw that I dismissed and other things I should have noticed." He closed his eyes. "I'm so sorry, *lieb*."

She pulled away from him and went to sit on the bed, weary. "Lukas, this is what I wanted to avoid, you taking on my blame. I wanted to spare you all of it. Instead, I hurt both of us."

He sat down beside her. "Now that's honesty."

"I suppose it is." Then she turned and looked at him. "So how do we get over this?"

He took her hand and entwined his fingers in hers. "We promise each other we'll face it together, with God's help. No more shutting each other out. No more lies."

"I promise I'll never lie to you again, Lukas."

"And I'll do the same. There's something else we need to do."

"What?"

"According to one very wise *mann* I know, we give ourselves time. Time to get angry and grieve." He cupped her cheek in his hand. "I love you, Anna. You have to believe that. I can't say I'm completely over what happened. I'm still hurting. But the only way I can get through this is with you."

Tears fell down her cheeks. How could he still love her after everything that had happened? Yet he did. God had worked a miracle but not the one she had asked for. He had given her Lukas, a man who accepted her unconditionally, who loved her in spite of it all.

He wiped the tears from her cheek with his thumbs, his own eyes misting over. "I want a new beginning for us. Our dreams about having our own children won't come true, but that doesn't mean we can't have new dreams to work toward."

"I want to share those dreams with you. I love you, too, Lukas."

Leaning toward her, she felt his lips press against hers gently, then with more intensity. After a long moment, he pulled away, his eyes darkening, showing her through his kisses and his gaze how much he wanted to be with her.

"Be with me," she whispered.

"Are you sure?"

Anna put her arms around his neck. "*Ya, mei* husband. I'm sure."

Chapter 21

For the third time that morning, Elisabeth sneezed. She snatched a tissue from the box in the living room and blew her nose.

"Feeling better?" Emma sat down in the chair opposite from Elisabeth, pale yellow yarn and knitting needles in her hands. Several days had passed since Elisabeth's dip in the Detweilers' pond, and since she'd last seen Aaron. Monday morning had been her day off, and on Tuesday she woke up with a slight fever so she couldn't go to work. Now it was Thursday, and she was just starting to feel herself.

"*Ya.* I think I can *geh* to work tomorrow."

Emma peered over her glasses. "I'm sure Gabe will appreciate that. I hope you learned your lesson about swimming in freezing water."

"The water wasn't freezing. It was only chilly."

"Still, it was cold enough for you to get sick." Emma picked up the needles and yarn and started knitting.

"I know, *Mami*, I know. Don't worry, I won't do

that again." She settled back on the couch, picked up her pen and writing paper, and continued her letter to Deborah. She filled her friend in on life in Middlefield since she'd left for Paradise, telling her in vague terms about Anna and Lukas's wedding and about Anna's surgery along with other trivial news. But concentrating on writing proved difficult. As she had since Sunday, all she could think about was Aaron and his kiss.

You won't believe this, Deborah, but I think I'm in love with Aaron Detweiler. I know, it's weird, but it's wonderful too. At first I wasn't sure I even liked him at all, then we became best friends. On Sunday he kissed me. And that's all I think about anymore.

Elisabeth reread the last four sentences, then balled up her letter. It felt foolish to put her feelings about Aaron in a letter. She wished Deborah was here to help sort things out. She had other friends, but she wasn't eager to share this with them. It was too important. Too personal. Too confusing.

"Mail's here." Stephen walked into the room, several letters in his hand. He handed them to their mother.

"*Danki.*" Emma put down her knitting and accepted the mail. She looked up at Stephen. "Are you ready for lunch?"

"In a little while." Flakes of sawdust dotted his angular face.

"Let me know and I'll bring out some meat-loaf sandwiches."

"Sounds *gut*." He held up two fingers. "I'd like two."

"I figured you would." After Stephen left, Emma remarked, "I don't know how that *bu* stays so thin; he eats as much as two men every meal." She thumbed through the letters, singling out one of them and handing it to Elisabeth. "From Deborah."

Elisabeth stood up and took the letter, then quickly opened it. Deborah had written her once since settling in Pennsylvania, and she had mentioned how homesick she was. Elisabeth hoped she was over it by now.

Dear Elisabeth,

I hope everything is good back in Middlefield. The baby's growing by leaps and bounds. I can't believe how big I'm getting! My aunt has been terrific, but I don't go out much, and I haven't made any friends yet. It gets pretty lonely. I thought it would be easier to live where people don't know me, but it's not. In a lot of ways it's harder.

I wish you could come visit me, even for a little while. If you were here we would have so much fun! Maybe you could get some time off work. I'd love to see you again. Write when you get the chance.

Deborah

Elisabeth laid the letter on her lap. She hadn't thought about visiting Deborah in Pennsylvania. She'd never been out of Ohio before, and the idea of a trip somewhere else sounded exciting. She had saved quite a bit of money from her job at Gabe's, more than enough for bus fare. The more she thought about the prospect, the more she was excited about it.

"Did Deborah send *gut* news?" Emma asked.

"Sort of. She wants me to visit her in Paradise. I'm thinking about going."

Emma looked at her. "What about your job?"

"Ruth is out of school now. Maybe she can take my place while I'm gone."

"What about her job at Anna's shop?"

Elisabeth tapped her finger on her lips. "I hadn't thought about that. But I can talk to her and Gabe and Anna and see if it will work." She smiled. "I really want to *geh*. It'd be a fun adventure."

Emma picked up her knitting again. "If you have the money and you've taken care of your job, then I don't see why you can't *geh*."

Jumping up from the couch, she hugged her mother. "*Danki*. I'm going to go over to Gabe's right now and talk to him about it."

"Why don't you wait until tonight? He and Moriah and the *kinner* are coming over for supper. Ruth will be here too."

"*Gut* idea."

Later that night, after Ruth said she would

cover Elisabeth's job and Gabe had agreed to it, she went upstairs and wrote a letter to Deborah. She'd decided to go the first of the week. After making a list of what she planned to take, she lay on her bed, excited about the trip and visiting her friend.

The only downside was leaving Aaron. She'd miss him, but it would only be for two weeks. It might be good for her to be away from him for a while, to get rid of the romantic feelings that she couldn't shake and start seeing him as her best friend again, instead of wishing for something she couldn't have.

Aaron came to work Monday morning, still fighting some of the sniffles that plagued him over the course of the week. From Elisabeth's absence at work he knew she had caught a cold as well. Swimming in a cold pond in the middle of April wasn't the smartest thing he'd ever done.

Neither was kissing Elisabeth.

Not that he didn't like it. The problem was he liked it too much, and he couldn't stop thinking about it. Or her. He'd been tempted to stop by her house during the week, but he didn't want to bother her if she was sick. Besides, he wasn't sure if he'd be welcome. The way she had run away from him the moment after he'd kissed her made him wonder.

He walked into the office, surprised to see she

hadn't arrived. Looking at the clock, he noticed she was running late, something she hadn't done since her first day of work. Maybe she was sick again. If she didn't come in today, he was definitely going to see her to find out if she was okay. Plus, he just plain missed her.

As he left the office, Gabe came into the shop, Elisabeth's sister Ruth behind him. "You can put your things in the office," Gabe told her. "I'll be there in a bit to show you around."

Ruth nodded to Aaron and went to the office. Puzzled, he turned to Gabe. "Why is Ruth here?"

"She's taking Elisabeth's place for two weeks."

"Her place? Is something wrong with her?"

"*Nee*. She's off to visit her friend in Lancaster. She was going to come in today, but there was a bus leaving this morning, and she wanted to leave right away."

Aaron stared at the cold forge in front of him, surprised at the news. Two weeks. It might as well be an eternity. And she hadn't even told him good-bye. Maybe her leaving didn't have as much to do with visiting her friend as it did with getting away from him. He reined in the thought. *Way to make it all about you.*

"Aaron?"

He turned around to see Ruth standing behind him. "*Ya*?"

"Elisabeth wanted me to give this to you. She said she was sorry she didn't get to see you before she left." Ruth handed him a folded piece of paper.

He took it, waiting to open it once Ruth was back in the office.

Dear Aaron,
    Don't forget me while I'm gone.
        Elisabeth

He tucked the note in his pants' pocket, smiling at her reminder not to forget her. As if he ever could.

Two weeks later on a Saturday evening, Elisabeth returned from her trip to Paradise. She'd enjoyed spending time with Deborah, who had reverted to the same girl she knew in school. It had warmed Elisabeth's heart to hear her friend talk about joining the church, which she wanted to do after the baby was born. Elisabeth also found Lancaster to be a nice place, if a little crowded at times. Still, she was glad to be home.

Being away hadn't extinguished her feelings for Aaron. If anything, the separation had intensified them, which she found annoying. Her plan to leave her attraction to Aaron in Lancaster had failed. The thought of seeing him again filled her with anticipation and dread. Somehow she had to figure out how to put a lid on her emotions. Problem was, she'd never been successful at doing that.

On Sunday afternoon, Moriah stopped by with the children for a visit. As her mother and Ruth watched the *kinner* in the living room, Moriah asked Elisabeth to sit with her on the front porch, a custom that the two sisters had enjoyed for as long as they could remember.

"Tell me about your trip," Moriah said as they sat on the wooden porch swing their father had installed a few weeks ago, the scent of fresh oak surrounding them.

Elisabeth fingered the metal chain that suspended the swing from the porch roof. "The bus ride was long and boring. Sitting in the same seat for twenty hours was dull, dull, dull. I even broke down and read the book *Mami* insisted I take, but I got a headache after page three. I ended up sleeping most of the way."

"I hope things were better in Lancaster."

"Oh ya. Much better." She shifted to the side to face Moriah. "Deborah's doing well, and the *boppli* is fine. Her Aunt Sadie is an odd bird, though. She wears the same necklace every day— these big red beads that match her big red lips."

Moriah frowned. "That's not nice, Lis."

"It's true! She even said she had big lips. Said that's why she wears red lipstick. 'Might as well show off what God gave me.' Her personal motto." She and Moriah laughed.

A small bird landed on the banister near Elisabeth and Moriah. Moriah looked at it for a moment before she spoke. "Did you hear from Aaron while you were gone?"

"Aaron?" Elisabeth's pulse started at the mention of his name. She looked away, hoping to sound nonchalant. "Why would I hear from him?"

"You two have gotten very close over the past year."

"We're friends." Her foot pushed against the porch, sending the swing into motion.

"That's all you're going to say?"

"*Ya.* What else is there?"

"Lis, you always have more to say. You're never at a loss for words." Her blue eyes twinkled. "I can think of only one reason you would clam up like this. He's more than a friend, isn't he?"

Elisabeth moved the swing faster. "I don't know what you mean."

"Oh, you know exactly what I mean."

She sighed. "Fine, you win. I like him. But it doesn't matter because he doesn't like me, not that way. Just because he kissed me—"

"Wait, he kissed you?" Moriah leaned forward in her chair, her expression filled with curiosity.

"Barely kissed me. And I think it was an accident."

"How do you accidentally kiss someone?"

"I don't know." She stuck out her heel and halted the swing. "But he sure wouldn't have kissed me on purpose."

"I can't believe you just said that. Why

wouldn't he like you, Elisabeth? You're sweet, kind, pretty—"

"You have to say those things, you're my *schwester*."

"I mean them. I'm sure Aaron thinks the same way."

Elisabeth threaded her fingers together. "I don't know."

"Then ask him."

"I can't do that!"

"*Ya*, you can." Moriah looked at her. "Remember when I was pregnant with Velda Anne? After Levi died, how Gabriel would come and visit and I'd send him away? I was falling in love with him even then, but I wouldn't tell him. I wasn't honest with him, or with myself."

"That's completely different. Your relationship with Gabe was complicated to say the least."

"And I made it more so by shutting him out."

"But you knew he loved you, Moriah. I have no idea how Aaron feels. You know how long it took for him to even smile at me?" A lump formed in her throat as she thought about the past year. He'd helped her with her nieces when she'd needed him. He'd taught her to ice skate. He'd saved her from possibly being arrested. Above all, he was willing to sacrifice his happiness and marry her when he thought she was pregnant with another man's child. "He's the best, and I don't want to lose the friendship we have."

"So what are you going to do? Ignore your feelings? Trust me, you can only do that for so long."

"I don't know," she admitted, just as confused about the situation as she ever was.

"Then think about it. Even better, pray about it. God will let you know what to do."

"I don't think it's as simple as that."

Moriah smiled and took Elisabeth's hand. "It is, Lis. It is."

For Aaron, the last two weeks had dragged slower than a turtle crossing a river of molasses. He'd missed Elisabeth more than he thought possible. Her image had consumed his thoughts, and he couldn't get the memory of their short, sweet kiss out of his mind. More than once he'd been tempted to go to her house last night, just to catch a glimpse of her. But he couldn't bring himself to do it. He wanted to see her, but the strength of his emotions for her scared him.

He'd been at loose ends today, trying to deal with the turmoil inside him. He decided to go for a walk, and now he was here at the shop. He unlocked the door and stepped inside, not bothering to turn on the light. Sunbeams streamed through the window, one illuminating the door of Elisabeth's office. His feet took on a mind of their own and he went inside and sat down in her chair.

Elisabeth had always kept a neat enough workspace, but since Ruth had filled in for her, the office had never been tidier. The only items on the desk were a blotter with the calendar on it, a pencil, and a small pad of paper. Usually Elisabeth left behind a coffee cup, a few pieces of unopened mail, or a couple of paper clips scattered around. Evidence she'd been there. He hadn't even realized he'd noticed those things until now.

He picked up the pencil and pad, tapping the eraser on his bottom lip. He thought about her note, which was still in his pocket. He had carried it with him. A corny gesture, but he couldn't help it. It made missing her a little more bearable.

He tore out one of the small yellow pages and wrote *I could never forget you*, then set it down on her desk. But as soon as he did, he regretted it. Talk about corny. He reached to take it back and throw it away.

"Who's in here?"

Startled, Aaron shot up from the seat at the sound of Gabe's stern voice. He opened the office door and came out. "It's just me."

Gabe's guarded expression relaxed. "Whew, I'm glad it's you. I thought somebody might have broken in. What are you doing here?" Gabe entered the shop, shutting the door behind him. "Don't tell me you're working on a Sunday."

"*Nee*. I wouldn't do that."

A puzzled expression crossed Gabe's face. "Then why are you here?"

Aaron's cheeks grew hot. He felt like he'd been caught with his hand in the cookie jar.

"Did you forget something?"

"I, um, I thought I did." Aaron bit his tongue on the lie. "My lunch cooler. But I couldn't find it here, so I guess I took it home."

If Gabe wasn't buying Aaron's lame excuse, he didn't let on. "Gotcha." He looked past Aaron's shoulders at the office door. "I'm glad Elisabeth's coming back tomorrow. Don't get me wrong, Ruth's a great worker. I've never met anyone more organized. But Elisabeth is more—"

"Fun?"

Gabe grinned. "Exactly." He looked up at the clock on the wall. "Moriah should be back with the *kinner* pretty soon. Do you want to stay for supper?"

Aaron shook his head. "I need to get going." He headed toward the door of the shop.

"Okay. You know you always have a standing offer with us."

"I appreciate that." And he did. For the first time in a long time he didn't feel like an outsider anymore. Elisabeth had a lot to do with that, but so did Gabe and the rest of the Bylers, along with his own family. They had put his past behind them, and finally, Aaron had too.

He left and headed back for his house, filled with peace and, as usual, thoughts of Elisabeth. After an interminable two weeks, he'd see her tomorrow. It was only when he was nearly home that he remembered he'd forgotten to grab the note.

Elisabeth yawned as she opened the door to the blacksmith shop. She had decided to come in to work early, just in case she had some catching up to do from her absence. Although knowing Ruth, everything would be completed to annoying perfection. But she still came in half an hour before her scheduled time.

It didn't help that her stomach had been swirling with butterflies since before breakfast. She'd contemplated Moriah's thoughts all night and had prayed about what to do about Aaron. Her sister had said it was simple, but Elisabeth still didn't see it that way. She also wasn't sure what to do. The only thing she knew was that she wanted to see Aaron. She'd worry about what to say to him later.

She flipped on the gas-powered lights. The shop still looked the same. And why wouldn't it? She'd only been gone two weeks. Never mind that it had seemed like forever. Elisabeth started for the office when she heard the door open behind her. She whirled around to see Aaron standing there, holding his blue lunch cooler, and looking more handsome than ever.

"Hi," he said, his gaze steady and connected with hers.

Her mouth went dry, and she squeaked out, "Hi."

They didn't say anything for a few moments, an unusually awkward silence stretching between them. This is what she had wanted to avoid, them feeling uncomfortable around each other. And clearly he felt uncomfortable, because now he was looking everywhere but at her. Maybe she had finally gotten her answer. If things were this strained between them because of a quick—and more than likely accidental—kiss, imagine how they would be if she told him the truth about her love for him. No, she'd keep that bit of information tucked inside.

Taking a deep breath, she gave him a tight smile. "I better see the disaster Ruth left for me."

As if her words had lit a fire under his feet, he dropped the cooler and darted in front of her. "You don't have to worry about that."

"Oh, I know. I was making a joke. Ruth would rather die than leave a mess. I'm sure my office is neater than a pin." She moved to walk past him, but he stepped in front of her.

"So, how was your trip?" He crossed his muscular arms, looking more like a guard than a blacksmith.

"Fine." She gave him an odd look. "Deborah's doing well, she has a crazy Aunt Sadie, and the *boppli's* healthy."

"*Gut, gut.*"

Elisabeth looked up at him, bewildered by the strained expression on his face. Any awkwardness she'd experienced a moment before disappeared, replaced by confusion. "Aaron, what are you doing?"

"What do you mean?" He smiled, but instead of looking pleased, he looked like his grandmother had stepped on his toe and he was trying to be polite about it.

"I need to get to my office. Do you mind?" She stepped to the side, but he followed her.

"You came in kind of early this morning. Have you had breakfast? I thought Gabe mentioned Moriah was making cinnamon rolls this morning."

Now he was really spouting nonsense. Elisabeth highly doubted Gabe knew what Moriah was planning to make for breakfast, much less that he would mention it to Aaron. "Just let me by, Aaron." As he opened his mouth again she dashed past him and went inside the office. *Finally!* She set down her purse on top of her desk and turned around to see Aaron inches away from her.

Was he blushing? "I can explain," he said.

Her brows lifted. "Explain what?"

He peered around her shoulder at her desk, then frowned. She turned around to see what he was looking at. All she could see was her purse, a pencil and a pad of paper, and the calendar. She turned and faced the desk completely. "I should have known Ruth would do this."

"Do what?"

"She can't stand to have anything out. She has nothing on top of her dresser, and when it's her turn to clean the kitchen, there's not a crumb left on the counters. Now she's done something with my pencil and pen can." Elisabeth picked up her purse and set it to the side. Where would her sister have put it? She had about twenty pens and pencils in an old pork 'n' beans can, which she had washed out and torn off the label. Elisabeth was always leaving pencils and pens everywhere, and having a stash on her desk prevented her from losing time searching for them.

She had started to turn away when she noticed a slip of paper on the desk. How could Ruth have left this behind? Shocking. Elisabeth picked it up.

"Elisabeth," Aaron said from behind her.

"I could never forget you," she read out loud. What a weird little note. She turned around and looked up at Aaron. "Who wrote this?"

But as soon as she saw the look in his eyes, she knew.

"Like I said, I can explain."

"You wrote this?" She glanced at the note again. She should have recognized the small, compact handwriting. She'd seen his writing on enough order forms before.

He nodded.

She read the words. *I could never forget you.* Then she remembered the note she'd left for him.

Don't forget me while I'm gone. A warm fuzzy feeling traveled from her head to her toes. "That's the sweetest thing anyone's ever done for me."

"Sweet?" His blond brow lifted. "I thought you'd think it was corny."

"Hardly." She brought the note to her chest. "You missed me?"

"*Ya,*" he said in a low voice. His eyes turned a smoky blue color, reminding her of the way he had looked at her that day on the porch, just before Kacey had arrived. "I missed you. A lot."

"I missed you too." At that point her confusion cleared. She had asked God for an answer regarding Aaron, and he had just given it to her. Now she knew exactly what to do. "Aaron, I—"

"Wait." He put his finger to her lips. "I need to tell you something first. And if you don't want to talk to me after I say it, I'll understand." She opened her mouth to speak again, but he stopped her with his words. "I like you, Elisabeth."

"I like you, too, Aaron."

He shook his head, hard. "I don't think you know what I mean. I don't just like you, I *like* you. A lot. I've liked you for a long time. Even before I kissed you at the pond."

"I thought that was an accident."

The tension suddenly drained from his face and he smiled. "Believe me, Elisabeth. I definitely kissed you on purpose."

"You did?"

"*Ya.* And I'd like to do it again." His smile faded. "But our friendship means a lot to me, and I don't want to screw that up. But I can't keep pretending that I don't have feelings for you." He leaned closer to her. "I can't lie anymore, Elisabeth. Not to you."

A hard knot lodged in her throat. "Oh, Aaron." Suddenly everything she wanted to say to him flew out of her head. She couldn't confess her love with words. Actions would have to do. She threw herself into his arms and hugged him tightly around the neck, placing a kiss close to his ear. She closed her eyes as his arms went around her waist, drawing her close.

"Does this mean what I think it does?" He whispered in her ear, sending tingles down her spine.

She released him and stepped away, nodding.

He waited for a moment, then grinned when she didn't say anything. "I can't believe it. Elisabeth Byler is *speechless.*"

"Stop!" she said, her voice sounding thick. She playfully tapped him on the arm.

The sound of the front door closing wedged them apart. Aaron peered out the office door. "Gabe's here. We better get to work."

Elisabeth nodded, still unable to say anything, the emotions flowing through her blocking her voice.

He moved closer to her and whispered, "I think

you're overdue for another rock-skipping lesson, don't you?"

"Are you asking me out, Aaron Detweiler?"

"Now she finds her voice." He smiled. "*Ya*, I'm asking you out."

"And does this mean you want to court me?"

He laughed. "I should have known you wouldn't make this easy for me."

She lifted her chin and smiled. "Nope. I'm going to savor the moment." Aaron liked her. Cared for her. Was looking at her like he couldn't get his fill. Never had she been so happy.

"Then savor this, Elisabeth. *Ya*, I want to court you. I want to teach you how to skip rocks and ice skate. And I want you to keep teaching me how to love life." His gaze softened. "So what do you say? Will you go out with me?"

"Of course." She'd wanted something to savor, and he had definitely delivered. "I thought you'd never ask."

Chapter 22

*A*nna tore off a brown tassel from an ear of corn, yanking down on the husk. She and Lukas sat on their small back deck, another improvement Lukas had added to the house. A stack of corn lay between them, and they sat in plastic chairs, shucking and preparing the corn for canning. She had been removing every last piece of silk from each ear before putting it in a large bin. Their garden had been plentiful that summer, and the corn was full and dripping with sweetness. It was a lovely September evening, and Anna couldn't think of a better way to share it than working side by side with her husband.

"I've been thinking," Lukas said, grabbing another ear of corn from the stack. He pointed to the back corner of the yard behind the house. "I think that's a *gut* place for a swing set."

Anna froze, stunned. Why was he talking about putting up a swing set?

"Stephen can help me dig a pit, and we can fill it with sand and put some timbers around it. I think with my *bruders'* help, we can build the set quickly. There'll be a tire swing, of course. And maybe a small sandbox right beside it."

"You mean for your nieces and nephews to play in?"

He shook his head. "Sure they can play when they come over, but that's not who it's for."

The peace she'd felt moments ago shattered. They hadn't talked about children in months, at least not directly. Moriah and Gabe's son had been born a few months ago, a plump healthy baby they'd named Caleb. Lukas had been so happy to hold his new nephew, and the familiar waves of regret had covered her when she saw her husband with the baby. She still felt a small measure of loss and failure. She knew it would take years before those feelings would die . . . if they ever did.

"Look at all this around us, Anna." Lukas stood up and spread his hands wide. Beyond their neatly mown backyard was four acres of grassy field, where their horses grazed contentedly. "We have more space than we need here. The house is too big, even for the four of us. And look at all this land." He stood up to another empty space next to the picked-over vegetable garden. "I'd like to put a trampoline over there. We had one when we were growing up, and it was a blast."

"Lukas." Anna rose from her chair, wondering if her husband was having a breakdown or something. "We don't need a swing, or a trampoline."

"We would if we had *kinner.*"

"Lukas, I . . ." She turned around, unable to speak.

He moved to stand in front of her. "I can wait, Anna. I don't want you to feel rushed into this. When you're ready to talk about adoption, we can."

"Adoption?" He had never said anything before about it, and she had always assumed that he would want his own children, not someone else's.

He nodded. "I've been thinking about this for a while. Like I said, we have more than we need and plenty to spare. We have enough money, space, land . . . and love . . . to provide for a *kinn* or two."

She grinned, excitement growing in her. "Or three."

"As many as the Lord wants us to have." He put his arms around her neck. "I think this is what he wants for us, Anna, to open our home and our hearts to the *kinner* who need them. It doesn't matter whether a *boppli* comes from us, or comes to us. We will still be a family."

"You know it's not that simple," she said, hating to put a damper on his enthusiasm. Or her own. But they had to be practical about this.

"*Ya.*"

"I've heard you have to go through a screening process. And that someone comes out and looks at the house. They'll probably check our finances too."

"I don't have a problem with that."

She moved away from him. "We might not be able to adopt right away. We might have to foster some *kinner* first."

"That's another thing I want to talk to you about. Dan Mullet came to see me in the shop today."

"Do I know him?"

"I don't think so. He was in a buggy accident last year, before you moved to Middlefield. He and his wife got four *kinner* and one on the way.

But it's been a struggle for them financially."

Anna's heart went out to his family. She and Lukas were blessed financially, and she assumed he wanted to help the Mullets out. "How much do they need? If we can provide it for them, we will."

His expression filled with warmth. "I knew you were going to say that. But that's not what he asked for. Remember that old barn that burned down a month ago? It was on a Yankee's property and had been abandoned for a long time."

Anna nodded. "I'm glad no one was hurt."

"*Ya*, it's a miracle because it turns out a teenage *bu* was living in it for a few months. A runaway. Dan's twin son and daughter were bringing him food and clothes without telling anyone. Turns out he had been living with cruel foster parents, which was why he ran away. When the barn burned down, the secret came out. The *bu* had to go back to children's services."

"To those same foster parents?"

Lukas shrugged. "I don't know. I have no idea how all that works."

"So what does Dan need from us?"

"He asked us if we'd consider fostering the *bu*."

"A teenager?" She'd always imagined that if they were going to adopt, it would be a baby, not a child nearly grown.

"Anna, if you don't want to, that's okay. Like I said, we can wait until you're ready. I didn't give

Dan an answer, I just said I'd talk it over with you."

Anna sat down in the chair and looked out over their property as the sun dipped below the horizon. "What do you want to do, Lukas?"

He knelt down next to her and took her hand. "I think the Lord wants us to take in this *kinn*, Anna. I know I want to."

Anna reached out and touched her husband's face, his thick black beard soft against her fingertips. As she looked into his eyes, all her doubts disappeared. "Me too," she said softly. "What's the *bu's* name?"

"Sawyer."

"Someone who saws wood," she said, marveling at the connection between the child's name and Lukas' vocation. "We definitely have to take him in, Lukas."

He kissed her, then pulled away, smiling. "I'll let Dan know in the morning. This won't be easy, Anna. We'll do whatever it takes. One step at a time. Together."

"I know we will. I love you, Lukas."

"I love you too. You're going to be a great *mami*, Anna."

"And you'll be a great *daed*."

He reached for her hand and she entwined her fingers in his. As they watched the sun set, their hearts were filled with hope for the future, and for their new family.

Acknowledgments

*T*his book wouldn't have been possible without the help of several people. Thank you to my editors: Natalie Hanemann and Jenny Baumgartner, whose insight and hard work on the story were invaluable. I can't thank you enough for everything you do! To Jill Eileen Smith and Jenny B. Jones for brainstorming with me; your chocolate is in the mail. To Tamela, my awesome agent who keeps me from worrying about business so I can focus on the story. A special thank you to the medical professionals and others who shared their expertise: Ronda Wells, James Morse, Harry Kraus, Kimberly Zweygardt, Kristen Ethridge, and Kathy Harris. And to you, dear readers, for allowing me to share Aaron, Elisabeth, Lukas, and Anna's stories with you. *Danki.*

Reading Group Guide

1. Elisabeth doesn't have much confidence in herself, something many of us struggle with. How can our faith help grow our confidence?

2. Aaron has difficulty letting go of his past and accepting God's forgiveness. Has there been a time when you had trouble accepting God's mercy? What made you finally accept it?

3. Anna is afraid to tell Lukas the truth about her possible infertility because she's afraid of losing Lukas. Do you agree with her decision? What should she have done?

4. Despite Aaron's warnings, Elisabeth attends the party at the Schrocks'. Have you ever been warned against doing something, only to do it anyway? What lesson did you learn from that experience?

5. At the party Elisabeth stood up for her beliefs, despite peer pressure. Share a time when you defended your faith.

6. After her procedure, Anna decides to put her faith in God's healing instead of seeking more medical treatment. That decision lands her in the hospital, and she has to accept the fact that she may never have children. Have you ever prayed for something and felt that God said no to your request? How did you respond?

7. The title, *An Honest Love*, is something the characters in the novel struggle with—honesty with each other and with themselves. Why do you think they had such a difficult time telling and accepting the truth?

Center Point Publishing
600 Brooks Road ● PO Box 1
Thorndike ME 04986-0001 USA

(207) 568-3717

US & Canada:
1 800 929-9108
www.centerpointlargeprint.com